An Ocean Apart

CAROL NIGHTINGALE

Copyright © 2024 Carol Nightingale
All rights reserved.
ISBN: 9798329663488

Acknowledgements

This book was inspired by my love for two very contrasting locations — one in the south of England on the Dorset coast, where I am fortunate enough to spend most weekends, and the other being the home of my brother, Paul. I have visited Delray Beach in Florida virtually every year since he moved there for work about 35 years ago — a place I have come to love and know well.

During my many visits to both locations on opposite sides of the Atlantic Ocean, I have witnessed the undeniable impact of climate change on the coast, with crumbling cliffs in Dorset and the threat of hurricanes and tropical storms caused by rising sea temperatures in Florida. This is where my inspiration came from for a subtle reference throughout to climate change, alluding to parallels to the human spirit when times are tough.

Huge thanks go to Mike, my partner, for his ongoing support and encouragement during the writing process. He makes it all possible.

I must also thank my Mum, Patricia, for being the first to read the book and give me her honest feedback; to my brother, Paul, for reading the first draft on his holiday and helping out with some minor edits — and for living in Delray Beach! A very special thanks must go to my sister, Helen, for her valuable feedback and support, and for being a sister who, despite living a few hundred miles away, is always there for me.

Introduction

West Bay, Dorset

West Bay is located on the English Channel, part of the Atlantic Ocean's broader system of seas and straits. The English Channel meets the open waters of the Atlantic Ocean near the southwestern tip of England.

The county of Dorset, situated in South West England, is bordered by Devon (west), Hampshire (east) and Somerset and Wiltshire (both north). Dorset's coastline is designated part of the Jurassic Coast World Heritage site.

West Bay, located at the western end of Chesil Beach was originally known as Bridport Harbour, sited at the mouth of the river Brit. Historically, Bridport needed a harbour to export its principal products – rope and nets – but its original harbour (one mile inland) kept silting up and became blocked by shingle from Chesil Beach, leading to a new harbour being built. By the 18th century, Bridport decided to rebrand the harbour as a resort and towards the end of the 19th century, West Bay was redeveloped with villas and lodging houses, cafés and shops.

In recent years, West Bay has been protected by a coastal defence scheme as it suffers from an eroding landscape. Facing southwest, in the direction of prevailing winds and towards the Atlantic Ocean, the coastline is subject to swell waves. A seawall was built in 1887 on West Beach, then rebuilt in 1982, aiming to interrupt the natural transport of protective sediment along the shore. East Beach has been artificially raised with shingle, yet the cliffs remain unstable with frequent rockslides - notably a 1000-tonne cliff fall at East Cliff in 2019. The sandstone East Cliff at West Bay (180 million years old) is protected a little by East Beach but continues to be eroded by wave attrition and pounding at its base, resulting in rockfalls. West Cliff is subject to slipping and slumping, caused by clay sliding over lower layers, exacerbating faults within it. Large, protective boulders on the foreshore, acting as coastal defences, are backed by a sea wall, promenade and artificial grass-covered slope.

Today, West Bay is a centre for fishing, tourism and geology. Visitors can enjoy crab fishing from the harbour, launching boats from the busy marina, or collecting fossils from the beach.

Delray Beach, Florida

Delray Beach is a small city in Palm Beach County, on Florida's southeast coast, and is one of South Florida's most popular beach destinations. It is located 52 miles north of Miami, nestled between Boca Raton (south) and Boynton Beach (north). Ocean Boulevard (or Florida State Road A1A) is considered to be one of the most picturesque drives in the county, designated a Scenic and Historic Coastal Byway. It hugs the coast for roughly 35 miles from Palm Beach in the north to Pompano Beach in the south. At the heart of Delray Beach is Atlantic Avenue, the primary east-west highway, running from Interstate 95 to the shore. Its cobblestone sidewalks are lined with oak and palm trees, offering plentiful unique boutique shops, fine dining experiences, watering holes and galleries.

The Intracoastal Waterway flows through Delray Beach – an inland, navigable route consisting of some natural inlets, saltwater rivers, bays and sounds, plus some artificial canals. Along its banks can be found jaw-dropping, exclusive multi-million-dollar properties. The Municipal Marina and drawbridge crossing over the waterway in the centre of the city are significant features of Delray Beach.

Delray Beach is in a very high-risk hurricane zone and has an Extreme Wind Factor rating based on the projected likelihood and speed of hurricane, tornado or severe storm winds impacting it. Average maximum wind speeds in Delray Beach are higher now than they were 30 years ago, and 100% of homes in Delray Beach have at least some risk of damage to properties, scattered debris, fallen trees and being cut off from access to utilities, emergency services and transport.

Today, the city's economy is based on tourism. Other economic activities include commercial flower growing, high-tech industries and the cultivation of citrus fruits.

Atlantic Ocean

The Atlantic Ocean - meaning 'Sea of Atlas' - is a huge body of saltwater, covering approximately one-fifth of the Earth's surface. It is bordered by the Americas to the west, and Europe and Africa to the East.

West Bay and Delray Beach are separated by this body of water. The distance is approximately 4325 miles – literally an ocean apart – and they occupy different time zones, Florida being 5 hours behind the UK.

PART ONE

Chapter One

West Bay

Opening the blinds, she blinked several times, trying to adjust her sleepy eyes to the bright summer sunshine that was keen to wish her a good morning. But it was too bright and the screeching seagulls were too noisy. It would take a while and several cups of strong coffee to persuade her to get dressed and start work today. Shuffling across the oak floor in her tired, old slippers, she made her way slowly from her sunny bedroom, through the open-plan living/dining room to the kitchen with its modern, sage-green units and supposedly clutter-free worktops. Glancing towards the kettle, she spotted the two wine bottles close to the sink – one half-full, the other empty. So that would account for her heavy head and lack of energy this morning. She had promised herself a night off; it was mid-week after all, with nothing to celebrate. So much for her good intentions. Well, today was a new day, and there was every chance of it improving. She just needed to take hold of herself and turn over a new leaf, starting with a pint of tap water and a mug of black instant coffee.

Ella had been living in her penthouse Quay West apartment, West Bay, for the past twelve months. She really couldn't complain: her waterside, second-floor accommodation offered stunning views of the Jurassic Coast from South Devon as far east as Portland, just about visible in the distance on a clear summer's day. Returning to the lounge with a strong, black coffee, she opened the blinds and then the patio doors onto the balcony and flopped into her favourite lounger, from which she was able to take in the full splendour of the panorama and reflect on its beauty. Known locally as the Golden Gateway to the Jurassic Coast due to the majestic glow of the sandstone cliffs and the shimmering radiance of Golden Cap, she realised that her decision to move to the South Coast was the right one. The need to get away and start afresh had been the driving force, and here was as good a place as any. There was something about the sea that she was drawn to. Maybe it was after a lifetime of living in various inland locations, with a rare trip to the coast being only an occasional treat.

Closing her eyes, she cast her mind back to the events that had brought her here, wondering how it was possible that life could turn upside down so dramatically, so quickly. Life had been almost perfect up until then – or so she thought – living with Marcus, her partner of ten years, in their three-storey townhouse in central Bristol. Yes, they both had time-consuming careers in the world of art and graphic design, but they had a great life – no money worries, a full social life and holidays abroad whenever they were able to take time away from work. Maybe something had been missing in their relationship that she hadn't perceived. Surely there must have been something wrong somewhere along the line for it to have happened. The memory of it gripped her heart like a vice – recalling the moment she discovered that she was no longer enough for Marcus. She hadn't thought anything about his weekends away with the boys – why should she? It's what he'd always done, and to be honest, she looked forward to some time to herself every now and again. Yet, it turned out that wasn't just the boys he was playing away with. Her eyes opened wide to erase the face of the woman who had taken him away from her - the image that haunted her regularly in her dreams and whenever she closed her eyes. The irony was that it was she who had employed her to help them out in the office. Gorgeous Maria, with her long blonde hair and her hourglass figure. What a cliché! And the way she found out - it was laughable. So clumsy. Wondering how to spend that particular Saturday evening when Marcus was away, she'd picked up her phone to call Maria. She'd always got on well with her and enjoyed her company both in and out of work and thought a few cocktails in Clifton would be the treat they both deserved after a really busy, successful week. What she didn't expect was the web of lies that followed: how she was at an art conference in Bath with Marcus and others; how she was sorry to hear that Ella wasn't feeling well and was therefore unable to attend the conference; how she could get Marcus to call her back if she wanted. Art conference? What on earth was she talking about? As far as she was aware, Marcus was in Torquay with his usual group of university pals, staying at The

Imperial. Fired up, Ella decided to check out a few details. Internet searches threw up no references to art conferences in Bath, and there were no reservations in the names of Marcus or his friends when she phoned the hotel, declaring a need to contact him urgently.

She remembered painfully the phone call that sealed her fate. He had picked up immediately and began to chat about the weather in Torquay and how chuffed he was with his performance on the golf course. At first, she let him talk without interruption to see how many lies he could pack into a few minutes, then she decided to play him at his own game, asking after his friends and where they'd dined. When she had heard enough, she simply ended the call.

On his return, he had begged her to forgive him, but she simply couldn't do it. He confessed to spending the weekend away with Maria, but explained there was nothing to their relationship. It had been a stupid mistake, he said. It would never happen again, he said. But Ella, having spent the remainder of the weekend reflecting on her childhood, her teenage years and the past ten with Marcus, was resolute about how to proceed. She wasn't prepared to give him another chance. He had broken the trust she thought was rock-solid, and knew she didn't have it in her heart to forgive him. She had always told him that she would never tolerate infidelity, and now it had happened, it made her question their relationship. Where were they heading after ten years together? They were seemingly drifting aimlessly, with no long-term plans for the future. Perhaps this was the wake-up call she needed.

Swiftly, she put their house on the market, which ended up being sold through closed bids due to its enviable location. Despite Marcus protesting, begging for forgiveness and declaring his undying love for her, she calmly asked for her share in the house so that she could move on. Within just a few months, she had left her much-loved job and house in her favourite city, and found herself relocated to the south coast, searching for freelance opportunities in graphic design from her own beach-front property.

Delray Beach

Opening the bi-fold doors onto the sundeck, she slipped on her designer sunglasses to protect her eyes from the harsh Florida sun. Sitting on the edge of the pool, watching the palm trees waft in the sea breeze, she reflected on the life of luxury that she was fortunate enough to wake up to each day, so far removed from her previous life back in the UK. This was her home – a luxury oceanfront penthouse condo – enviably located on Ocean Boulevard, with its private beach only steps from the Atlantic, accessible via a private elevator. Much as she had loved Bristol and her parochial existence there, she adored the contrasting life she experienced in Delray Beach – a charming, vibrant city of dynamic and diverse communities. How she loved the sophistication of Downtown Delray with its art scene – murals and art installations, galleries and upscale shops. In contrast, yet literally on her doorstep, was the wide, sandy sprawl of powdery white sands lined with grasses and palm trees, and the sun-soaked shoreline of cosmopolitan trendy beaches. As art enthusiasts, they had been drawn to Delray Beach, famous for its Pineapple Grove Arts District, packed with galleries and performance art, and the Arts Garage, home of live theatre, musical concerts and a multi-media arts venue.

Greg, a US citizen, born and raised in Boca Raton, had been keen to move back to Florida with his new bride. They met in Bristol six years ago, when she was working in her father's Clifton art gallery, managing day-to-day operations whilst he planned to ease into retirement. She was fresh out of university, having studied art history, and was keen to gain experience in the art world before deciding on her career path. It was love at first sight – something of a cliché – but it truly was. Greg, with his tousled blonde hair, blue eyes and sun-drenched golden skin, his athletic body and sexy American drawl. How could she resist, that day he'd walked into the gallery, seeking an opportunity to showcase his latest artwork?

It had been something of a whirlwind romance. Following just a few work-related meetings, their relationship began to extend beyond the world of art and it wasn't long before business turned to pleasure. He owned his own gallery in an exclusive art district of Delray Beach and was planning to travel between the UK and the States to establish business links, but ultimately, he wanted to settle permanently in Florida, and he was keen to take Freya with him. She was easily convinced and quickly fell under his spell. What else held her in Bristol, after all? Within months, they had made plans to move. During a trip to his hometown – Boca Raton, Florida – he asked her to marry him. Freya was seduced by the Florida sun, the white sandy beaches and palm tree-lined avenues. Driving along the A1A beachfront highway in his open-top Cadillac, to the sound of the Beach Boys 'Good Vibrations', she felt as though she had never been happier. She said yes.

    That was five years ago. Five long, glorious years ago. On the surface, her life was perfect; yet lately, she had wondered whether it really was. Surely she had everything and more she could ever have dreamed of? Looking around their luxury penthouse condo, with every conceivable mod-con, positioned on its own private beach, she asked herself what more she could possibly want. Greg was perfect too. Gorgeous Greg. Everyone loved him: his model looks, athletic physique; his gregarious personality – friendly, funny, kind and caring; his talent and business acumen. Greg was a good catch, there was no denying it. And yet there was a void. Something was missing. Yet she wasn't sure what it was.

Chapter Two

West Bay

Sunday afternoon. End of the school holidays. Although she accepted it was thanks to the influx of tourists during the past few weeks that business was booming, she was relieved to be able to walk along the harbour walls without weaving in and out of hordes of visitors dripping melting ice creams along the pavements, stuffing their faces with paper-wrapped fish and chips and taking up far too much room with their dogs and pushchairs. Alongside her freelance graphic design projects, she had been selling her art on the quayside – modern takes on the iconic views of Golden Cap and nearby Colmers Hill on the Symondsbury Estate. Commercial stuff, but it sold well. Probably the sort of thing that would end up gracing the walls of a cloakroom or guest room in a modern four-bed detached. Not that it mattered, so long as she was earning.

Early September glorious morning sunshine – it seemed, typically and ironically, that the best weather had waited for the tourists to go home. The past few weeks had been miserable, with constant cloud, drizzle and some high winds, although the holiday-makers were not deterred. The amusement arcade had been packed, the cafés crowded and the mackerel fishing trips ever-popular, despite the poor weather and disappointing catches. The adrenaline-inducing rib rides, offering fast-paced, sightseeing tours of the Jurassic coast from the marina, had been cancelled more often than they'd been chartered this summer.

For once, she was able to find a table on the marina, outside her favourite kiosk – a perfect spot for her to settle for a short while and take in the atmosphere created by the colourful bobbing boats against the backdrop of the shimmering sandstone cliffs. As she waited for her coffee and croissant, she reflected on the crumbling coastline. It seemed that it was wearing away in front of her eyes despite all the sea defences doing their best to prevent further rockfalls. Only a few weeks ago, part of East Beach had to be cordoned off following a cliff collapse causing chunks of rock to hit the beach, narrowly missing holiday-makers. Selfishly, she turned her thoughts to herself. She felt as though she was crumbling away. This isn't what she had planned for herself – to be sitting alone on a Sunday morning reflecting on the dramatic effects of climate change, with no one to talk to. She wondered what Marcus would be doing at that very moment. Probably still in bed with Maria and the Sunday papers, alternating sex with coffee, just as they had done. Had she given up on Marcus too readily? Sometimes she thought she had, but at other times she realised they had been existing mainly in parallel universes incapable of converging. They had no real direction in life. Is that why he had started a relationship with Maria? Perhaps they would have been fine if she had never found out about her.

Deciding to prolong her musings in the autumn sunshine, she turned her thoughts to her childhood. It had been happy, but complex. Her parents had separated when she was about five, but her mother had never wanted to say much to her about what happened between them. She remembered visiting her father every other weekend in the company of her grandparents for several years, but then the visits stopped as quickly as they had begun. She had no idea why and her mother offered her no explanation. Aside from the mystery surrounding her father, her family life with her mother, step-father and half-sister was a happy one. Their home was close to Bristol – a chocolate-box, thatched cottage in a much sought-after village on the outskirts of the city. She was fond of her stepfather, who treated her as his own, and her sister was good company – most of the time – although they were five years apart and inevitably clashed over different interests and age-related abilities.

As the years rolled by, the age gap widened as Ella went off to university and became an independent adult. Sadly, time had not really filled that gap; there still remained a distance between them.

Delray Beach

Sunday afternoon. Hurricane season. It was unbearably hot and humid with temperatures well into the high 80s. Thank goodness for air-conditioning and a chilled, private pool. The latest news bulletin warned of a tropical depression threatening Florida in the form of a hurricane in the next few days, originating in the Caribbean and set on a path to threaten Florida, although there remained hope that the path could change. She listened carefully as the weather bulletin continued, describing an above-normal level of activity expected for the hurricane season, and record warm sea surface temperatures. She listened to the explanation of how hurricanes draw their power from the warmth of the sea and ocean surface temperatures, which have climbed to unusually high levels, boosting the potency of storms. They spoke of a 60% chance of an above-normal hurricane season. More evidence of climate change.

Sitting on the edge of the pool, her feet dangling in the shimmering, cooling water, she sipped a chilled glass of her favourite Californian white wine. The condensation forming on the outside of the glass dripped down her lower arm onto her bronzed thigh – a welcome freshener in the oppressive heat – causing her to snap out of her musings about the effects of climate change which were clearly exacerbating the threat of hurricanes. It seemed inevitable that each year, the prevalence of stormy weather increased during the hurricane season, causing her to wonder whether they should relocate to somewhere safer, somewhere inland, or even a different state.

As her thoughts turned from climate change to herself, she asked herself whether she was truly happy. How could she not be? Yet this question remained unanswered. Greg was everything to her. He was perfection personified; he could do no more for her in her pursuit of true happiness and fulfilment. Yet looking around her idyllic home, she acknowledged that one thing was indeed missing – the one thing that would make everything perfect: Greg. He was hardly ever there. His life was 90% the gallery and 10% home. She missed him. Yes, she could fill her days with the gym, the pool, and the mall. She could wander up and down Atlantic Avenue, with the means and freedom to purchase anything she wanted. She could lie on her sun lounger or meet up with friends at the members-only tennis or beach club, every day of the week. Yet it wasn't enough – in fact, it's not what she wanted. She lacked company – proper company. She missed Greg; she wanted to spend more time with him. Or maybe she needed a job – something more meaningful to occupy her than shopping and sunbathing. Since moving to the States, she hadn't worked; Greg said there was no need for her to do so. He thought she needed time to settle into her new home and lifestyle in Florida, make friends and take things easy – he earned more than enough to pay the bills. She reflected on the short time she had worked in her father's Clifton gallery and often wondered why Greg repeatedly refused her offers to help him out in his own gallery when he complained of being so busy.

Sipping another glass of wine from the comfort of her shaded sun lounger, her thoughts turned to her childhood. It had been a very happy one. She loved her parents dearly, although missed them now that they were so far away. She missed her sister too – her half-sister, five years her senior. She smiled as she recollected happy times trying to win her approval and join in her games. They were as close as sisters could be bearing in mind the age gap and the fact that they were now geographically separated.

Chapter Three

West Bay

Early December. The interminable approach to Christmas and its tedious traditions. Ella was not in the mood for it one bit. For some reason, it didn't feel 'Christmassy' at the coast. She thought back to her previous life in Bristol – the city lit up with lights, candlelight concerts in the cathedral, street markets selling mulled wine and mince pies. How could she not miss all that? Walking around the harbour, she smiled at the contrast – a lopsided Santa dangling from a lamppost, closed shops and boarded-up food kiosks, boats covered over in the harbour for the winter. She wondered what would happen if she popped into the pub seeking a mulled wine around an open fire – an unlikely prospect, she felt. Yet she needed to make plans for the festive season; it was not going to do her any good ignoring it and hoping it would go away. Her parents weren't bothered about Christmas these days and had booked themselves onto a six-week cruise of the Southern Hemisphere to escape the festivities, and her friends, who were far and few between, were busy doing their own family things. The way things were looking, she would be on her own for Christmas.

Returning to the warmth of her apartment, she logged on to her laptop. She would send her sister a message. At least then she would feel better for having reached out to her. If she didn't, another month or two would roll by. After ten minutes, her fingers remained frozen on the keyboard. What did she have to say to her without sounding pathetic and lonely? Pushing her chair back somewhat aggressively, she stomped into the kitchen and pulled out a half-opened bottle of wine from the almost empty fridge. Pouring herself a large glass, she returned to the laptop, took a gulp and let her fingers do the talking:

Hi! How are you both? Hope you enjoyed Thanksgiving. Are you up to anything special for Christmas? Things are going well here. I'm feeling more settled although it's rather quiet at this time of the year and the weather makes everything seem a little bleak. As I look out of the window at the angry, grey waves, it's hard to imagine that you have calm, blue waters on the other side of the ocean!

Work is reasonably steady. I've got some regular business with a local magazine and I've managed to get some of my pieces in a gallery in Bridport. Everything's ticking along pretty well.

No plans for Christmas, but you know me, I've never been the greatest fan! It will probably be me and an M&S lunch, but that's fine. PJs and a bottle of wine, with a pile of my favourite films – sounds perfect!

Hope to hear from you soon.
Lots of love,
Ella x

Reading it back before pressing 'send', it all sounded pretty glum. She didn't want sympathy; she was fine. Absolutely fine. It was true – she'd never particularly enjoyed Christmas, even as a child. It was something to be endured: gimmicky gifts in the shops since September; Christmas songs on the radio since the end of November; supermarket shelves filled with chipolata sausages and stuffings, tubs of chocolates and selections boxes. She tried to imagine a Christmas she might enjoy. Perhaps a snowy scene, somewhere in the mountains. Sleighbells and gluhwein. Fur-trimmed coats and sheepskin gloves. Something on the lines of those final scenes of 'White Christmas': skiing in Vermont, matching Santa suits, pine lodges, log fires and freshly cut pine trees surrounded by well-chosen and perfectly-wrapped gifts. She smiled thinking about the reality that would be her Christmas – a stroll around the empty harbour in the fog, central heating on full, old pyjamas and her snagged towelling dressing gown, an artificial tree on top of the nest of tables decorated with tinsel and half a dozen cut-price baubles. It sounded glum, and it was. She pressed 'send' and closed the lid of her laptop, returning to the kitchen for just one more glass of wine.

Delray Beach

Early December. Her favourite time of year. Thanksgiving was over and it had been a good one. She loved the traditions – the turkey feast served with pumpkin pie, green bean casserole, cornbread and candied yams – shared with close friends whose families, like theirs, lived elsewhere. She enjoyed having Greg for the whole day, snuggling up to watch Macy's Thanksgiving Day Parade on TV, followed by his favourite movie 'Planes, Trains and Automobiles', the daft tale of John Candy trying to get home for Thanksgiving. Now it was her turn to share her own much-loved Christmas traditions she'd enjoyed as a child. The next few weeks would be filled with hours in the malls, stocking up with garlands, lights, candles, wreaths and tree decorations. Somehow, she'd managed to persuade Greg to take her to the traditional lighting celebrations of the 100-foot Christmas tree and yuletide street fair in Downtown Delray at the weekend. She'd dragged him up and down Atlantic Avenue and Pineapple Grove, buying unnecessary but beautiful gifts and treats for each other, stopping only to listen to musical performances at open-air bars. She'd loved it – mostly because she'd managed to tear him away from work and have a whole evening with him. His gallery in the Pineapple Grove Arts District was doing incredibly well, hosting contemporary art, abstract paintings, sculptures and fine photography, yet he seemed incapable of leaving it in the hands of anyone else, even for a few hours. Delray Beach came to life in the evenings, especially at this time of the year, and he was keen to keep the gallery open later than usual to capitalise on the busy streets and booming business.

Although their home would be Christmas-ready by the weekend, she felt there was still something missing. Something that money couldn't buy. Much as she enjoyed the company of friends, she yearned for a family Christmas. She had already mentioned her wishes to Greg and he was happy to go along with whatever she wanted. She guessed he would be immersed in work and it would be down to her to make any arrangements.

Opening up her laptop, she decided to contact her sister, only to discover that she had received an email from her. It made her feel sad and led her to reflect on her own enviable situation in comparison. It was enough to make up her mind:

Hiya! So good to hear from you. I'm glad to know you're settling into your new surroundings and that work is going well, although I'm not at all surprised - you've got such a talent.

Reading your email has made me wonder whether you would be up for a trip to Florida. We'd love you to visit. It's been ages since you were here and Christmas is a time for family after all. Give it some thought – serious thought! Come for as long as you like, to fit in with flights and so on.

Why don't you swap those angry winter waves for the sunshine shores of Delray Beach? Book your flight over the Atlantic and come and spend Christmas with your little sister. Please!

Much love, always,

Freya xxx

Oh well, it was worth a try. Maybe this year, now that she was on her own, she might make the trip. She closed the lid of her laptop, grabbed a chilled beer from the cooler and settled down in her favourite poolside lounger with a glossy magazine.

Chapter Four

West Bay

One week until Christmas and she had so much to do: a few loose ends to tie up with her regular magazine contract - although her laptop would be going with her so that she could be on hand should the need arise; an art commission to be finalised for a local client; a few small but carefully selected gifts to wrap; last-minute cleaning, washing and packing to be done. She hadn't accepted the invitation immediately, but after sleeping on it, decided it was an offer she couldn't refuse. As it turned out, the timing was just right. She acknowledged that she had been sinking into something of a depression lately, turning to alcohol to boost her mood, then discovering it was having the opposite effect. And it was true, she hadn't seen her sister for ages. She and Marcus had visited Delray Beach once during a fortnight's holiday touring Florida, but it had been a flying visit and they hardly saw anything of Greg. Then a couple of years later, Freya had flown back to the UK on her own to spend some time with their parents. Maybe it was time to get to know her sister better, now that she was single. Marcus had never been supportive of her fostering a closer relationship with Freya, declaring that he had no plans to revisit Florida – once was enough, he said.

The prospect of Christmas in warmer climes had boosted her spirits massively. She even caught herself humming along to 'Last Christmas' when it came on the radio for what must have been the fourth time in as many hours. Her suitcase lay open at the end of the bed, packed with brightly coloured summer dresses and swimwear purchased specifically for the trip. She glanced at herself in the full-length mirror, feeling satisfied for once with her reflection. Stroking her hand down the back of her new short haircut, she wondered why she hadn't opted for this style before – a layered pixie cut that magically added texture and volume to her silky, straight dark hair. Without even trying, her weight had plummeted since leaving Marcus, necessitating a new wardrobe for this trip. She felt happier and more positive than she had for several months. Yes, she was looking forward to jetting off to the Sunshine State tomorrow.

Delray Beach

One week to Christmas and just a few days until her sister's visit. Ella was due to arrive in Miami on Saturday afternoon; Greg had generously agreed to take time off to collect her from the airport. She felt genuinely excited at the prospect of seeing Ella after what had been far too long. A proper family Christmas for once. It was a pity their parents couldn't join them, but they would be somewhere in the Pacific enjoying what had become their favourite pastime – cruising around the globe. Friends would be joining the sisters for the festivities, but there would be plenty of time during the fortnight to really get to know each other all over again.

The spacious guest room was now ready for her sister with its panoramic views over the sapphire ocean and soft white sandy shores, with its huge floor-to-ceiling windows framed by waving palm trees. Turning her back on the view, she caught sight of herself in the mirrored closet doors and studied her reflection closely. The time, effort and money she spent to maintain her enviable figure and appearance were immeasurable – she spent every waking moment obsessing over her weight and looks. Weekly appointments at the beauty bar for either hair or nails; daily trips to the sports club for tennis, the gym or spa treatments; early morning sessions in their home gym and pool – a constant pursuit for perfection. Perhaps it was just as well she didn't go to work – how would she fit everything in?

Wandering into the suite of rooms at the end of the long glass corridor, she entered her huge closet to choose from the rows of designer clothes organised according to style and colour. She was planning a special evening with Greg, who had promised to be home early. The finest champagne to start, followed by his favourite rib-eye and salad, a bottle of Shiraz and whatever else he wanted... Deciding upon a cerise chiffon kaftan, she twisted her long blonde hair into a loose knot and applied another coat of lip gloss and a spritz of Chanel.

She was intent on making it a much-needed night to remember.

Glancing at the kitchen clock, she began to wonder what had held him up. He was now an hour later than expected. She picked up her phone and promptly put it down again, believing he would have a good reason to be delayed. He didn't need her checking up on him; it would ruin the mood before the night had begun. Dinner could wait, but she felt the need for an aperitif. She could always open the champagne – there was plenty more where that came from. As she struggled to release the cork, she changed her mind, knowing that once it was released, the bubbles would die down – a bit like her spirits. Perhaps she should stick to wine until he arrived. After pouring herself a large glass, she wandered out onto the sundeck. The winter sun had set over an hour ago, but the air was still pleasantly warm. As she sat down, her mind began to wander as it seemed to do more and more these days. She felt so lonely and unfulfilled; it was time to share her feelings with Greg, but maybe not tonight. Just as she was mulling things over, she heard his car pull onto the drive, then doors opening and closing. Standing up, ready to greet him, she instantly forgave him. Nothing would spoil their evening.

"Hi, darling. So sorry I got held up. I planned to close up a bit earlier, but..." He began, after kissing her affectionately.

"It doesn't matter. I understand. Shall I fetch you a drink?" Not wanting to hear whatever excuse had delayed him.

"I think I'll shower and change first if that's ok."

"No problem. Take your time. Then you can tell me how your day went."

"You too, my love. I won't be long. You look gorgeous by the way, as always."

Freya chose not to respond, although she was grateful for a compliment after making such an effort. She would pour herself another glass of wine whilst she put the final touches to dinner preparations and decide what she had to tell Greg about her day. It wouldn't take long – nothing of any significance to report, as usual.

Half an hour later, they were seated opposite each other at the outdoor dining table which offered spectacular views of the ocean. Gentle mood music was playing in the background, as they began to sip champagne and enjoy each other's company. A rare moment.

"Well, this is just about perfect. Thank you."

"No need to thank me, Greg. I just wanted us to have some special time together. You've been so busy lately. I'm not complaining, but I feel we have so little quality time these days, just the two of us."

"I know it's been ultra busy lately. Bound to be, what with the holiday season upon us. But business is booming and that's something to celebrate, surely?"

"Absolutely. It really is. It's just that the days seem so long with you working such hours. We've hardly seen each other lately."

"I understand what you're saying, Freya, but that's the way it has to be for now."

"What do you mean? I don't understand why you won't have some help in the gallery. Surely you could employ someone to enable you to have some time off every now and again?"

"Why would I do that? It would mean paying a salary and commission. And, to be honest, it's really only me who can make the decisions."

"So, what about me? Couldn't I help out? I've got experience of the art world and working in a gallery. And you wouldn't have to pay me!"

"How would that solve the issue you have about us not spending more time together? So, whilst I'm taking time off, you would be in the gallery? That makes no sense at all."

"True. Maybe I'm trying to say something else."

"Like what? We've got a perfect life here, haven't we? Just look around you – at all this. It's what most people can only dream of. We have an exclusive property in an idyllic location, with no money worries and lots of friends."

"Friends we hardly get to see."

"Freya, come on. You're out most days with your friends, aren't you?"

"My friends, yes. But Greg, I'm spending all day, every day, merely whiling away long hours wandering around the mall or passing time at the club. It has no meaning, does it?"

They fell silent for a while, their eyes cast down towards their empty glasses. Eventually, Freya stood up to return to the kitchen. The evening wasn't turning out exactly as she had planned after all. Greg chose not to follow her.

Fifteen minutes later, she returned with the steaks and salad. Greg hadn't moved; he was gazing out across the turquoise pool, illuminated by solar lighting around its perimeter.

"Do you want to choose the wine, Greg?"

"OK. And then we need to talk."

As he left the table, Freya began to regret opening up to Greg so soon in the evening. Clearly, the mood was spoiled. She appreciated that the holiday season was upon them and things would quieten down after Christmas. Yet, she'd clearly pushed his buttons and now she needed to face the consequences.

In silence, the wine was poured and the salad served. It appeared that Greg was happy to finish his meal before embarking upon the conversation he planned to have with her. Eventually, once dinner was over and glasses refilled, he sat back and began to speak, looking directly into her eyes. "Are you happy, Freya?" he began somewhat bluntly.

"Of course I am! That's not what I was saying, at all."

"So, what do you want? You've got your sister coming to stay in a matter of days. Let's have this conversation before she arrives."

"I'm so incredibly grateful for my wonderful life with you here in Florida. Yes, I miss my family, but that would be the same wherever we lived – Mum and Dad are always away, and I've never had the closest of relationships with my sister. It's more about my own self-worth, I think. I know my life is incredibly privileged and I have a totally indulgent lifestyle, but I think I need more. I don't mean money or material things – you provide for us amply. It's more about living a meaningful existence. I suppose I mean a job."

"I'm hearing what you're saying but you work incredibly hard to maintain this house and create such an amazing home for us. The house is perfect because of you. We have a wonderful life because of you. I'm so grateful that you are highly organised and capable of managing this property to such a high standard. You manage everything here, Freya – our finances, the maintenance contracts for the house, garden and pool, the shopping and our meals – the list goes on."

"But it's not hard, Greg. It doesn't challenge me. I need more."

"Such as what? How about talking to your sister about her freelance work?"

"Maybe."

"What is it, Freya? There's something on your mind. What is it you're not telling me?"

Silence fell between them, with Greg believing that he had said enough, and Freya wondering exactly what was missing in their relationship. As the minutes rolled by, it suddenly dawned on her. She knew what would complete them.

Chapter Five

West Bay

Ella's mood had continued to brighten and, as she waited for her taxi to take her to Heathrow, she felt genuinely happy and excited for the first time in ages. Her almost ten-hour flight to Miami would present her with the opportunity to watch a couple of films and read her book, hopefully with a glass or two of complimentary wine to help her nap in between. Looking out of the window, before closing the blinds for the fortnight, she cast her eyes over the angry, grey waves threatening the crumbling coastline. They posed a very serious threat to the cliffs that seemed to be disintegrating in front of her eyes. Another portion of the beach had to be cordoned off only two days ago due to a small but nonetheless, serious rockfall that posed a threat to walkers along the shoreline.

Her suitcase, packed tightly with Christmas gifts and possibly too many clothes, stood close to the front door. She checked her handbag for her passport for the umpteenth time – it was still there. Then she wandered around her apartment, double-checking that everything was left perfectly in readiness for her return, two weeks later.

Checking her watch, she leaned forward to try to spot the taxi before it arrived at her door. After a few minutes, once it appeared on the far side of the marina, she began to make her way to the ground floor with her heavy luggage and hopeful heart.

Delray Beach

"Are you sure you don't mind going to the airport, Greg?"

"It's the least I can do. You do realise I can only take a few days off while Ella's here - not the whole fortnight."

"Sure. That's fine. We've got lots to catch up on."

"So, do you want to come with me?"

"I think it makes more sense for me to get everything ready here if you don't mind. I know she'll be tired, but I still want to make a good impression. I expect she'll be tired and hungry."

"Fair enough. The flight is on time according to the tracker app, but I think I might as well factor in a bit of time for her to get through immigration. You know how long it can take."

"Good idea. Probably allow an hour for her to get through and collect her luggage."

"That's what I was thinking. However, it's a busy time of day on the I-95, isn't it? It will probably take a good hour."

"Whatever you think. By the way, are you sure you'll recognise Ella?" asked Freya giggling. "It has been a while."

"Good point! You'd better remind me. I haven't seen her for a few years and that was only for a couple of days. Perhaps you'd better let me have a photo," he said, continuing the humour.

"Well, I haven't got a recent photo, but here's an old one. Shoulder-length dark hair, healthy build, a bit shorter than me." She'd been scrolling through her phone to find a photo from the time she visited the UK, a couple of years ago. He glanced at it, not taking a great deal of notice.

"I'll recognise her, but let me have her mobile number just in case. Now what else do I need to know? What's been going on in her life lately. It could be a long journey home if the traffic's bad."

"Well, let's see. She's had a difficult year; she's no longer with Marcus and she's living in a small seaside resort called West Bay on the south coast. She's still working in graphic design and now she paints in her spare time, I think. Will that give you enough to talk about?" Freya smiled at her wonderful husband, who always wanted to please.

He was right, the I-95 was just as congested as he feared. Thank goodness for the express lane; he should arrive just in time. As he motored along, he reflected on his recent conversation with Freya. Whilst he understood what she was trying to explain to him, about a somewhat empty existence, he hoped that a fortnight with her sister would distract her over the holiday season while he was busy and make her see that life wasn't so bad after all. Yet, even though the evening turned out well in the end, he couldn't help but feel there was something she was holding back. During the evening, he noticed a positive shift in her mood, as though it had suddenly dawned on her that she had nothing to complain about after all. Perhaps the conversation was enough to clear the air for now; she certainly seemed much more content. Hopefully, with her sister arriving, her mood would only improve further.

As soon as he pulled into the parking lot, he checked to see whether the Heathrow flight had landed. Discovering that it had arrived half an ago, he decided to make his way leisurely to arrivals. He would sit at a table with a coffee while he waited for her to make her way through the lengthy queues at immigration; hopefully, it wouldn't be too long before she appeared. Eventually, passengers from the flight began to make their way through the gates. He stood up and wandered closer to the throng of tired-looking holidaymakers dragging luggage and clutching British passports, scanning them for a sole female traveller in her early thirties, with shoulder-length dark hair and of medium build – a bit non-descript from the photo that Freya had shown him. As the minutes rolled by, he wondered whether he should text her. Once or twice, he thought he had spotted her, but there had been no look of recognition in response to his smile. Yes, he would let her know where he was waiting; it would make things simpler. As he began to type out his message, he suddenly felt a hand on his arm.

"Greg?" Before him, stood a petite brunette with stylish short hair and the most beautiful big brown eyes he had ever seen.

"Ella? Hello! I was just about to message you to meet up. How was the flight? Here, let me take your case." He was waffling nervously, taken aback by the sudden appearance of his sister-in-law, looking nothing like the person he was expecting.

"Thank you," she responded, keen to offload her luggage. "The flight was pretty good. I watched a couple of films and had a few hours' sleep. Before I knew it, we were landing! How are you? And Freya?"

"We're both fine, thanks. Do you need a drink or anything before we leave the airport?" He was keen to leave the busy terminal and make a start on the journey home, but felt he should make the offer.

"I'm fine thanks. Happy to head off, if that suits you."

Chatting amiably about nothing in particular, they made their way to the parking lot. Once in the car and on the northbound stretch of the I-95, their conversation developed into something more meaningful. Greg asked Ella about her work but avoided any mention of Marcus. Ella asked Greg about the gallery and asked after Freya. Every so often, Ella glimpsed across at Greg; there was no doubt about it, he was a fine-looking man. It had been a few years since she had seen him and at that point in her life, she had eyes for only Marcus and hadn't even noticed or remembered his athletic physique, blonde tousled hair, and striking blue eyes. Since becoming single, she had begun to take a renewed interest in men, wondering whether she would ever meet anyone again. There was no doubt about it, she missed male company, having a soul mate, a partnership, and intimacy.

"Do you have any ongoing commissions?" asked Greg suddenly, glancing across at Freya, who appeared to be gazing out of the window in a world of her own.

"Er, sorry? I must have dozed off. What did you say, Greg?" Freya shook herself out of her reverie, ashamed of herself for contemplating the attractiveness of her brother-in-law.

"I'm not surprised. It's quite a trip across the Atlantic, isn't it? You've been travelling for hours. I was just going to ask you about your commissions, but we've got plenty of time to talk about that over the next couple of weeks. Why don't you close your eyes again? It should take about another half hour, all being well." Greg had to admit to himself that Ella was not as he had remembered, or indeed bore much resemblance to the photo he had seen that morning. Gone was the unflattering shoulder-length hair; her delicate features were enhanced by the short, layered cut that framed her undeniably pretty face. She was of a slight build – petite yet shapely. He was drawn to her fresh-faced, natural appeal, from her pale English rose complexion to her casual, yet stylish attire.

As predicted, after just under half an hour, they were making their way slowly down Atlantic Avenue - the vibrant, bustling epicenter of Delray Beach with its brick-paved sidewalks lined with palm and oak trees, twinkling fairy lights creating a magical festive atmosphere for the crowds of happy shoppers and diners. As they turned onto Ocean Boulevard, Ella felt excited at the prospect of staying with her sister in her luxury beachfront property; it was exactly what she needed.

As she stepped out of the car, she couldn't help but feel a mix of emotions: excited yet a little nervous about seeing her sister after such a long time, especially as they had become somewhat distant from each other over the past twelve months; overwhelmingly joyful at being in such an idyllic beach setting after the bleak, grey weeks leading up to Christmas back in the UK; bewildered and bemused at her reaction to Greg and how he had stirred up feelings she thought she had packed away forever.

"Ella!" cried Freya, skipping down the white marble stairs from their large foyer to greet her. "You made it. Come on in." She slipped her tanned arm through her sister's and led her into their incredible contemporary condo with panoramic oceanfront views from every window.

It was like stepping into the most tasteful Christmas grotto ever with its flickering fairy lights; the glow and fragrance of cinnamon candles; festive background music emanating from hidden surround speakers; twisted garlands and glittery baubles adorning the centerpiece that was a floor-to-ceiling fresh pine tree surrounded by gifts of all sizes perfectly positioned and wrapped in matching paper, ribbons and bows. Everything was exquisite and magical. After taking in her surroundings, her eyes eventually settled on Freya, standing opposite her in all her glory. She too was every bit as perfect and polished as her magnificent home. A vision in emerald green, her long blonde hair falling over her shoulders like a satin curtain, and a face that would not be out of place on the cover of a magazine. When she smiled, her eyes twinkled as bright as the festive fairy lights surrounding her. And then, completing the scene, in walked Greg with a tray of champagne and crystal flutes. It was like a scene from the pages of a glossy magazine.

Ella was entranced yet amused by the contrast with her own life back home. She imagined what she might be doing if she were still at home just days before Christmas. A small, artificial Christmas tree with its branches still twisted and uneven; a string of old fairy lights, half of which no longer worked; a burnt-out cheap candle pretending to have something to do with frankincense and myrrh and an old snow globe from her childhood containing a fat Santa.

"Welcome to Delray Beach!" interjected Freya, snapping her out of her reverie. "Here's to us. Happy Christmas!" she continued, passing a glass of celebratory bubbles from the tray.

"To us," Ella responded dutifully, avoiding eye contact with Greg for some reason. "Thank you so much for having me. I can't tell you how grateful I am. Even though it's supposed to be the festive season back home, it's so cold, dark and glum. It's as though everyone is hibernating from the cold."

"Do you think it's because you live at the coast? I don't suppose you get many tourists in December."

"You're right. All the action is in the towns and cities – packed shops and Christmas stuff going on. Not really my scene anymore, to be honest."

"Well, let's hope this is! We have a few things arranged if that's OK but feel free to relax and enjoy some winter sunshine. We'll have something to eat shortly and then I bet you're ready for an early night."

"That would be lovely. Thank you." Freya guided her sister outside onto the sundeck, where Greg was sitting gazing across the pool illuminated by festive lanterns and festoons of fairy lights in the palm trees.

"This is simply beautiful," sighed Ella, sipping her champagne.

"Well, make yourself at home. It's your holiday," responded Greg. His generous smile lit up his whole face. They certainly made a gorgeous couple, Greg and Freya – the American dream. She felt so ordinary and plain in their company.

Chapter Six

Delray Beach

"Happy Christmas!" greeted Ella as Freya walked down the twisted wrought-iron staircase into the open-plan reception room, with two carefully selected and exquisitely wrapped gifts for her hosts. Freya looked stylish in a festive red silk trouser suit; her hair effortlessly twisted into a low knot. Greg was sitting at the long white marble kitchen island with a mug of freshly brewed coffee, looking as if he had stepped out of a fashion magazine with his tailored shorts and winter white designer shirt.

Thankfully, Ella had decided to make a concerted effort to present herself with equal care and attention, having chosen a new dress from an over-priced boutique on Atlantic Avenue and invested in some new makeup on Freya's recommendation. Several close friends were due to arrive from midday and Ella was keen to make a good impression. It had been a very long time since she had dressed up for a special occasion and could hardly remember the last time she'd been invited to a party. She was feeling both nervous and excited at the prospect of such an occasion but was determined to enjoy herself, especially now that she was feeling more self-confident and reasonably happy with her appearance for the first time in ages.

"Happy Christmas Ella! You look gorgeous. Doesn't she Greg?"

"That colour certainly suits you. Merry Christmas. Too early for champagne?" Ella didn't dare to look in his direction, feeling self-conscious and a little embarrassed at the attention she was receiving.

"It's never too early," giggled Freya. "Then we could open some presents!" Ella smiled, remembering her younger sister's excitement and impatience when they were small children. It seemed that some things never change.

"What about prep for lunch? What can I do to help?" Ella enquired, mindful that she had done little to help since arriving three days ago.

"Nothing at all. It's all under control but thanks for the offer." Ella was aware that there had been a delivery of festive food, mostly pre-prepared dishes requiring nothing more than heating through, and the table had been dressed the night before with an elaborate floral centrepiece, silver runners and matching folded napkins. Something of a contrast to the microwave tray meal for one that she would have ended up with should she have stayed at home!

Soon after midday, the first of their ten guests began to arrive. Freya explained to her that they were close friends and neighbours - four couples and two of Freya's girlfriends from the tennis club – with whom they socialised regularly. Ella began to feel self-conscious and uncomfortable as the remainder of the guests continued to arrive; she felt like retreating to the kitchen to help with the catering rather than trying to make small talk with strangers.

"Wondered where you'd got to." Greg had entered the kitchen to fetch more wine, only to find Ella staring out of the window by the kitchen sink. "What are you doing? Washing up?" he joked.

"Oh! You made me jump. I'm fine thanks. Just having a glass of water," she explained, grabbing a glass from the draining board.

"How about a glass of wine instead?"

"That's great. Thanks." He made her feel nervous for some reason, and for a moment, she felt lost for words.

"There's someone I'd like you to meet. Let me introduce you." Obediently and wordlessly, she followed him back into the gathering of strangers, wishing she could slope away unnoticed.

Yet Greg soon made her feel valued and worthy of being amongst this small group of wealthy, yet welcoming individuals. It became clear that he had taken an interest in her work back home, introducing her as a freelance graphic designer and professional artist. Conversation flowed effortlessly with genuine enthusiasm being shown for her career, resulting in Ella feeling more confident and relaxed in their company than she imagined possible. Even though she was busy chatting, she was aware that Greg was watching her from across the room, having retreated as soon as he knew she was in good company. He had shown her genuine kindness and concern, ensuring she was comfortable and fully integrated into his group of friends. She was grateful to him, especially as she had hardly seen Freya since the first guests had arrived.

☐

After a leisurely lunch, the guests gradually drifted outside onto the sun terrace for more drinks. The warm winter sun was still shining brightly on the ocean as it began its descent in preparation for an early sunset, and a comforting breeze wafted gently through the palm trees surrounding the pool creating the most perfect temperature for relaxation. Standing alone in a sheltered corner, Ella reflected on the past few hours. Although the day had begun as something that felt like a test of endurance, it had developed into a pleasant occasion. She had enjoyed meeting Freya's friends and was flattered that Greg's colleagues from the art world had shown such interest in her work. She had spent very little time with either Freya or Greg at the party, but that was to be expected; she had more than a week left of her vacation, plenty of time to enjoy their company once the festivities were over.

"There you are," remarked Greg, suddenly standing beside her, and handing her an exotic-looking cocktail. "Are you enjoying yourself?"

"I certainly am," she responded, feeling unaccountably awkward in his company. "How about you?"

"It's been great – more Freya's sort of thing, to be honest – but we have some good friends. Just between you and me, I'm ready for a quiet evening. Maybe the three of us could watch a cheesy Christmas movie later?" he suggested, smiling from ear to ear, his aquamarine eyes twinkling with mischief.

"Sounds like a plan."

And as swiftly as he had appeared, he left her to chat with a couple standing on the other side of the pool. She couldn't stop herself from watching him; he had incredible charm and charisma. As soon as he joined them, she noticed how he brought energy and good humour to their conversation from the smiles, laughter and relaxed body language she observed from her vantage point. She had to admit that it would be good to end the day watching a movie and hoped Freya would agree.

In the following hour, just as the sun began to set, their guests began to drift away a few at a time, and by early evening, it was just the three of them left with some clearing away to do. It didn't take long to restore everything to normal, thanks to the dishwasher and a bit of teamwork.

"There we are. All done!" said Freya, looking happy and relaxed and every bit as perfect as she did several hours earlier, despite having been on the go all day. "How about a swim?"

"A swim?" Ella was taken aback by the suggestion, especially after all the alcohol they had consumed during the day. She glanced over at Greg who was lounging on the couch flicking through the TV channels.

"Come on. Just one more cocktail, but this time in the pool! How about a cranberry mimosa – my favourite. Greg, are you going to join us?"

"Not for me, darling. I'll make the drinks while you get changed."

It seemed the deal was done. The girls were to change into their swimwear whilst Greg got to relax and watch a movie. She knew what she would have preferred.

☐

She couldn't deny it – relaxing in the pool with her sister on Christmas Day evening was a perfect almost-end to the day. Freya seemed high on happiness, having deemed the party to be a great success. Ella felt as though she could stay here in Florida forever; it was the epitome of perfection, or so it seemed. Freya and Greg possessed everything and more – an amazing home in an idyllic location, no money worries, delightful friends, and most importantly, each other. Freya appeared to be living a life of leisure with her time spent between the beach club, gym and beauty salon. Greg appeared to be happily immersed in the world of art, with his own gallery and ambitions, proud to be able to provide the life of luxury they both evidently enjoyed.

"Thank you so much for such an amazing day, Freya. I don't know how you do it."

"What do you mean?"

"Well – everything! After hours of entertaining, you still look amazing. You're the perfect host and you keep a wonderful home."

"And husband!" she added with a laugh. "Don't forget about him."

How could she? Ella had purposely omitted to mention Greg; she had been trying to focus purely on her sister, even though her mind had been flitting constantly to him. "Of course, Greg too. You make the perfect couple."

"Do you honestly think so?" she asked somewhat unexpectedly. "I'll be frank with you, Ella, we spend very little time together. Just lately, I've felt there's a problem developing between us."

"What do you mean?" she added to fill the silence that followed.

"I realise it sounds incredibly ungrateful of me to complain, and I know I appear to have everything and more: a beautiful home and a life of leisure, plenty of money, and loads of friends. I'm very fortunate in so many ways. But, Ella, material things aren't everything, are they?"

"Very true. But you have your health and a happy marriage too, don't you?"

"Yes. I have good health and a husband who loves and provides royally for me. But at times I feel lonely. Greg is so busy with work, my family lives miles away and I miss you all."

"Oh Freya, I'm sorry to hear you feel this way. I understand how hard it must be. Being here with you now makes me realise how much I miss you too. And our parents – they are always away!" At this, they both laughed and the mood lightened as they went on to discuss the possibility of Facetiming them on their latest cruise, trying to work out the time difference between Florida and Australia and when best to contact them.

"I think I'm ready to go indoors now, if that's OK, Freya. It's been a long but fabulous day. Thank you so much."

"Me too. I'm starting to feel tired now. I might have a soak in the tub and have an early night. I think Greg's waiting to watch a film, but I might have to take a rain check on that plan."

"And me. I'll have a shower and read my book for a while if that's ok."

"I don't think Greg will be too happy with you if you do that! He's going to need someone to watch his favourite Christmas movie with."

"Really? I thought you said you don't spend enough time with him." Ella couldn't help herself. Why would Freya want to have an early night when they had a rare opportunity to spend time together? It would surely make more sense for Ella to have an early night and leave them alone for the remainder of the day.

"I know Christmas won't be complete for Greg until he's watched 'The Holiday' for the umpteenth time. And I know my Christmas will be ruined if I have to watch it one more time! You'll be doing me an enormous favour if you'll agree to sit through it with him."

It seemed the decision had been made for her. Ironically, it was her favourite festive film too. It would be the perfect end to the day.

☐

After a shower and changing into modest shorts and a baggy t-shirt, Ella wandered downstairs feeling in two minds about a movie night with Greg. She appreciated that it was Freya's wish, yet she couldn't help but feel it was odd, or did her reservation stem from the way Greg made her feel?

"There you are!" he exclaimed, pouring wine into the empty glass next to his full one, as she entered the expansive room, wondering where best to sit.

"So, this is your favourite movie?" she responded, settling down into the large leather armchair adjacent to Greg.

"Not exactly my all-time favourite, but it's become something of a longstanding tradition at Christmas. You'd be better sitting over here with your wine and a more comfortable angle to view the TV screen." He patted the space close to him.

Deciding to avoid making a fuss, Ella sat at the opposite end of the couch and pushed her wine glass along the table towards her.

"Are you telling me the truth about this being your favourite festive movie? Or is this some kind of joke? It seems an almighty coincidence that this movie is about two women on opposite sides of the Atlantic arranging a home exchange over Christmas!"

Greg laughed at the suggestion. "I agree it seems like a coincidence, but it's true! Anyway, Cameron Diaz lives in California, not Florida, so it's totally different," he continued, seemingly enjoying the situation.

"Hmm…" Ella was not convinced. She couldn't help but spot the similarity in appearance between Freya and the dazzlingly beautiful Ms Diaz; she certainly felt empathy for Kate Winslet in her role as the English girl whose ex-boyfriend had cheated on her and so decided to take a trip to the US to escape heartbreak over Christmas.

As the movie began, memories of Marcus cheating on her came flooding back, as well as overwhelming feelings of relief and gratitude that she had been able to escape the depressing weather back in the UK, not to mention the loneliness she was bound to feel at this time of the year. She wondered how Freya would cope with a house exchange. Maybe a couple of weeks in West Bay, looking at the angry winter waves smashing against the crumbling coastline, with nothing much to do other than walking around the lifeless, hibernating harbour was exactly what she needed; it would certainly give her the experience of a contrasting lifestyle and make her appreciate just how privileged she was.

Despite her reservations, Ella found she was having the perfect end to what had been an excellent day. During the movie, they managed to polish off the bottle of wine, making her feel a little light-headed but happy. Even though she believed Freya should have spent the evening with them, she had enjoyed chatting with Greg during the boring bits of the movie. It turned out that they had a great deal in common through their connections in the art world and a mutual interest in certain styles of painting. He was easy to talk to and she enjoyed his sense of humour.

"And they all lived happily ever after! Did you enjoy it?" asked Greg as the credits began to roll.

"Very much. A bit cheesy but it's got a good festive feel, hasn't it? Especially the ending. Anyway, time for me to go to bed," she replied, jumping up from the long, leather couch. "See you in the morning. Happy Christmas and thank you for a lovely day."

"Happy Christmas to you too, Ella," replied Greg, resting his arm on hers as she walked past him on her way to bed. "I'm so glad you've come to stay."

Chapter Seven

Delray Beach

"I'm planning to take Ella into the gallery today," announced Greg over breakfast.

"I see," responded Freya abruptly.

"Is that ok? I thought you'd appreciate a break. Maybe you wanted to go to the gym or something."

"Have you asked Ella?"

"Not yet, but she seems interested in that new artist we've just commissioned. I was telling her about him last night. He specialises in modern seascapes, that sort of thing."

Silence fell between them. Freya was lost for words. How many times had she tried to show an interest in the gallery? He made her feel inferior and almost invisible at times.

"I could come too," she ventured. "I'm not bothered about the gym today. I'd much rather spend the day with you and Ella."

"Really? After today, I'll be back at work and you two will have plenty of time together, just the two of you. Let's stick to my plan for today. We'll only be an hour or two; it will give you a break."

It seemed that his mind was made up and there was no point in arguing with him further. "Well, I'm off out then," she announced, feeling rattled. She jumped off the bar stool and left the kitchen without another word.

Minutes later, Ella appeared, looking refreshed and radiant after another good night's sleep. "Morning! Isn't Freya up yet?"

"Oh, she had to go out this morning. She was hoping I'd be able to entertain you. Is that ok?"

"Really?" Ella couldn't help but think this was a little unexpected, especially as Freya had explained how busy Greg always was. She had confided in her about how little time he took off work. "I'll be fine here if you need to get on with things. I can read my book or go for a walk."

"I was hoping you might want to see the gallery. I would value your opinion on those seascapes I was telling you about."

"Oh! Well, so long as you don't mind and can spare the time, I'd love to," responded Ella, somewhat taken aback by his offer.

"Sorted then. Half an hour?" he asked, placing his empty mug in the dishwasher before leaving her alone.

How odd, thought Ella. It seemed strange that Freya hadn't mentioned Greg's plan to take her to the gallery. However, she must have her reasons, and Ella was most certainly interested in seeing the gallery. Perhaps Freya had plans for them during the afternoon.

⌑

Located in the trendy Pineapple Grove Arts District in the heart of Delray Beach, Ella felt a sudden surge of excitement at viewing Greg's contemporary gallery, specialising in the modern seascapes that she had heard so much about, and featuring a small but careful selection of paintings and sculptures by established and emerging artists. Stepping inside, she was impressed by the complementary lighting and layout of the gallery – plain white walls with one or two anchor pieces accompanied by supporting works. Greg left Ella to wander around his collection, interested to hear her feedback, whilst he appeared to be sorting through a small pile of paperwork.

"It's beautiful, Greg. I love the lighting and placement." She was entranced by every piece gracing the walls of the gallery. "This one is spectacular," she remarked, stopping to stare at a large impressionistic seascape, admiring the loose, fluid brushstrokes with its focus on the overall mood of the scene.

"How about this one?" he asked, directing her to a surreal seascape with elements of the bizarre with dreamlike and fantastical elements.

"Stunning. I'd like to know more about it."

"Well, I'll have you know, I'd like to know more about your work, Ella. As you can see, I specialise in seascapes, hence my interest in your opinion as a seascape artist yourself. Maybe a commission from you could grace my walls?" he teased, or so she thought.

"Very funny. I cannot think of anything more unlikely than my paintings gracing the walls of a trendy gallery here in Florida!"

"I'm being serious, Ella. From the photos you've shown me of your work and the stories you've told me about the crumbling Dorset coastline, I would be extremely interested in discussing a possible commission. Doesn't it fascinate you how the ocean is destroying the coastlines on both sides of the Atlantic, albeit in different ways?"

"It fascinates me a great deal. That is precisely the reason why I've chosen to live on the coast and focus on painting dramatic seascapes. It's just that lately, I've been concentrating on small, commercial pieces to sell locally. It's been a case of trying to bring in extra income alongside my freelance graphic design work."

"Well, think about it. You can see the prices clients are willing to pay for quality artwork. We need to talk seriously about whether it's something you would like to embark upon; it would be highly remunerative. Talking to you these past few days has given me an idea for the gallery. I'm envisaging a large painting of your Dorset coastline, depicting perhaps one of those landfalls you told me about. I want to show the dramatic contrast between the coastal landscape here in Florida and your coastline on the other side of the ocean, both under threat through climate change."

Ella was lost for words. It would be a once-in-a-lifetime opportunity – assuming he was serious. She loved the prospect of investing all her time and effort into one important, potentially lucrative commission. "I would consider it if you're serious, but I already have plenty of questions and maybe a few reservations about such an undertaking."

"Of course. But we have time to discuss it further before you leave. Please think about it, Ella. I think it would be an amazing opportunity for both of us."

For the next half hour, Greg left Ella to wander around the gallery to allow her to spend time studying each painting in depth. He knew it would help her make up her mind. It would be an exciting prospect for each of them – something no other local gallery had caught onto – capturing the effects of climate change on the ocean and its coastline, with its warmer surface temperatures and increased storm activity.

Ella was deep in thought as they left the gallery and wandered back to the car in silence. Driving down Atlantic Avenue, she reflected on the artistic influences everywhere she looked: the endless patchwork of up-market shops and restaurants; colourful murals splashed across trendy buildings; quaint brick sidewalks and gaslight-style street lamps. It was a truly inspirational backdrop for an artist. As they reached Ocean Boulevard, Greg suddenly turned right into a parking lot rather than taking the left turn homeward.

"As we're in no rush, I thought we could manage a celebratory drink and maybe a spot of lunch before heading back," suggested Greg, implying a decision had already been made and the deal was done. "This is my favourite watering hole – Boston's on the Beach. I usually sit up at the bar, but I think you might prefer it in the Sandbar." He led her into the oceanfront tiki bar nestled at the side of the restaurant, with its sandy floor, shady palm trees, tropical background music and beachside breezes.

"Well, this is gorgeous. I love it. So, what exactly are we celebrating?" she teased.

"Our new business relationship of course. Your first large commission. Need I continue?" he asked, handing her the menu.

There was so much to choose from: craft beers, hand-muddled cocktails, tiki specials and frozen concoctions. "Just a beer for me please," she requested modestly.

Raising his eyebrows dismissively, he ordered for them. "Two Tropical Storm Daiquiris, please. Another minute or two for our food order, if that's ok. Thanks."

Ella couldn't help but smile at his choice of cocktail – typical of his sense of humour, she was beginning to observe. "That's an odd-sounding beer, I have to say," she teased, joining in with his playful mood.

"And to eat? I recommend the conch fritters or the mahi mahi."

"I like the sound of the tacos – served with lemon-cilantro slaw and smoky chipotle aioli," she announced, reading from the menu. "I do love a fish taco. Do you know, I can get one of those in a food kiosk just outside my front door back home?" It was true. All around the harbour in West Bay was a collection of shed-like structures selling the usual seaside delicacies – fish and chips, hot dogs, ice cream – but her favourite one, on the corner of the marina, specialised in seafood: fish chowder, tacos, tempura prawns and beer-battered goujons.

Relaxing in the Florida sunshine, sipping a cocktail, she wondered how she would be able to face going home in just over a week; she could easily stay here for longer. She questioned what she was rushing home to. Certainly not to a meaningful relationship, her comparatively modest apartment or the dismal weather back home. Maybe she could arrange a house exchange, like Kate Winslet in The Holiday! However, in reality, there would be no way Freya could ever adjust to the stark contrast of life back in the UK – the very thought of it made her smile, thinking of her wrapped up in a thick jumper rather than a floaty kaftan, swapping her beach club for a dip in the local municipal pool, and wandering up and down the vintage market stalls in Bridport rather than the vast, all-singing all-dancing Florida shopping malls. Nothing was a more unlikely prospect.

Chapter Eight

Delray Beach

New Year's Eve. From Ella's point of view, it had been a very relaxing, eventful week. Over the past few days, particularly since her visit to the gallery, her head had been filled with thoughts of Greg's proposal. Yet for some reason, she had decided not to discuss it with Freya, sensing it was best to keep it to herself for now. Greg had returned to work as planned, appearing only for dinner each evening. When Freya was out of earshot, he reminded Ella that his offer was serious and he would like to know her feelings about a possible commission before she returned to the UK. Meanwhile, Freya had not enquired what Ella thought about the gallery or mentioned Greg's name, despite her revelations earlier in the week. Instead, the two sisters had enjoyed each other's company each day by walking along the beach chatting about their childhood memories or mooching around the shops, stopping only for coffee or an occasional light lunch.

"I can't believe how quickly the time has gone," said Ella, taking a sip of chilled white wine. "It's been fantastic. Thank you so much for making me so welcome."

"It's been our pleasure. I only wish you could stay longer."

"Me too. I can't say I relish the prospect of the next few dreary months back in the UK. I always struggle with January and February."

"I can imagine. So, have you got plenty of work on back home?"

"Some regular graphic design work, but not much else. How about you? What are you planning for the new year?"

"Oh, Ella! That's the million-dollar question, it truly is. Returning to what we were talking about before, something needs to change. You can see how it is for yourself. Now Greg's back at work, I have hours every day to waste."

"To waste? What do you mean?"

"Yes. Much as I've enjoyed a life of luxury and leisure for the past five or six years, you can see that it's a pretty empty existence. I don't spend many meaningful hours in a typical day."

"I suppose so – but surely, it's a lovely life here in this gorgeous setting with such a supportive husband? Have you thought about working? To give you more fulfilment, I mean."

"I have, but Greg's not supportive in that sense. He likes things just the way they are."

"So, what's the answer, do you think?"

"Oh, I know exactly what the answer is! I want a baby, Ella. More than anything in the world."

"A baby?" Ella tried to disguise her surprise, as it was not what she was expecting to hear. She couldn't imagine how a baby would fit into her somewhat materialistic life of shopping, wining and dining. "But what about Greg? Is that what he wants too?"

"We've never discussed it. Can you believe it? I don't know why. I think it's because he's so wrapped up in the gallery and has got into a pattern of coming home late each day. There never seems to be the right time or enough time to talk about something so important. And he doesn't appreciate all the empty hours I struggle to fill."

"You have to talk to him, Freya."

"I know. I will."

Before visiting Freya, Ella had half-expected news of a baby, knowing that Greg was doing well with the gallery and Freya wasn't working. But having now seen their Floridian lifestyle first-hand, she had begun to wonder how a baby would fit in. When they were younger, it was clear that Freya was more maternal than Ella. She had always shown more interest in babies and spoken of her dream to become a mother one day, whereas Ella hadn't felt the same desire herself and put it down to her own experience of family life. Although she'd had a happy childhood in many ways, it had been different from Freya's, and a little more complex. Her mother had separated from her father when she was very young and all she remembered of him, was visiting him every so often with her grandparents. The visits stopped abruptly when she was about eight or nine, but she never knew why. There was so much about her father that she didn't know. What she remembered most about her childhood was her stepfather, who she grew to love very quickly. He had made her mother so happy and treated Ella as his own, but it wasn't long before they added to the family with a sister for Ella – baby Freya. Much as she loved Freya, she had always had the feeling that she was their favourite. Ella was, she perceived, the product of a failed relationship and therefore a reminder of the past.

"What better way to start the new year than to have that conversation as soon as possible?" suggested Ella, pulling herself away from her reflections on the past.

"You're right. The sooner the better. By the way, we've all been invited round to Jacqui's for drinks to see the New Year in, and then I think it's time to make some resolutions."

"That's a great idea, but maybe just the two of you should go out tonight. I'll stay behind. You don't need me tagging along, and I'm not fussed about seeing in the New Year."

"Absolutely not! I won't hear of it. I want you there and so does Jacqui. Let's make it a night to remember."

Ella remained silent, mulling over the prospect of another evening in Greg's company.

[ ]

"Ella! You look stunning," cried Freya, as she made her way somewhat slowly down the spiral staircase showcasing an emerald green satin dress, purchased specifically for a special occasion such as this one. They were waiting for her in the hallway. There was no denying it, the sun had brought colour and life to her pale, tired skin, and the dress complemented her shiny brunette hair and enhanced her enviable figure. She had never felt better.

"You look amazing too, as always," responded Ella, keen to return the compliment. Freya always looked perfect and tonight was no exception. Her silky blonde hair fell in loose waves over her bare shoulders, skimming the top of the black velvet bodice of her maxi dress. Her eyes glanced briefly over to Greg, who was opening the front door in readiness for their departure. Even though she knew it was totally inappropriate, she was taken aback by the way he made her feel. He was everything and more. Only two more days, she reminded herself, and she would be back in the UK and thankfully, he would be a mere memory. She was determined to distance herself from him tonight and enjoy the company of others.

☐

"Ella? Are you trying to avoid me or something?" Greg suddenly appeared on the rattan bench beside her. She had tried to find a quiet spot around the pool, away from the crowds, having begun to feel overwhelmed by the pressure of making small talk with strangers for the last few hours. Champagne had been flowing all night and her head felt fuzzy; she needed fresh air and a break from conversation.

"Hi. No, of course not. I just needed a bit of a break for a moment or two," she replied honestly. "Is it nearly midnight?"

"Five minutes to go," he responded glancing at his watch.

"You'd better find Freya then."

"Why? To be honest, I haven't seen her all night."

"You need to be with your wife at midnight, Greg," she responded, stating the obvious.

Laughing dismissively, he placed his hand on hers. "I've really enjoyed getting to know you, Freya. I do hope we can do business together."

Snatching away her hand, Ella leapt up, startled by the fact that she was feeling a forbidden attraction towards her brother-in-law. "Come on, let's find Freya," she suggested, desperate to shake off the frisson of temptation she was experiencing.

Standing beside her, in the dark corner of the dimly lit poolside, he grabbed her hand again and kissed her playfully on her burning cheek. "Let's not," he suggested.

"Greg…"

"C'mon. Let's head down to the beach. It's just down those few steps behind us. No one will miss us."

"No, Greg. That is not a good idea. And you know it isn't."

"I think it is. I just want to sit on the sand with you and clear my head. I want to forget about everything. To be honest with you, having you stay these past couple of weeks has given me food for thought."

"What do you mean?" she ventured, instantly regretting asking and dreading his response.

"You've made me acknowledge how Freya and I have begun to drift apart these past few months." It was exactly what she had feared. Ella couldn't help but notice during her stay how dismissive they were of each other; they seemed to be existing in parallel universes with very little common ground between them.

Knowing how Freya was feeling, Ella understood the importance of her response. "Maybe you just need to spend more time with Freya. Perhaps she could help you out at the gallery in some way?" Sensing his aversion to this suggestion, she tried again. "Or maybe you two need a holiday. A total break away from everything so you can spend some quality time together."

"I don't think that's the answer. Freya's changed. Maybe it's my fault."

"Talk to her, Greg. Make it your New Year's resolution. Please."

At that very moment, Jacqui came out of the house to gather everyone inside to toast in the New Year in time for the countdown to midnight. "Come on inside everyone! One minute to go."

In silence, the two of them followed instructions and returned to the party, Ella's head filled with questions, doubts and confusion.

"There you are!" cried Freya from across the large room, waving her arms wildly. It was obvious that she had had one or two glasses too many from the way she staggered towards them. "I haven't seen you all night!" Leaning heavily against them, she draped her arms around both of them for support.

"Are you OK?" asked Ella, feeling a little concerned to see her under the influence of alcohol.

"I'm fine. What do you mean?" she responded, her eyes blurry and unfocused and her speech a little slurred.

"Come on. Let's see in the New Year and head home," interrupted Greg, seemingly embarrassed by Freya's lack of composure.

Crystal champagne glasses were handed around in time for the toast at the stroke of midnight, then raised and clinked enthusiastically during

Jacqui's toast with well-wishes for health, happiness and success for the coming year. Festive fireworks along the beach lit up the sky as they exchanged traditional kisses of good luck and affection, bidding farewell to the old year and welcoming in the new one with optimism and joy. Ella was able to avoid Greg, who was thankfully preoccupied with Freya.

Ten minutes after midnight, the three of them said their goodbyes and made their way home – just two houses away on Ocean Boulevard. It was an uncomfortable walk home, with Freya requiring support to stay upright on her heels; Greg seemingly embarrassed and annoyed with Freya, and Ella wishing she could disappear into thin air.

As soon as they arrived home, Greg escorted Freya to bed and returned to the kitchen five minutes later, where Ella was pouring herself a glass of iced water from the cooler.

"Happy New Year," he remarked somewhat sarcastically, his voice flat with disappointment.

Ella knew not to respond. It felt as though the night had ended on a bad note; it had not gone as planned for any of them. She wished she had gone straight up to bed to avoid any further contact with Greg. Now, it was too late, and without asking, he poured two glasses of wine and led her out onto the sundeck.

"Now you know why I wanted to escape onto the beach. I feel trapped, Ella."

"You just need to talk to each other," she offered, trying desperately to appease him.

"I just need to have a break. Walk onto the beach with me, Ella. Please. I just want to breathe in the sea air and forget everything."

She knew her decision was wrong. She knew she should persuade Greg to stay at home and convince him that Freya needed him. She could explain to him how Freya was feeling. Yet, she stood up and followed him as they took a few fateful footsteps onto the soft, white sands of the midnight beach.

☐

The shimmering reflection of moonlight shone like a torch on the ocean, illuminating the shore as they wandered barefoot along the beach, the deep indigo skies glistening with twinkling stars. The rhythmic pulse of the waves matched her heartbeat and the light breeze rustled the fronds of the palm trees – the first and only sounds of the New Year.

"Let's stop here," suggested Greg, as they approached some dunes, colonised by sea oats, sand spurs and beach morning glory, creating a nest-like hideaway on the expanse of the beach. They had walked for a while and it seemed natural to stop and take in the magical atmosphere created by the sights and sounds of the shoreline.

Sitting side by side in silence, Ella was filled with mixed emotions so complex that she felt she must be on a film set or in a dream. This moment was so far removed from anything she had ever experienced – it was utterly perfect. The whispering breeze and shimmering waves; the horizon merging seamlessly with the ocean, soft powdery sand between her toes. And then the man sitting beside her...

"Thank you, Ella. This is exactly what I needed."

"Don't thank me. Let's just take in the air and then walk home."

Silence fell between them again and neither made a move. Then suddenly and unexpectedly, Ella felt his hand on hers. She snatched it away and turned to him in surprise. Their eyes met and melted into each other. "I'm sorry," he uttered. "It's just that I'm going to miss you."

"You won't, Greg. You've got things to sort out here. That should be your priority."

"I will miss you, Ella," he repeated, leaning towards her as though to kiss her.

Looking back, there was no excuse or explanation for what happened between them. She knew it was so wrong, yet she simply couldn't help herself. In hesitant, slow motion, their hungry lips met and, in that instant, she was lost in him. Why had she allowed it to happen? A question she would ask herself over and over again. Surely it was the influence of alcohol? She'd been drinking all night and seemed to have lost all inhibitions. Or was it the potency of the magical atmosphere, a moment of escapism for them both, or had she dreamt it? No. It had happened, of that, she was in no doubt. She had not resisted one bit – more than that, she felt she had encouraged his advances - and much as it was the most wonderful experience of her life, it was also the very worst. His hands were everywhere as he gently eased her down into the dunes. Her body responded like never before as he pushed up the satin fabric of her dress roughly and took her in his arms. Responding with every fibre of her being, she tugged at his clothing as they rolled over in the dunes. Her mind emptied of any logical thought as she succumbed to his overwhelming physical presence.

Afterwards, lying beside each other, their bodies no longer touching, they looked into the starlit skies in silence as their racing heartbeats finally settled. What had they done? Immediately, she knew she could never forgive herself for these selfish moments of madness. Was it her fault? Had she led him on? Her mind was racing with shame and guilt. And what of Greg? What must he be thinking? He had put so much at risk. She would not wait to find out. Rearranging her ruined dress, she staggered to her feet and stumbled back along the beach without a word, leaving Greg alone to his musings.

Chapter Nine

Delray Beach

New Year's Day. Freya tried to open her bleary eyes, yet everything prevented her from doing so. The bright sunlight was shooting parallel tracks across the room through the slight gaps in the shutters, and her head was pounding like a drum. She closed them again. Sliding her arm across the bed, she discovered that Greg was not beside her. It was probably mid-morning and he was most likely spending his rare day off around the pool, hopefully entertaining Ella. Her throbbing head told her she shouldn't have drunk so much last night; she could hardly remember a thing past midnight, and certainly not how she had got home. Reflecting on the evening, she realised she couldn't remember spending much time with Greg or Ella – she was too busy having fun with her girlfriends from the beach club and had hardly laid eyes on them all night. It suddenly dawned on her that she had promised to talk to Greg about what was on her mind. Today was the day for that before he returned to work. New Year's Day. New beginnings.

Ella had tossed and turned all night; she hadn't slept a wink, going over and over the events of last night in her head. She contemplated packing her case and leaving without a word, but that would only cause Freya concern and confusion. Yet how could she face her? She was wracked with guilt and remorse. And what about Greg? She must never lay eyes on him again.

Unable to deal with the consequences of his actions, Greg had spent a few hours on the couch on his return from the beach in the early hours of the morning and then left early for the gallery. He simply couldn't face anyone and wondered whether he ever would after last night. Going over and over what had happened led him to wonder how and why it had happened. He loved Freya with all his heart and yet he had cheated on her in the most despicable way. Yes, Ella had captivated him during her short visit with her elfin appearance, gentle charm and modesty, and he had thoroughly enjoyed her company and conversation, her shared interest in and knowledge of the world of art. But nothing excused his shameful behaviour. He decided to opt for the coward's way out for a day or two and lie low until Ella returned to the UK.

By midday, Ella realised she had no choice but to make an appearance, dreading what she might face; she couldn't stay in her room until her planned departure date two days later. Tentatively making her way down the spiral staircase into the open-plan kitchen diner, it became apparent that no one else was around. She had spent the past hour researching the possibility of making her own way back to Miami on the train from Delray Beach. She could go today, making up some reason for departing early – meeting up with a friend or spending some time perusing the galleries in Downtown Miami. The train journey was regular and direct, taking only one and a half hours – that would be her best option. The idea of Greg returning her to the airport was unthinkable. She had also begun to pack and tidy her room; she had to go home. The sooner the better.

Deep in thought, she stood at the open bi-fold doors, taking in the breathtaking beauty of the ocean for possibly the last time. She would miss seeing it from this side of the coast with its turquoise waters glistening in the bright sun by day and the moonlight by night. She would have to make do with angry, grey waves and the blurred horizon on the other side of the ocean for the next few months until the return of Spring.

"Ella! Happy New Year to you." From behind her, Freya's cheery voice took Ella by surprise as she entered the kitchen from the lounge. "How are you this morning?"

"Oh hi. Happy New Year to you too," responded Ella somewhat meekly. "I'm fine thanks. How about you?"

"A little jaded, I have to say. Can't say I remember a great deal about last night!" she laughed, sitting down on a bar stool next to Ella at the kitchen island. "I think it was a good night from the headache I woke up with this morning."

Keen to change the subject, Ella decided to broach the subject of heading home earlier than planned. "I'm thinking about heading back today, Freya. Whilst I'm over here, I'd love to spend some time in the art districts of Miami. I've already looked into getting the train from Delray in an hour or two."

Taken aback by Ella's sudden change of plan, Freya launched into a long list of reasons why she should stay. "Don't go. It looks as though Greg can't keep away from the gallery – even on New Year's Day – so I'm on my own as usual and I'd love to spend the last couple of days just you and me – a bit of quality time before you go back. It could be ages till we see each other again. Please reconsider."

It was clear that Greg had decided to keep a distance until she left, but he would have to return home to Freya in the evenings – something she simply could not face. "I am keen to go to Miami, Freya. There are a couple of exhibitions I'd love to see."

"How about I come with you?" suggested Freya.

"Please don't worry. I'm happy to go alone. I know it sounds selfish, but I don't think I'd be much company. I enjoy studying art on my own."

"It sounds as though your mind's made up. That's a pity. I've loved spending time with you. Could we at least have lunch together before you go?"

"Of course we can." It was the least she could do. "I'll get the train late afternoon."

"But you won't get to say goodbye to Greg. He won't be back until dinner – about seven. Are you sure you can't leave it until the morning?"

"I think my mind's made up. I've already booked a room for tonight. Let's go out for lunch – my treat to say thank you. Somewhere special. You choose."

|.|

She found herself back in the Sand Bar at Boston's on the Beach. Out of all the places Freya could have chosen, this was the one place Ella had no desire to return to. It was the very place where it all began – that first flickering of attraction between her and Greg. She wasn't sure that

Greg had told Freya that he had taken her for lunch that day, so she would have to tread carefully.

"What do you think?" asked Freya. "I wanted to share our favourite bar with you before you went home. Isn't this a great spot?" Clearly, she was unaware that Ella had been here before.

"It's perfect, Freya." She wasn't in the mood for talking or eating for that matter. Yet maybe a drink would help her to relax and see out the next hour or two. "Do you fancy a cocktail?"

"Absolutely. I think you might like Sex on the Beach."

"Sounds good." Ella felt herself flush at the memories of last night. The irony.

"Then to eat? Calamari, conch fritters, wings, tacos?"

"Maybe the calamari," Ella offered, feeling no appetite whatsoever.

Whilst waiting for their drinks to arrive, the conversation between them centred on Ella's visit and when they might see each other again. They discussed the possibility of Freya and Greg visiting the UK and having a family get-together if they could pin down their parents in between their travels. Ella had no choice but to go along with every suggestion that was made, knowing deep down that she would never want to lay eyes on Greg in the future, and feeling certain that if Freya knew what had happened, she would never want to see her ever again. Everything was ruined.

"So, tonight's the night," said Freya suddenly changing the subject. "If it's going to be just the two of us for dinner, then I'm going to talk to Greg about you-know-what tonight!" She was clearly very excited by the prospect. Ella's heart sank even further, wondering how Greg would react to the news that Freya wanted to start a family, amid the feelings of guilt that he must surely be experiencing.

"I hope it goes well," she responded somewhat blandly, her mind full of fears of how the news might be received by her cheating husband.

Chapter Ten

Delray Beach

Freya and Ella sat together in silence on the uncomfortable wooden bench at the Tri-Rail Station, both subdued and saddened by Ella's visit having come to an end. A dusty wind whistled down the shadowy tracks creating a stark contrast to the calm winter warmth outside the station.

"Thank you again, Freya. I've had a wonderful time. I'm sorry to be going home, leaving this gorgeous weather behind."

"I've loved every minute of your visit. We mustn't leave it so long next time. Maybe we will make that trip to the UK to see where you're living now. And Greg tells me he's commissioned you to do a painting for the gallery, so we'll need to keep in touch a bit more."

Ella was somewhat taken aback to hear that Freya knew about the commission. Surely, after what had happened, it was no longer on the cards. "Yes. We must keep in touch. Although I'm not sure how realistic the chances are of me finding time for a large commission what with my freelance work. We'll have to see."

Returning to silence, Ella willed the train to arrive as quickly as possible. Within minutes, her wish was granted. They kissed and embraced before Ella stepped onto the train, her heart heavy and her eyes filled with tears.

[]

"Sorry I'm late, darling," said Greg, as he entered the kitchen where Freya was waiting for him, the table laid for what appeared to be a celebratory dinner. "I'm so glad I went into the gallery today. I had some important matters to deal with, and I thought you wouldn't mind a quiet day with your sister being as it's coming to the end of her stay." As he spoke, he noted the table was set for two rather than three.

"She's already gone – she went this afternoon. It's all a bit odd. She suddenly announced she wanted a few days in Miami on her own to look at the galleries. I wonder what brought that on?"

"Really? That's rather sudden. Had she told you about her plans?" Learning that she had gone filled him with a complex mix of emotions – sad that he had not had the chance to say goodbye, sorry that he would not see her again, and relief that he wouldn't have to face her after what happened on New Year's Eve. Overall, maybe it was for the best. It was something he needed to put behind him and keep firmly in the past.

"No. It was unexpected. She seemed rather quiet today, to be honest. Maybe she was sorry to be going home – back to the gloomy British weather."

"Maybe..." He felt it best to leave it at that and quickly change the subject.

☐

As the evening wore on, Greg began to feel much more relaxed than he had earlier in the day. In all honesty, he had been dreading coming home to both of them, wondering how he would deal with the difficult situation he found himself in. Yet everything seemed fine. Ella had gone home, much to both his relief and disappointment, and Freya appeared to be in a particularly buoyant mood, totally unaware of his deceit. In fact, she was unusually happy. Just lately, he had felt worn down by her constant complaints about her boring life, but this evening he couldn't help but feel that something was brewing – hopefully something good.

"Let's go and relax by the pool, Greg," she suggested, taking him by the hand. *What is going on?* he wondered, feeling somewhat suspicious of her uncharacteristically cheerful mood. "There's something I want to talk to you about."

Sitting side by side on the edge of the pool, Freya turned to kiss him gently. "I love you so much Greg, but I know I've been a bit difficult to live with just lately. Over the past couple of weeks, having spent time with my sister, I've come to a decision. There's something I want to ask you." She seemed nervous and hesitant as she delivered the speech she had clearly rehearsed beforehand.

Greg's mind began to spin. He couldn't imagine what she was about to say. Did she want to move back to the UK? He hoped not; he couldn't imagine selling the gallery. Did she want to visit her parents or invite them over to stay? It was clearly something to do with family, triggered by spending time with her sister.

"I've realised what's missing. I want a baby, Greg."

Before responding, he attempted to process what he had heard. *A baby?* Despite having been together for several years, it was a topic they had never discussed, although he didn't know why. A baby would fulfil Freya in all the ways that she desired; he knew she would make a wonderful mother. A baby would mean that they stayed in the States. A baby would cement their relationship. A baby could be the answer to everything.

"Freya, this is wonderful news. It's exactly what I want too. Why have we waited so long?" He took her into his arms, believing in that moment that everything would be all right after all.

Thrilled and relieved by his positive reaction, Freya beamed, her heart full of love for her husband. What he didn't know couldn't hurt him, she believed: she had already been trying for a baby for over a year.

Chapter Eleven

West Bay

As it turned out, Ella had been able to fly home a day earlier than planned. She was keen to get back. During the nine-hour overnight flight, she had been unable to sleep, her mind too troubled by how her visit had ended. She was devastated by what had happened – it had changed everything. Whilst it had been wonderful to stay with Freya and Greg in their beautiful home and spend quality time with her sister, she knew that it could never happen again. She had loved the vibrancy of Delray Beach with its trendy beach bars, independent shops and art galleries. She would miss the warmth of the glorious Florida sun and the luxury of daily pool and sea bathing. What did she have to look forward to for the next few winter months back in the UK? At least three more months of cold, dreary weather. Thick jumpers, thermal vests and woollen scarves. Dry skin and chapped lips. Expensive central heating and warm baths. She would have to immerse herself in her work and try to move on somehow. But what about Freya? She wouldn't be able to distance herself from her sister forever. As for Greg... she had no choice but to block him out of her mind completely; in the grand scheme of things, he wasn't important. Too bad about the commission that had been so tempting. She would have to pick up local projects instead.

As the plane touched down, she felt an overwhelming sense of relief at being back on home territory, almost five thousand miles away from the turn of events that would haunt her forever - on the other side of the ocean.

Delray Beach

Sitting on the edge of the pool, Freya reflected on the success of her sister's visit. It had been great to reconnect with her properly after a couple of years apart. Even though they were very different in so many ways, she loved her dearly and was particularly pleased with how well

Greg had got on with her too. Before Ella arrived, Freya had expected Greg would do anything to avoid spending time with her. Yet he had been generous with his time and had taken several days off over the festive season joining in, helping out and getting to know her better. He'd collected Ella from the airport, taken her to the gallery and spent quality time with her at their Christmas and New Year gatherings. Freya couldn't have asked for more.

    She also had Ella to thank for what was hopefully to be a new chapter with Greg. Opening up to Ella had given Freya the chance to reflect on her marriage and the confidence to broach the subject that had been on her mind for many months. She wondered why she hadn't been able to talk to him about starting a family before now. Maybe because he was so engrossed in the gallery. He had been unsympathetic when she had tried to broach the topic of her unfulfilling existence, leaving her feeling ungrateful and pushing them both further apart at times. She wished she had been open and honest with him from the start - over a year ago - when she had taken it upon herself to stop taking the pill. Deceit and deception were not the best ways to embark upon starting a family, yet she had not been able to find the right moment to talk to him properly. Now she knew for sure that Greg wanted a baby too, she wanted it to happen straight away, and wondered why it was taking such a long time to get pregnant. Was twelve months a long time? She would need to research it. To be honest, their sex life had dwindled dramatically over the past few months due to their recent bickering and Greg spending more and more time at the gallery, leaving him tired at the end of the day. Surely there was nothing to worry about.

    Wandering into the kitchen, she decided there was no time like the present. She would research the facts now that she knew she no longer had to be secretive about her desire for a baby. Sitting at the kitchen island, she logged onto the internet, searching *How long does it take to get pregnant?* The results came flooding in, with the word *Infertility* catching her eye. She would read on before panicking:

90% of couples will conceive within 12 to 18 months of trying.

Infertility is defined as the inability to conceive after 12 months of frequent, unprotected intercourse, if under the age of 35. Evaluation of infertility is usually not done until a full year has gone by. This is because most people will conceive by then.

This was not reassuring information. She was only 27 and had been having unprotected sex for a full year. What was the definition of *frequent* though? Sometimes a week or more went by when Greg was particularly busy at work and fell asleep the moment his head hit the pillow. There was no need to worry just yet, she thought. She read on:

Infertility results from female factors about one-third of the time and both female and male factors about one-third of the time. The cause is either unknown or a combination of male and female factors in the remaining cases.
Female infertility causes can be difficult to diagnose. There are many treatments, depending on the infertility cause. Many infertile couples will go on to conceive a child without treatment.

So, if a problem existed, it could be due to either of them and surely it would be possible to fix whatever it was. The first hurdle was letting Greg know that she hadn't been taking any contraception for a year; it was not going to be an easy conversation. Why hadn't she been open and honest with him from the outset? She would leave it for a few more months, hoping that a revived sex life might result in a pregnancy. Then he need never know that she had been keeping a secret from him.

Chapter Twelve

West Bay

The weather was beginning to improve at last; spring was finally on its way. Opening the curtains, she looked optimistically across the bay. The days were beginning to lengthen and become a little warmer, and the loss of heat from the Atlantic over the winter months had led to less heat and moisture being transferred to the atmosphere. The sun, high in the sky, was enabling temperatures to rise during the day but stay cool at night due to the moderating effect of the ocean temperature. The skies held the promise of a lovely day.

So why did she feel so out of sorts? Just lately, she felt constantly weary and couldn't focus on anything for long, finding herself falling asleep at every opportunity. Feeling weak and dizzy, and suffering from heartburn, her appetite had vanished; she could only face dry toast in the morning and plain suppers in the evening. As for alcohol, the very thought of it made her feel ill. She must be coming down with something, although she hadn't felt particularly well for the past couple of months since she returned from Florida. Perhaps it was something she'd picked up over there or maybe it was some new strain of Covid. Whatever it was, she wished she could get over it and return to her normal self.

Since her return from Florida, she had spoken to Freya a few times via Messenger. She seemed happy enough as they chatted amiably about everyday trivia – what they were watching on Netflix, the weather and Freya's recent purchases from her favourite boutique on the Avenue. To her relief, they discussed nothing of any real significance: news about Greg and pregnancy plans were clearly off-limits. She didn't mention to Freya that she was feeling out of sorts and tried her best to sound cheerful and positive about work and the improving British weather. As they chatted about their parents, who were currently on a three-month holiday in the Canary Islands, staying in their friends' villa, they wondered whether there would ever be a chance for a family get-together. Thankfully, they were in good health and certainly living life to the full in retirement.

Today, on this beautiful spring morning, she decided to take herself off for the day. Somewhere to improve her mood and hopefully make her feel a little better. She decided to take a trip to Abbotsbury Subtropical Gardens – one of her favourite places on the Jurassic Coast – a garden with its own micro-climate in a sheltered woodland valley with its special plant collection of rare and choice varieties from all over the world which had been growing in harmony in its tranquil setting since the late 18th century. She loved the mixture of formal and informal flowers; the viewpoint of the Jurassic Coast from the top of Magnolia Walk; the Burma rope bridge and the lily ponds. On her way back, she would stop to take in the breathtaking views of the Fleet Lagoon at Chesil Beach.

Yet as she began to make the short car journey into the picturesque village of Abbotsbury, she began to feel nauseous and lightheaded. She had hoped to be feeling better now the weather was improving, but instead, she felt worse. Perhaps it was time to visit the doctor. Once there, she hoped that the fresh spring air would make her feel better. She was looking forward to seeing the signs of new beginnings – fresh white snowdrops emerging from the depths of winter; yellow primroses popping up along the woodland walk; clumps of gelatinous frogspawn just below the surface of the ponds, holding the promise of birth and renewal. As she pulled into the carpark, she was suddenly struck by a shocking realisation – it had been a while since her last period. Why hadn't it occurred to her before now? Probably because they were mostly light and irregular – they always had been. But surely it was virtually impossible to fall pregnant after just one dreadful mistake? For some reason, it hadn't even occurred to her at the time that she had put herself at risk; she had been so caught up in the guilt and sense of urgency to get herself back home.

As she wandered through the magnificent camellia groves, she tried hard to focus on their bountiful blooms in shades ranging from snow white to pastel pink and blood red, grouped together with their dark, dense foliage. Yet her mind was wandering too, contemplating whether her worst nightmare was about to become a reality and if so, what she would do about it. Strolling onto the West Lawn, she made her way to her favourite swing seat in the arboretum – a plantation of mixed pines and deciduous trees – where she would try to make sense of her predicament. Firstly, she must establish the facts; she would stop at the chemist on the way home. Then she would have to make plans, serious life-changing plans, for how on earth she was going to deal with the unthinkable.

Delray Beach

Early March and the onset of probably the most pleasant season in Florida, with its cooler nights, warm days and lower humidity, Freya was feeling more hopeful about life in general. Her marriage had taken a positive turn, with Greg being much more attentive towards her. Whilst the gallery was still taking up several hours a day, he was now coming home much earlier, involving her more than ever before in what was happening at work, and making a greater effort to spend quality time with her each evening. Consequently, they were enjoying each other's company more than they had for a good while, and their sex life had certainly stepped up a notch or two, back to how it was in the beginning. Freya felt sure it would only be a matter of a month or two before she would finally become pregnant – she had decided to conceal from Greg the fact that she had not taken any contraception for over a year. She knew he would not react well to her deception, plus she didn't want to worry him unduly.

To improve her chances of becoming pregnant, Freya had decided to modify her usual routines – fewer boozy lunches with the girls at the beach club, more frequent exercise classes at the gym and a diet of nutrient-rich health food aimed at boosting fertility. Today she was in the mood for a day of quiet contemplation in her favourite place – the Morikami Japanese Gardens – located west of Delray Beach in Palm Beach County, with its six distinct gardens, museum and tea house. How she loved wandering around the lakes surrounded by cascading waterfalls, rock formations and pagodas, inviting her to stop and ponder on life. It was claimed that these peaceful gardens were designed to speak to its visitors of timeless truth and rhythms, offering therapeutic insights, hope and inspiration, and enduring qualities of health and wholeness, integrity and renewal. It was exactly what she needed.

As she wandered into the Modern Romantic Garden – her favourite of the six – she was drawn to the long-legged kotoji lanterns, symbols of friendship and drawing together the sea to the shore, leading her to think about Ella and how close she had felt to her during her visit. Now though, they seemed miles apart once again, not only separated geographically by an ocean, but by the lack of communication between them; she had hardly heard from her since her visit. Strolling on dreamily through the masses of irises and camellias, the lighter, more open feeling of this garden reflected in its freer choice of planting led Freya to reflect on the love she felt for her sister; she was determined to build their relationship rather than allow them to drift apart all over again.

Chapter Thirteen

West Bay

She had known for a fortnight now, recalling the dreaded moment the two red lines appeared on the strip. She had sat motionless for what must have been several hours, looking out to sea, feeling completely numb. Nothing made any sense to her. She couldn't even believe it was possible to be pregnant after just one reckless, meaningless encounter – surely the chances of that happening were incredibly slim? But the solid lines told her there was no mistake; she was expecting a baby, and doing the maths, it would be due at the end of September. In the meantime, she would have to deal with not only carrying a new life but the dreadful guilt of betraying her sister. She had no idea what to do. Should she keep it a secret from her altogether, hoping that she could lie her way out of the situation when she had to, pretending the father was someone else? That surely wasn't the answer in the long term. Yet how could she explain why she hadn't told them she was pregnant? Lying about the baby's father was one thing, but there was no way she could pretend the next however many months were not happening to her. She would end up having to tell Freya something but was terrified of implicating Greg as the father, especially knowing that she was trying for a baby herself. She hoped and prayed that the next time they spoke, Freya would have the joyful news that she was pregnant too. Yet there was absolutely no doubt about it that if Freya knew what she and Greg had done on New Year's Eve, their relationship would end forever.

On a positive note, if that were even possible, Ella was beginning to feel a little better health-wise. The pregnancy symptoms of the first trimester had passed over, and other than a slightly rounded abdomen and heavier, tender breasts, she was feeling much more like her former self, with more energy and an improved appetite. She was able to put her mind to her freelance work with renewed focus and relished the fact that it took her mind off her predicament for the hours she was immersed in it. However, she was acutely aware that she hadn't spoken to Freya for a few weeks, even though it wasn't particularly unusual for them to have periods of no contact. Yet there was an expectation that they would keep up with each other's news at least once a month, often through Messenger. Perhaps she would message her later on – just a quick catch-up, nothing more.

Delray Beach

Another month filled with bitter disappointment. Fifteen months without success, or three as far as Greg was aware. Surely there was no option now; she would have to seek medical advice. Yet how should she deal with her deception? Looking across the ocean for the answers, she realised she had two stark choices: either to come clean and tell Greg that she had not been taking contraception for all these months and admit that she had deceived him, or pretend that she was disappointed that three months had gone by and tell him she was going to have a health check to increase her chances of getting pregnant. The latter seemed the more favourable option. Things had been much improved between them just lately – better than ever for some reason - and she didn't want to jeopardise or jinx anything. A few tests should put her mind at rest. She would make an appointment and decide later what to tell Greg, depending on the outcome.

☐

Scrolling through the lists of local fertility clinics, Freya's heart began to race with the sheer panic that there might be something wrong with her after all. Troubling medical words jumped off the screen - fertility, sterility, IVF, impotence, PCOS, egg donation, low sperm count – surely none of them were relevant to her – or Greg for that matter. She was young and healthy, fit and slim, a non-smoker, and only a moderate drinker. As for Greg, he was the picture of health too, and full of energy - especially in the bedroom. For the next hour, she read and tried to take in as much information as possible about all the possible causes of infertility in men and women. She'd never given it much thought in the past, but there appeared to be all sorts of reasons why problems might exist. She wondered how far she would be able to investigate matters on her own, without involving Greg, as according to her research, there was an equal chance of their lack of success being down to Greg. Under normal circumstances, they should be facing the situation as a couple; it wasn't something she could pursue fully without Greg's involvement. Plus, there was the matter of medical insurance. How would she be able to arrange appointments without Greg knowing, when the policy was jointly held? After much agonising and searching the Internet for the answers to some of her questions, she decided to arrange an initial fertility consultation with a local clinic. Apparently, she would need to download a questionnaire to prepare for the meeting – all about her physical and sexual history. Reading through the questions made her feel overwhelmingly anxious – there were so many possible causes of infertility, some relating to a range of medical conditions, none of which she felt were relevant to her. Yet something was evidently wrong somewhere along the line.

Suddenly, a notification popped up in the corner of the laptop: a message from Ella. About time, she couldn't help but think. It must have been weeks since she last heard from her.

Hi Freya. Hope all is well with you. Sorry I haven't been in touch for a few weeks. Work has been really busy lately and I've been feeling a bit under the weather. Thankfully, I seem to be over the worst and the weather has really picked up. Spring has sprung! What's it like in Florida? Lots of love, always. Ella xx

Brief and to the point. It could have been a message from an old aunt or some distant relative. No personal touch asking how things were between her and Greg, which would surely have been an obvious follow-up to all the conversations they had had when she was staying with them. Perhaps that was something they would be able to talk about some time, over Facetime or Zoom rather than via messages, although that was not something that happened regularly between them. And what about the commission she was supposed to be working on for Greg? Maybe she had messaged him separately about that. She must ask him later. For now, she would compose a suitably neutral message in return; she had no plans to mention her own health concerns.

Hi! Good to hear from you. It's been a while! Good weather here at the moment – probably the best time of year. Not too hot or humid. Sorry to hear you haven't been feeling too well lately, but glad to hear you're on the mend and that work is keeping you busy. Life is much the same for me over here – Greg's busy at the gallery and I seem to find plenty to keep me occupied. Let's try to Facetime soon. Maybe at the weekend? Lots of love, Freya. xx

Send. Her equally bland response felt like a box-ticking exercise, but to be honest, her mind was elsewhere today. She was keen to start preparing for her consultation early next week by completing the questionnaire and doing more research, hopefully to reassure herself that help would be available to her once the cause of her problem was discovered.

"Hi, darling!" Greg called out cheerily as he opened the front door, arriving home from the gallery at his now regular and earlier time of around six.

"Hi, my love," she responded warmly, looking forward to another relaxed supper and an early night as he entered the kitchen, where she was sitting still browsing through her Internet searches. "Good day?" she asked, closing down her laptop hastily.

"A really good day. In fact, business has picked up since Christmas. I wondered whether it might tail off as it often does. A few lucrative sales today and a request to source some pieces portraying the British coastline for some expats."

"That's fantastic news, which reminds me… I heard from Ella – at last. It was just a really brief note with no real news. Well, she did mention she'd been feeling out of sorts. She's okay now though. By the way, she didn't mention that commission you wanted her to do – surely that would be ideal if you've got clients already lined up?"

It may have been her imagination, but Freya sensed a look of awkward unease come over Greg for some reason at the mention of Ella's name. Choosing not to respond, he turned away from her abruptly and walked across the kitchen. "Glass of wine?" he offered.

"Not for me thanks – trying to be good." Keeping off alcohol was one of the many strategies she was following to improve her chances of becoming pregnant. "So, what about that commission? You should get in touch with her," pressed Freya, sensing something was amiss.

"Maybe I will. Although I'm not altogether sure she was overly keen. I expect she's too busy. Anyway, what's for dinner?"

Freya sensed Greg's unease at talking about Ella for some reason and therefore decided not to pursue the topic any further, noting he seemed a little odd. She thought back to Ella's visit just a few months ago and how well the two of them had connected on so many levels, especially through the world of art. Now it seemed it was yet another topic of conversation that was off-limits.

West Bay

Reading Freya's brief response to her message for the hundredth time, she sensed an uncomfortable breakdown in communication gradually forming between them. In the first few weeks after returning from her wonderful, bonding holiday with her sister, their messages had become much more frequent, chatty and newsy. Now their correspondence had returned to being sparse and somewhat dull, reporting nothing of any consequence. The obvious geographical distance between them was, and had always been, significant in keeping them apart both physically and emotionally. Not only were they separated by thousands of miles of ocean, but their lives were very different in every way. Glancing around her apartment, she reflected on the contrast between her home and Freya's - both desirable in their own ways – and their lifestyles. Freya, with her husband and life of luxury; Ella - single, lonely and now pregnant.

Pregnant. What did that really mean to her? She hadn't even thought about the impact this baby was going to have on her life. In all honesty, she had been in denial, unable to face the ramifications of what was happening to her. Perhaps it was time to do so. Grabbing a notebook lying open on her desk, she decided to put pen to paper and face up to the consequences of her situation by listing everything that was going on in her mind:

1. *Am I ready to be a mother? – not yet, maybe not ever.*
2. *Does my baby need a father? – not one who belongs to someone else.*
3. *Guilt – I will never be able to forgive myself.*
4. *Betrayal – I hate what's happened.*
5. *Secrets – too many.*
6. *Grandparents – they can never know.*
7. *Work – no time for a baby.*
8. *The future – a baby changes everything.*
9. *Me – not good enough, too selfish, too busy.*
10. *Freya.*

So, ten powerful reasons for not becoming a mother. Yet, there was no choice. There never would have been a choice; abortion was out of the question for her. She had made a massive, life-changing mistake and she had to face up to it and deal with it somehow.

Chapter Fourteen

Delray Beach

"What are your plans today?" asked Greg as he finished off his breakfast.

Freya flinched. Today she was preparing for her first fertility consultation. She had decided to keep it to herself for now and involve Greg further down the line if need be. "Oh, not a great deal today. Probably a stint in the gym this morning, then meeting up with the girls for lunch. A busy day for you? Have you thought any more about contacting Ella about the commission?"

"I haven't done anything about it yet, but maybe it's worth mentioning it again to her. Do you think she was interested?"

"Well, I didn't really get involved in much conversation about it with her, but there can't be any harm in asking her. I know how impressed you were with the samples of her work, and now you have a client lined up, she would surely be of help. Why don't you get in touch with her today?"

"Maybe I will," replied Greg quietly.

It felt daunting to be attending the consultation alone, but there was no alternative. Heading to a fertility clinic just south of Delray Beach in Boca Raton, just off the I-95, she knew from her research what to expect: a meeting with a doctor to review her medical history; a physical examination including a pelvic ultrasound; a series of blood tests and a discussion about potential fertility treatments available. Upon arrival, she sat nervously in the parking lot, clutching the paperwork she had brought with her. The white exterior of the modern building looked cold and sterile, yet the palm trees and potted plants created something of a welcome as she slowly walked up the wide stone steps to the glass entrance. She was immediately greeted warmly by a friendly nurse who ushered her into a patient waiting area with comfortable seating and refreshments. Within minutes, she was shown to a private room where the nurse explained the process involved with the initial consultation, offering her a meeting with an in-house financial counsellor to go through the tests, procedures and medications covered by her insurance plan. Freya felt immediately flummoxed by what she considered to be an overload of information, and decided to worry about the financial aspect later.

Then it was time to meet the doctor, who could not have been more welcoming, warm and friendly. The appointment began with a comprehensive overview of her medical history, lifestyle and discussion about any existing health conditions, before introducing her to the small team of fertility specialists. As they went through her details discussing family planning goals (one baby, sooner rather than later), previous attempts to conceive (none), menstrual history (erratic) and any emotional concerns (none), Freya felt reassured that her problem must be one that could be fixed. Then they would test hormone levels and carry out an ultrasound to view her reproductive organs, before following up with further testing, most likely involving Greg. Depending on the outcome of their findings, there would be follow-up consultations to explain the potential causes of fertility challenges and treatment options, which might include lifestyle changes, fertility medications, assisted reproductive technologies such as IVF and other personalised treatments.

An hour later, Freya was escorted back to the private room where her consultation had begun for a final meeting with the fertility nurse. Pending the results of the tests, the nurse discussed regular and timed intercourse and ovulation-inducing medication, before scheduling her next appointment. As she left the clinic, Freya felt overwhelmed by a mix of emotions: pleased that she had begun the process of finding out what was wrong – if indeed there actually was something wrong; disappointed that Greg was not involved at this stage; sad that she was not able to be open and honest with Greg, especially that now she needed to keep diaries, check her temperature and engineer best times to have sex. It was bound to create tensions between them. Hopefully, there was nothing seriously amiss and she would be pregnant within the next few months.

West Bay

Ella was aware she needed to see her doctor or midwife as soon as possible; some of the tests should have been done ten weeks into her pregnancy, and between 11-14 weeks she was due for an initial scan to confirm the baby's due date. She knew the exact time and date of conception of course, but she appreciated it was still important to have an ultrasound to check the physical development of the baby, and screen for possible conditions, including Down's syndrome. She'd spent ages on the Internet researching how the baby develops during pregnancy, nutrition and diet, pelvic floor exercises, antenatal screening tests, care and potential risks during the pregnancy. There was so much to think about, to worry about, and she had to do it all alone. She was experiencing such a mix of emotions, likely to be heightened by pregnancy hormones: scared that her life was about to change forever and be taken over by a baby she had not planned for; sad that the baby would be born amid lies, deception and secrets; worried about how she would cope with everything ahead of her all on her own. She felt no flashes of happiness whatsoever about bringing a new life into the world. All her thoughts were negative ones.

Delray Beach

The blood test results were in and Freya was on her way to the clinic to discuss them. She had been recalled for additional tests, which had inevitably given her cause for concern, even though the nurse assured her it was only to establish hormone levels at a different point in the month. At home, she had been struggling to stay positive and upbeat with Greg and he had started to come home a little later each day, clearly picking up on her change in mood. It was the last thing she wanted to happen, but she had begun to feel negative about the outcome of her tests. She sensed there was going to be no happy ending for her.

As before, she was greeted warmly and ushered into a consultation room off the main waiting room. Within minutes, she was joined by the fertility doctor she had seen previously, and after an initial spiel about the outcome of the results, he began to explain the findings.

"The blood tests have revealed high FSH and LH levels. Let me explain: FSH stands for follicle-stimulating hormone. This helps regulate the menstrual cycle and stimulates egg growth in the ovaries. LH is what is called the luteinising hormone, which is needed to trigger ovulation and also helps the egg to mature." Freya's mind became blank. All she could hear was bad news; his words meant nothing to her. "Now unfortunately, the results are also indicating low levels of an oestrogen hormone known as E2 which prepares the endometrial lining - the lining of the uterus - for ovulation by thickening it ready for egg implantation."

"What does all this mean?" asked Freya, her heart sinking. "It's a lot to take in."

"You're absolutely right, so I'll try to explain. As the FSH and LH levels are high, while E2 is low, it may indicate something called premature ovarian insufficiency or failure." *Failure.* That's all she could take in. "We'll refer to it as POF from now on. It's a condition where the ovaries fail to develop and stop functioning normally. It means the ovaries do not produce normal amounts of oestrogen or release eggs regularly. It's a rare condition, caused by a number of reasons, often as a result of autoimmune conditions or genetic causes."

"Is that why I've always had irregular periods?" His words were beginning to sink in and make sense. "Can it be cured?" she asked desperately.

"That's exactly the reason why, Freya. There are treatments, as you have some eggs and follicles that may mature and result in normal ovulation. It may also be possible to undergo successful fertility treatment such as egg donation and IVF treatment."

"Is it similar to the menopause?"

"It is. Premature menopause. You may have experienced other symptoms associated with the menopause."

"I haven't. I've always been fit and well. I've never had regular or heavy periods, but just thought I was lucky. But I'm not, am I?"

"It is a rare condition, as I said before, yet a small proportion of women with POF do become pregnant naturally. I'm going to do further tests, give you some literature to read on the condition and make another appointment for you in a month's time. Maybe you would like to bring your husband next time. It's good to have the support of a partner, I'm sure you'll agree."

"Maybe," she murmured, too upset to speak further.

West Bay

Sitting in the busy waiting room at Dorset County Hospital's Maternity Unit in Dorchester, she glanced around the large, brightly painted room, observing that she was surrounded by happy couples, chatting and holding hands. How on earth had she ended up in this condition, in this place, all alone? She didn't even have a parent, sister or friend to bring along to keep her company and offer support, or share the 'joy' she was supposed to feel at her first ultrasound scan.

After a twenty-minute wait, her name was called out from the reception desk and she was ushered into a dimly lit room to meet the sonographer, who after taking some basic details from her, asked her to lie on her back and reveal her tummy. She felt so disconnected from the baby as the cool gel was smoothed over her gently rounded abdomen. It didn't seem real; she felt nervous and daunted by the whole experience and wondered whether she would feel differently in a few moments once she met her baby for the first time. Maybe she would be overwhelmed by the miracle of reproduction and fall in love instantly and unconditionally, just as she knew she was supposed to.

"Now, Ella, if you would like to keep an eye on the screen, a picture of your baby will appear when I pass this probe over your tummy. You might feel a slight pressure, but that is only so that we can get the best views of baby." After a minute or two, her baby's first image appeared on the screen. She experienced no rush of maternal love or happiness. Nothing. Just an oppressive sensation of guilt and betrayal that she knew she would always carry with her. "There we are. Everything is looking very good, I'm delighted to tell you," the sonographer announced, glancing at Ella in anticipation of some reaction or response. "Now I'm going to take some measurements and then I can let you have your due date."

Well, there would be no surprise there; she could tell the sonographer the exact date of conception and save her the bother. How was it even possible that the tiny human form on the screen belonged to her and a man whom she planned never to see again who was on the other side of the ocean? It was miraculous – in every sense of the word – but she felt no part of it. She didn't deserve a baby; she didn't want one and she knew would make a dreadful mother. Yet even though she didn't have a maternal bone in her body, she would not be terminating this pregnancy. For Ella, that simply wasn't an option.

Chapter Fifteen

Delray Beach

"Have you heard anything from Ella lately?" asked Greg over breakfast, without taking his eyes off his laptop screen. Her name hadn't been mentioned for a few weeks and he was wondering how to move forward after what happened on New Year's Day. Should he just carry on as though nothing was up? It seemed odd that Freya hadn't mentioned her lately either. She'd been pestering him repeatedly a few weeks ago to contact Ella about the commission he'd promised her; she knew he needed to sort something out urgently for some pressing clients.

"Only the usual. A message now and then about nothing in particular. Why? Do you still want her to produce that seascape for you?"

"Possibly." A brief response indeed. End of conversation. Freya contemplated pursuing the topic further but then wondered what the point was. She felt as though she'd lost proper contact with her sister, which seemed odd after the happy time they'd spent in each other's company over Christmas. Surely Ella would want to know how things were going pregnancy-wise? The reason she had confided in her sister was so that she would have someone to share her concerns with. Although maybe it was just as well she hadn't asked; another month of failure, despite efforts on her part to maximise the chances around the most fertile days of her cycle. She was due to return to the clinic next month, although the nurse had reassured her that she could contact them at any time. For now, she would carry on as she had been doing for the past sixteen months, hoping the hormones and medications she had been prescribed to encourage the growth and release of eggs might actually work.

"I'm off," Greg announced, closing the lid of his laptop and tucking it under his arm. "Do you fancy going out for dinner tonight?" he added as he kissed the top of Freya's head somewhat chastely on his way past her in the kitchen.

"That would be good. We haven't been out in a while. Have a good day, my love."

As he left the house, Freya realised it would present her with an ideal opportunity to have a heart-to-heart with Greg about her concerns. She might even broach the subject of her having seen a fertility doctor now that four months had elapsed. Perhaps today was also a good day to contact Ella to seek her advice. She glanced at the clock; the five-hour time difference meant that lunchtime might be a suitable time to contact her. She would FaceTime her and see if she could get their relationship back on track.

It was a quiet day in the gallery, possibly due to the weather being more conducive to a day at the beach rather than shopping, giving Greg plenty of time for contemplation. He'd had a lot on his mind lately and today he was in the mood to sort things out. Firstly, he had decided to contact Ella about the commission. He had loved what he'd seen of her work and he knew that she would be the perfect artist for the seascape the expat couple were after. Coincidentally, they were from Dorset too, and had specifically requested a painting depicting either Chesil Beach or Golden Cap to remind them of home. Given the delicate situation between him and his sister-in-law, he had tried to source a painting from elsewhere, without success. The couple were, quite understandably, very specific about what they wanted and had a generous budget in mind for this particular large-scale commission. Secondly, he wanted to talk to Freya about their baby plans. He sensed something was amiss; she had been behaving oddly and somewhat suspiciously. He shouldn't complain, but she had been incredibly assertive in the bedroom just lately – unusually so – and at times he was even struggling to keep up with her demands. Perhaps there was something they needed to talk about, something she was keeping from him?

First, an email to Ella. It took him about half an hour to compose a suitably worded message to her, requesting her help in a business-like but brother-in-law-friendly tone. Brief and to the point, with a slightly casual undertone – a tricky balance. His finger hovered tentatively over the keyboard, checking and rechecking the contents of the email, deliberating the repercussions of making contact with Ella after four months of silence. Yet it needed to be done - whatever the outcome. The guilt and deception he had felt since New Year was overwhelming at times. If only he could forget about it and move on, without hurting Freya along the way.

After lunch, Freya sat down at the kitchen table determined to finally have a decent exchange with her sister. During the morning, she had spent time thinking about what she wanted to say to her, keen to sort out some of the issues that were on her mind. Opening up Messenger, she clicked on Ella's name and tapped the phone icon to start a voice call. Within seconds, Ella responded.

"Hey! How are you? It's been a while," began Freya. "Actually, shall we do a video call instead; it would be good to see you."

"Hi, Freya. Lovely to hear from you," she responded, her heart racing as the panic set in. "I think there's a problem with my laptop camera. I think we might have to stick to a voice call instead." There was no way she could face looking at her sister's innocent face or letting her see her guilty one. It was going to be enough of a challenge to maintain a normal conversation without the extra complication of a face-to-face encounter.

"I was wondering how you are and what's been going on in your life since we saw each other at Christmas," Freya ventured, anticipating very little in response.

"I'm fine thanks. Not a lot to report really. Work keeps me busy."

Exactly as predicted, she was giving nothing away. "One of my reasons for calling was that I was wondering whether you'd be able to help Greg out with that commission he mentioned. I know it's not really my place to ask, but for some reason, he seems reluctant to ask you himself. He's got some clients keen to get hold of a seascape. I think they've mentioned Chesil Beach to him."

"Well, I am rather busy at the moment, Freya. I might struggle to fit it in."

"I understand. But perhaps if I tell him I've spoken to you, then you could discuss it with him. You need to talk to him about fees and timescales. I know he's keen for you to do it and there's a generous budget for the project that might just persuade you."

"Ok. Perhaps I might be able to help out if there's no rush for it. Anyhow, what about you?" Ella was keen to change the subject. Any form of contact with Greg was unthinkable.

"Not so bad." She didn't know how to answer. There was so much to say.

"Not so bad? That sounds a bit cryptic to me."

"You're right. I could have said, *not so good*, as it turns out." Silence fell between them for a few seconds, neither of them knowing how to follow up on the admission that something was amiss.

"Do you want to tell me?" Ella ventured, feeling deeply concerned. What was she referring to? Had Greg confessed to her? Probably not, judging by Freya's friendly tone. Something else must be troubling her.

"I'd love to tell you, Freya. How much time have you got?"

"I've got as much time as you need. What's up?"

Freya breathed a sigh of relief that at last she had someone to open up to. "Oh, how I wish you were here. I miss having someone to talk to. I can't share all this with any of my friends. It's just too sensitive and personal." Her voice was filled with emotion and she sounded somewhat tearful as the words poured out.

"Tell me, Freya. You can tell me anything. I'm here to help." What a fraud she felt. *Tell your lying, cheating sister your secrets. By the way, she slept with your husband and is expecting his child. She's clearly the perfect person to open your heart to.*

"Oh Ella, where to start?" She had begun to sob gently through her broken words. "I don't think I'm going to be able to have a baby."

Ella felt sick with shock. This was the very worst news ever. "What do you mean? Surely, it's early days, isn't it? It can take a while, Freya."

"It's been longer than you think. I kept it to myself – from you, from Greg, from everyone. I've been trying for ages; I just knew something was wrong."

"Tell me more. Have you done anything about it yet?" Ella couldn't believe what she was hearing. How was it possible that she had become pregnant after a one-night stand, yet her younger sister had been trying for months?

"Oh yes. Plenty. I've had a few consultations at a fertility clinic in Boca and loads of tests."

"Oh, Freya. I'm so sorry. Do you know what the problem is?"

"It's something called Premature Ovarian Insufficiency. Basically, it means my ovaries aren't working properly. They're not producing the right amount of hormones or releasing eggs regularly, which means the chances of me getting pregnant are virtually non-existent."

"Surely there's something that can be done?" Ella simply could not believe what she was hearing. It was the worst possible news.

"Well, I'm on hormones and medication to hopefully encourage the release of eggs. Although, I've got another problem too. In simple terms, I've got low levels of the hormone that prepares the lining of the uterus for a pregnancy. Basically, even if an egg was fertilised, the chances of it embedding itself are virtually non-existent. It's not good, Ella. Realistically, there's very little chance of me ever getting pregnant. And it's all my fault. There's nothing wrong with Greg."

With every sentence, Ella felt as though she was sinking deeper and deeper into a black hole. *Nothing wrong with Greg.* She could vouch for that. The words stabbed her like a knife. *Say something, Ella.* "Oh Freya. I'm so sorry to hear this. I'm lost for words, to be honest."

"The thing is, I don't know what to say to Greg. I've deceived him, haven't I? He's not going to be happy about that. I didn't tell him I'd been hoping to get pregnant the whole of last year and now I've had to be secretive about the fertility treatment."

"Why? You need to tell him so he can support you."

"Well, he thinks we've only been trying for four months – not sixteen. Anyway, I think it's come to the point where I'll have to say something. He must suspect something's going on, especially around the middle of the month when I have to step up the action in the bedroom!" Freya laughed at herself; she wasn't really comfortable about revealing such personal information, but she felt it was relevant to her confession to Ella. "Plus, there are the costs involved. We have medical insurance but it won't be long before Greg finds out exactly what's going on."

"You need to tell him, Freya. This isn't something you should be facing alone."

"So how do I explain that I've been to a fertility clinic? I should have told him from the start, shouldn't I?"

"Maybe you could tell him you went for a few tests in view of the problems you've had in the past. You've never had a regular cycle, have you?"

"You're right. I hadn't thought about that. I went from having irregular periods to taking the pill, so I've never had a proper cycle." Now Freya came to think about it, the writing had always been on the wall. "We're going out for dinner this evening, so I'll tell him then."

"I think you should. It will only get harder as time goes on, and you need his support."

"Definitely. I can't stand the lies and deception." Freya's words hit Ella hard; she was not the only one living a lie. They all were.

West Bay

Ella sat back in her favourite armchair, the evening sun creating a comforting warmth and glow in the lounge, and reflected on her lengthy and candid conversation with her sister. There were no easy answers; the situation was unbearable. Indeed, it could not be worse. Placing her hand on her rounded abdomen, as though to remind herself this nightmare was in fact a reality, she tried to unravel the complex web of lies they were all caught up in. The basic, indisputable truth was that she was pregnant by her sister's husband after a one-night stand, whilst her sister was unlikely to be able to have a baby of her own. Ella did not want a baby, yet Freya was desperate for one. Greg had betrayed Freya and Freya was keeping important truths from Greg, whilst Ella was concealing the biggest secret of all. If she could wave a magic wand, how might the situation be resolved?

She had already looked into a solution: surrogacy. She could carry the baby for them. The implications were huge though, not to mention the ethical, legal and emotional considerations involved. Yet the deed had already been done. She had already been impregnated by her sister's husband without her knowledge. She tried to envisage the range of emotions Freya would experience if only she knew – shock, anger, betrayal, hurt and sadness. Her relationship with her sister would surely be destroyed forever unless they sought counselling or family therapy. It was such a complex and emotionally charged situation. The alternative was to continue the lies and live with a secret for the rest of her life: she would not reveal the true identity of her baby's father. No one need ever find out; the repercussions would be far less damaging. Yes. That is what she would do. It was probably the kindest solution - one that would prevent the destruction of her sister's marriage and enable her to remain in Freya's life.

She was glad she had spoken to Freya at last; it had cleared the air and made her face up to her dreadful dilemma. After several weeks of agonising over the best way to deal with the situation, she felt she had finally come to a decision – a huge, life-changing decision that would have lasting implications for everyone, but minimising the massive inevitable hurt that would follow should the truth be revealed.

The sunset had taken with it the last dregs of light and warmth of the day and now she was ready to retire to her bed with a book. How she needed a glass of wine after the emotions she had experienced over the past few hours. As she eased herself out of her comfortable recliner, she decided to check her emails and diary one last time. There was one notification…

> Hi Ella
>
> Hope all is well. Freya may have told you that I'm keen to follow up our discussions about the commission we spoke of. I've

researched other options locally but feel that your work best matches my clients' requirements. Timescales and budgets are generous, so I am hopeful that you will give it serious consideration.

I look forward to hearing from you so we can discuss the project in more detail.

Regards,
Greg

So, Freya had clearly spoken to Greg before or after their conversation. The tone of his message was suitably neutral – formal but friendly – with no hint of what had happened between them. In many ways, it helped to reassure her that her decision to pretend nothing existed between them, either now or in the past, was the right one. She would take on the commission. It was the least she could do.

Delray Beach

Sitting on the deck of their favourite beachfront restaurant, they gazed at the burnt orange sunset settling over the ocean, gently cooled by the refreshing sea breeze. The setting was perfect for some honest exchanges about what was going on in their lives. All too often at home, the evenings were absorbed by watching the TV and everyday chat about nothing in particular. This evening, Freya was determined to open up to Greg and put an end to all the secrecy and deception that was weighing her down. Greg too had something significant to tell Freya – that, after months of deliberation, he had decided to contact Ella.

"Well, this is perfect," murmured Freya, her eyes cast over the moonlit ocean, her fingers wrapped around the stem of her fruity 'mocktail'.

"It is. We should do this more often," agreed Greg, following her gaze. Comfortable silence fell between them for a short while; it was clear that they both had something to say to each other. Easing his hand apart from Freya's and sitting back in his chair, he looked directly into his wife's eye. "Guess what? I decided to contact Ella about that commission today. You got me thinking this morning. She's the one for the job."

"That's brilliant! What has she said?" Freya was genuinely delighted that he'd taken the plunge. To be honest, she hadn't understood his hesitancy these past few months, especially as they seemed to have got on so well during her visit.

"Oh, I haven't heard back yet. I only sent it a couple of hours ago. She probably won't read it till tomorrow."

"Well, that's good to hear. I was hoping you'd ask her, especially as you'd virtually promised her the work when she was here. I know she's busy with her freelance work, but I reckon she'll be able to work with that generous timescale you mentioned."

"Let's hope so. How about you, my love? You're clearly looking after yourself," he remarked, nodding in the direction of her alcohol-free cocktail. "Anything to tell me?" His knowing, playful wink seemed to suggest she had some exciting news for him.

Anything to tell me? She had so much to tell him. Too much. It was a question of how much. Her eyes fell away from his, unable to hold his questioning gaze. Eventually, allowing her breathing to settle in time with the rhythm of the waves, she reconnected with him and placed a reassuring hand on his. "I have, Greg. That's why I was keen to have this chance to talk to you properly." She watched the colour drain from his sun-drenched complexion.

"What is it? You're making me feel worried!" he exclaimed, attempting to lighten the mood a little.

"I'm not going to beat about the bush, Greg. I'll just come straight out with it. It's what you deserve." Greg's mouth fell apart, clearly dreading what he was about to hear. "I've been trying to protect you from some really important things that have been going on these past few months. I just didn't want to worry you, especially with everything you have going on at work."

"What is it, Freya?" His mind was racing over every possibility. Was she about to tell him she was planning to leave him? Did she have a lover? Was she ill? He just wanted to know.

"I'm not sure that we're going to be able to have a baby." There, that was it in black and white. No messing around. After a few moments, in the absence of a response from Greg, she decided to press on. "I've been concerned for a while that something's up, so I've been to seek advice at a fertility clinic."

"But it's only been a few months!" exclaimed Greg, clearly shocked by her admission.

"More than a few months, Greg. I decided to come off the pill last year to give my body a chance to settle to its normal rhythm, if you like. I knew then that things weren't quite right. Anyhow, I thought I'd get a few tests done before involving and worrying you. So that's what I've done."

"But you've gone through this all alone. You should have told me, Freya. The problem could lie with me, you know."

"It's not. It's me. My test results have thrown up all sorts of hormone problems, meaning that there's virtually no chance I'll get pregnant naturally."

"Surely there's something that can be done though?" Greg felt shocked and frantic about wanting to solve the problem there and then.

"Well, medication can be used to boost hormone levels, which is what I've been taking the last couple of months. But still, the chances of conceiving are low."

"Oh Freya, I'm so sorry. I wish you'd told me before now. I would have supported you from the outset, you should have known that." He was genuinely saddened by the fact that she had tried to protect him, especially at a time when he knew he owed her so much in reparation for his own sins.

"I'm just so relieved that you know now. It's been tough, but I suppose I was hoping that everything would be OK and you wouldn't need to know how worried I've been. The hormones might work, after all. I think we've got to give it a few months before we decide on our next move."

"So, what would come next, if the hormones don't work?"

"We're talking IVF I suppose. Egg donations. I don't want to think about that too much at the moment. I'm still hopeful that it won't come to that."

"I'm going to be right by your side from now on. No more going behind my back. I don't need to be protected. I'm your husband for god's sake! I love you so much." As he said the words, he realised just how much he did love her, especially now, looking into her troubled eyes. She was his world. Why the hell had he risked everything with her sister? Drink, excitement, opportunism? Nothing that meant anything at all. All that really mattered was that he supported his wife now and helped her on what was likely to be a very difficult and emotional journey through fertility treatments and options for the future, fraught with cycles of expectation and disappointment, frustrations and sadness.

PART TWO

Chapter Sixteen

West Bay

Late September. Two days past her due date. According to her recent ante-natal appointments, everything was on course for a textbook birth. The baby's head was positioned downward, and Ella could feel it dropping lower into her pelvis, pressing hard onto her bladder. In the past couple of days, she had experienced some painful contractions as her body prepared itself for the birth. She hadn't wanted to know the baby's gender; in fact, she didn't want to know much about the baby at all, other than that it was healthy. She was understandably nervous about the birth, especially with having to cope with it all alone, and reflected on her decision to isolate herself from everyone. The past few months had flown by, with only sporadic contact with Freya and her parents, who were still travelling around the world but keen to have a family reunion around Christmas.

Just as she planned, her sister remained unaware that she was pregnant; there was no way she would ever be able to explain her decision to keep such huge life-changing news from her. Only she knew the reason for keeping it to herself of course, as Freya's monthly updates continued to be depressingly disappointing. The hormone treatment hadn't proved successful so far and discussions were now moving towards assisted reproductive procedures such as IVF, involving placing sperm closer to the egg. However, in Freya's case, the likelihood was that her eggs weren't of sufficient quality for successful conception, leaving three main options open to her: donor eggs, adoption, or surrogacy. Ella was dreading the day when Freya decided to discuss these options with her – it was surely imminent.

Closing her tired eyes for a moment, Ella placed both hands over her huge, tight abdomen. Her baby's movements had become more frequent and intense over the past few hours, squirming and trying to turn, getting ready for birth. She wondered how would she feel once she met her child. An unplanned pregnancy, a fatherless child, and an unprepared, reluctant mother. Not a great start in life. What could she offer a baby? Selfishly, she wanted to build a career and hopefully, one day, meet someone to share her life with once more. A baby would only stand in her way.

And Freya… How unfair life was. It broke her heart to think of what she was going through. Her lovely sister – so kind, loving and generous-hearted. She wanted a baby more than anything in the world and would do anything to have one. Anything.

☐

It was a textbook birth: a tough but safe labour of several hours, requiring only the help of a little gas and air, culminating in Ella pushing her healthy son into the world without any complications. Holding her newborn baby to her breast, her exhausted body allowed her mind to take over. What was she feeling? A complex mix of emotions for sure: a profound sense of relief that the birth went well and her baby was healthy, and overwhelming exhaustion mixed with concern about her ability to be a parent. Was she experiencing that immediate rush of love and attachment that she'd heard and read about? No. She felt vulnerable and uncertain, with only the absence of pain following the birth bringing any relief and comfort. Above all, she felt desperately lonely and scared. As she glanced down at her swaddled newborn, she allowed tears of self-pity to flow. Her life had changed forever.

Delray Beach

"I'm sorry to tell you, Freya, but IVF is not the solution in your case. I regret to inform you that the hormone therapy and medications have been unsuccessful in developing eggs."

She already knew what he was about to tell her. She had read everything and more on the subject and understood exactly what her problem was. She was also aware of what options remained available to her. Remaining silent, Greg by her side, she allowed the doctor to continue to explain the inevitable truth of her depressing failure to produce a child.

"However, there are still options open to you: donor eggs being one of them." Freya's heart sank; she knew what was to follow. "Another option is surrogacy, where, as you will be aware, another woman would carry the pregnancy to term for you. Finally, if you choose not to pursue further medical interventions, you might want to consider adoption. There is a lot for you to discuss with each other, but we are here to provide you with personalised guidance and support. It is important that you take the time to consider your emotional, physical and financial well-being as you decide on the next steps of your fertility journey."

Greg squeezed her hand reassuringly as Freya dropped her head and allowed her tears to flow. Even though she knew what was coming, his formal rehearsed spiel broke her heart. She felt like jumping up and screaming, "Why me?" but there was no point. *Donor eggs, surrogacy, adoption.* She wasn't convinced that any of these were viable options for her. She wanted her own baby – her and Greg's baby.

West Bay

After just two days, Ella and her son were discharged from the hospital. Ella felt she would never be ready for the role that was now expected of her. She hadn't even prepared a nursery for him yet, just a Moses basket, pram and a car seat. It was only at the eleventh hour when she realised she had to face up to reality and prepare herself for the baby's homecoming that she eventually ordered sets of clothing, nappies and other essentials. A taxi came to collect them, which surprised the midwife in charge, and saddened Ella that she was all alone in this. She hadn't told anyone where she was; there had been no need. Her friends back in Bristol were none the wiser and she still hadn't made any close friends in West Bay. Work, being freelance, had not been problematic either. She had managed to fulfil her regular local commitments but had not taken on any extra work in recent weeks. Of course, there was the seascape – Greg's commission – which she had finally agreed to take on following his emails several months back, but there was no urgency where that was concerned. Now she needed to settle into new routines and get used to being a mother.

Being a first-time, reluctant mother was not easy; she didn't expect it to be. Ella was experiencing a whirlwind of emotions and physical challenges alongside the weight of new responsibilities, leading to constant exhaustion and anxiety. His demands were relentless – nappy changes and erratic sleep schedules – indicated by bouts of crying that were impossible to ignore. It was overwhelming at times. She slept when he slept, ate once he was fed, and shed hormonal tears of self-pity in between.

What she was missing, and what she was waiting for, was the rush of maternal love and bonding she had read all about. She had not felt it. Not yet. Even though she had never possessed a maternal bone in her body, she had seen it in others – a powerful and overwhelming surge of emotions; an instant attachment and profound emotional connection; strong feelings of protectiveness and tenderness; a primal desire to care for and nurture baby's needs. Perhaps her feelings would grow, especially once she was in a position to share her son with others. For now, it must be just the two of them – it had to be – but it was incredibly lonely and isolating.

After a long, tiring week since giving birth, some semblance of daily routine began to emerge, with feeding and sleeping patterns starting to settle down a little. Ella was gradually getting to understand her baby's needs and her feelings toward him were growing each day, but nothing felt natural. She cared deeply that his basic needs were met, ensuring he wanted for nothing and monitoring his feeding and sleeping patterns religiously, but it felt as though he didn't fully belong to her, that she was his carer rather than his mother. Holding him closely to her whilst she wandered around the apartment to settle him after his feed, she decided the time had come to name him. Looking across the sea, she thought fleetingly about his father on the other side of the ocean; she would connect them through her choice of name. She had researched the options over the past few days and as she held him close, gazing into his aqua-blue eyes, she named him Kai, meaning 'sea'.

Chapter Seventeen

Delray Beach

The festive season was approaching again and the magnificent, towering Christmas tree was up in all its glory in the centre of Delray, meaning a whole year had elapsed since Ella had stayed with them. So much had happened since then, or rather - more accurately - nothing at all had. The fertility treatment had failed and due to her overwhelming desire for a biological child, she had been unwilling to accept surrogacy as a viable option. She was struggling to reconcile her own beliefs with the idea of it, feeling uncomfortable with the ethical and moral aspects, not to mention the obvious unlikelihood of finding a suitable surrogate.

Married life had sadly reverted to much the way it had been twelve months ago, with Greg spending more time at the gallery and Freya feeling as though she was wasting away the hours each day on futile shopping trips and endless lunch dates with her friends, who remained none the wiser about what she had been facing all year. Much as she enjoyed the company of the girls in her friendship group, there was no real closeness between them and she couldn't imagine ever asking them what their views were on life-changing issues such as infertility, surrogacy and adoption. Conversations between them tended to be superficial, light and fluffy, hardly ever touching on problems any of them may or not be encountering in their seemingly perfect lives.

Unsurprisingly, contact with Ella had reverted to messages rather than calls after a short while. She blamed herself for that; she couldn't face telling her how devastated she felt about her infertility and had tried to make light of it, explaining they were considering other options. She was however pleased to hear that Ella had been working on Greg's seascape commission since the summer. She liked to feel there was some sort of connection between them, yet she sensed there was something amiss with Ella. She had hoped that they might plan another reunion this year, maybe in the UK this time, or even with their parents, but Ella was non-committal as always.

During the summer, she and Greg had finally managed to meet up with her parents when they flew into Fort Lauderdale before the start of their Caribbean cruise. They spent several hours with them catching up on all their travels over a long, leisurely lunch on the waterfront. Retirement was certainly suiting them – they seemed years younger than their ages, healthy and happy, and clearly still very much in love. They spoke of Ella but seemed disappointed that they had tried to arrange a visit to see her on a couple of occasions during the summer but she had put them off.

"Let's make sure we have a family reunion early in the New Year," suggested Freya. "It's been far too long. I know it's hard with us living thousands of miles apart, and you two always being away, but we need to make it happen. It was so lovely to have Ella to stay last year."

"We would really love that," agreed her mother. "It's probably just as easy to meet out here in Florida, being as you're in a position to accommodate us. We can always see if it works out with one of our trips. And Ella, she told us what a wonderful time she had with you. I'm sure she'd be keen to come over again."

Maybe, thought Freya. She wasn't so sure. She sensed an awkwardness had developed between them lately, creating a distance that prevented them from confiding with each other in the way they had done a year ago. She had expected Ella to enquire how her fertility treatment was going, but she hadn't asked.

West Bay

How was it that she felt even lonelier than she had before Kai came into her life? It didn't make any sense. Fortunately, Kai had settled into feeding and sleeping routines that freed Ella up for a few hours every day, giving her time to work on the seascape. The painting was progressing well, but she was taking her time with it, especially now that she had Kai to consider. It relaxed her mind as she sat before the canvas with a focused gaze, layering shades of cerulean and aquamarine, the bristles of her brush rippling with each stroke, echoing the movement of the ocean.

Greg and his clients had given Ella a free rein as to what to paint and she had suggested the iconic sandstone East Cliff at West Bay, characterised by its layers of rocks in vibrant hues of rust-red and orange. Over time, it had been sculpted into a series of jagged peaks and valleys, with evidence of recent rock falls caused by wave attrition and pounding at its base. To view it in all its glory, Ella merely had to saunter across the beach road from her apartment to the pier to see the cliff ignited by the sun, radiating a golden glow, and providing a fiery foreground to a fantastic view stretching around the coast to Portland.

Today, she had decided to venture out along the pier with Kai strapped securely to her body in his snuggly carrier, shielded from the brisk sea breeze and the bright winter sun. The absence of crowds at this time of year made for a more tranquil and peaceful ambiance with only the occasional screech of gulls and cormorants interrupting the serenity of their stroll. Stopping at the end of the pier, she took in the dramatic view of the rugged cliffs and open sea, the low-angled sunlight casting striking shadows on the rocks, and tried to envisage what the future held for her and her son. Placing her hand protectively on his head, she couldn't deny the growing feelings she had towards her baby, yet she was unable to move beyond the guilt, lies and deception surrounding his existence. She knew that she had some serious, potentially life-changing decisions to make - sooner rather than later – including how and when to break the news to Freya and her parents that she had become a mother. Then she would need to create a story about his father. A one-night stand would be the simplest explanation, in the absence of any previous or present relationships in her life. At least that part was true. Why was life so unfair, that she had been blessed with the gift of a child whilst her sister had been denied that opportunity? Her pregnancy was unplanned and unwanted whilst her sister had experienced months of heartbreaking disappointment and failure. Worst of all was the fact that her baby's father belonged to her sister. There were no easy answers.

Chapter Eighteen

West Bay

"Happy New Year my darling! How are you? What are you up to?" asked her mother in a series of excitable short bursts, delighted to have finally managed to contact her daughter. They were holidaying in Madeira this year, home of one of the greatest fireworks displays in Europe according to her parents – a magical spectacle of lights on the skies of Funchal.

"Happy New Year to you too," replied Ella, smiling to herself at their obvious enthusiasm for life. "Were the fireworks as good as you hoped?" she continued, aiming to divert the attention away from herself as quickly as possible.

"They were amazing, Ella. We were able to watch them from the ship with the bay of Funchal and the hills in the background. You should have joined us; you would have loved it."

"Maybe next year. I've been busy just lately and I haven't really had a break."

"Well, you should make time for a break, Ella. I know we've been away such a lot this year, but we really must arrange a get-together. I've been talking to Freya and she agrees. What do you think? What could you manage?"

"You're right. It's been too long. We'll have to put our heads together and see when we're all free, won't we? What were you thinking? When are you next back in the UK for a longer spell?" So many questions. So many obstacles.

"We're back soon and don't have much planned until April. If Freya and Greg aren't able to visit the UK, then we must meet up soon and then try to take a trip out to Florida later in the year altogether. How does that sound?"

"That sounds good, Mum." The remainder of their conversation was taken up with more about their holidays and tittle-tattle about their numerous friends. Nothing more was said about Freya, much to her relief. She assumed that Freya had not spoken to their mother about her fertility treatment, and understood why, in the same way that she had said nothing about having given birth to a child only a few months ago. These were not topics of conversation to be had casually, amid excitable descriptions of Funchal and its famous fireworks. And yet, she could not imagine a time when she would ever be able to have that conversation with her mother. How would she ever be able to explain what had happened and why she had kept such a massive secret to herself?

Delray Beach

"Happy New Year, Ella. How are things?" She was expecting a call from Freya today. Exactly one year to the day. The day her life changed forever.

"Hi. Happy New Year to you too. What are you up to?" She tried to match Freya's enthusiasm for the festive season, but her mind was flitting frantically from this year to the last.

"Oh, you know, the usual. A party last night with the neighbours – same as last year. Only this time I actually remember the evening!" She laughed, which pained Ella as she reflected on what happened last year, mainly because Freya had drunk so much and went straight to bed as soon as they got home. She wasn't blaming Freya of course. Freya was totally innocent. She had only herself to blame; she was a willing participant. And Greg. He was guilty too.

"That's good," she responded neutrally, keen for the conversation to move on.

"So how about you? Did you see the New Year in?"

"Not this year. It's a busy time of year for me and I was glad to go to bed if I'm honest."

"Oh Ella! That's sad. Don't you have a group of local friends or work colleagues? You never talk about anyone."

"I'm fine. Honestly. I keep myself busy and I'm getting on well with the painting."

"Greg will be pleased. How much longer will it be?"

"I'm nearly there. Just some finishing touches. It's quite a project, you know."

"So, when are we getting together? Mum and Dad are keen for us to have a family gathering. I'm not sure how easy it would be for us to visit the UK at the moment, what with the gallery and everything, but you're very welcome to come out here again for some Florida sunshine."

"That sounds great. We'll sort something out," responded Ella non-committedly. "More importantly though, Freya, how are you? I have to ask."

"Not great, to be honest. Greg's become a bit distant again, always busy with the gallery. We don't even talk about it now."

"Oh, Freya. That's so sad."

"I've got to come to terms with it somehow. We've talked about other options, but I don't think they're for me. Does that seem selfish to you? I'm not sure I'm strong enough a person to deal with those options."

"Do you want to talk about it?"

"I'm not sure. Maybe voicing my views might help me come to terms with things a bit better."

"I'm more than happy to listen, Freya. You're right. It might help." The hypocrisy of her offer felt shameful, but what else was she to do?

"Thank you, Ella. I'll try to explain the way I feel." For the next few minutes, Ella listened intently as her sister opened her heart to her, about her strong desire to carry and give birth to a biological child belonging to her and Greg, and her concern about a lack of genetic connection. She described her feelings of inadequacy and loss at finding out she was infertile, and her deep fears of the unknown associated with surrogacy and adoption. Ella could feel her pain and understood her reservations more than Freya would ever know. Yet there she was, at the end of the phone, on the other side of the ocean, gazing at Greg's son sleeping peacefully in his Moses basket.

Chapter Nineteen

West Bay

The moment a massive rockfall took place on Dorset's Jurassic Coast has been caught on camera. The first sign of the collapse at West Bay began with puffs of dust before a large section of cliff crumbled onto the beach. The fall, which was described as 'significant', happened on 18 January at 11.30 am, and was captured by a camera placed on a pier to monitor the beach by the Environment Agency. It has blocked access to a section of the beach in both directions between Burton Bradstock and West Bay. The public is being urged to avoid the area. A spokesperson for Dorset Council said, "Please stay away and do not attempt to clamber over the pile. You would be putting yourself and others at risk. The heavy rain we've had over the last few weeks has made cliffs right along the Jurassic Coast unstable and more prone to rockfalls. Keep away from the base of the cliffs, and if walking along the top of the cliffs, keep well away from the edge."

News of the rockfall featured in the national headlines as well as the local bulletins. Viewing the collapse from the pier was truly shocking with piles of scattered debris and rocks strewn across the beach below. Thank goodness, at this time of the year, the beach was relatively free of visitors or dog walkers, so no one was harmed. Ella wandered down the pier, Kai strapped to her in his carrier, swaddled protectively from the icy air, where several onlookers stood with binoculars and cameras, capturing the devastation before the clear-up operation began. She would photograph it too. So much for her painting of the cliff – it no longer resembled what lay before her eyes today. Caused by changing environmental conditions, rising sea levels, and erratic weather patterns, these rockfalls were becoming increasingly frequent along the coastline.

Heading home, Ella reflected on the crumbling cliff and how it resembled her life, or more precisely, how she felt inside. She no longer felt solid and strong; she had been worn away these past couple of years by everything that had happened to her – her failed relationship and a moment of utter madness that would impact her life forever. Month by month, she felt as though she was crumbling away, eroded by the lies and deception, and worn down by the weight of responsibility of raising a child she did not deserve, clueless as to how she could move forward and rebuild her life. Something would need to happen sooner rather than later. She could not hide away forever, or conceal the fact that she was now a mother.

Delray Beach

It was inevitable that the pressure would get to them both in time. Freya's feelings of disappointment and sadness had morphed into ones of failure and inadequacy. Greg was at a loss as to how to deal with her constant low moods of depression and despondency, and although it pained him to admit it, he coped best when he was at work, immersed in his world of artistic creations. Away from home, he could take a break from it all. With increasing frequency, he would make an excuse to leave the gallery late, often stopping off at Boston's for a beer on the way home. Sometimes, when she was at her worst, he would stay at the bar to watch live football or basketball for an hour or two, hoping that she would have taken herself off to bed before he got home. He no longer knew how to console her or move forward.

Over the past few weeks, he had tried to talk to her about surrogacy, but she wouldn't discuss it in a calm or measured way with him, always reverting to the fact that it was all her fault; her eggs and womb were useless and so she didn't deserve to be or was destined to be a mother.

"Just go!" she screamed at him the last time he'd tried to broach the subject.

"Go where exactly?" he yelled back. "Leave my house? Leave you here? Talk sense, Freya. This isn't getting us anywhere. I'll do anything I can to support you, you know I will."

"There's nothing you can do, Greg," she uttered, tears streaming down her pale face. "You need to find someone else, someone who can give you a child."

"It's you I want. I want you more than I want a child, Freya."

"So why do I feel that you're avoiding me as much as you can? It doesn't feel as though you want me anymore."

"That's not fair and it's not true. I love you so much. It's that I'm not sure how to handle this anymore. I've tried my best but it's not enough. I'll be honest with you Freya, much as I would love a child, I would never let anything jeopardise our relationship. You mean more to me than anything and I will love you and look after you forever, but you've got to love yourself too."

"It's hard to love myself when I'm a failure."

"You're not a failure in my eyes. Don't let this change you, Freya. I want you back. What can I do? Is there anything I can do? I feel useless and inadequate and that's why I've kept my distance just lately. It's as though you don't really want me around, that I'm just making things worse."

"I don't know what I want. At the moment, I'm still trying to process my infertility. It feels like I'm grieving and it's going to take time."

"It is. It's like a bereavement. But I do have an idea. Why not help me out in the gallery?" he suggested. "You need something else to focus on."

"But you've always said you don't want that. I've offered in the past."

"That was the past. Things are different now. Maybe it's time for a change. You need a distraction and I need some help. I'm sure we could work something out."

For the first time in ages, their conversation had ended on a positive note. Greg was right; she needed a reason to get up in the morning, a reason for being.

The prospect of working in the gallery had given Freya the boost she needed. Greg said she could join him in the gallery and take a look at the books for him. It was a start; it also gave her the incentive she needed to contact her sister. She would email her and try to arrange the family get-together they had talked about over Christmas. There was every possibility of getting the family gathered before Easter. Opening up her laptop, she wondered how best to approach the subject. The best option was to invite Ella and their parents out to Florida again.

West Bay

Hi Ella. How are you? It's been a few weeks since I heard from you. Everything is much the same here, although things might be looking up a little as I'm going to start to help out in the gallery. Greg thought it would give me a new focus.

What would make me really happy is if we could get something in the diary for us all to get together. Mum and Dad are keen and, just for a change, they happen to be in the UK until April. Please give it serious thought, Ella. I'd love it if you could all come out to Florida again. The weather's perfect around Easter and we can accommodate the three of you. Nothing would make me happier. It's exactly what I need at the moment. Being surrounded by my family will make me appreciate that life can be full without a child. PLEASE COME! Love you, Freya.

Ella read the email and slammed down the lid of her laptop, her heart racing. Her time was up. She couldn't carry on like this, hiding herself away, pretending nothing had happened. But what should she do? She couldn't just turn up with a baby – *Oh, by the way, I'm bringing someone with me.* Yet she couldn't leave him behind; the absence of family and close friends left her without that option. And to be honest, she wouldn't want to be apart from him for any length of time. Much as she still felt distanced from Kai, her feelings towards him were growing steadily. She was getting used to him. He gave meaning to her lonely life.

There was just one more option. She could come clean and let her family know that she had given birth in September, but how would she ever be able to explain why she had kept it a secret? She had placed herself in an impossible position.

She tried to imagine their shock and surprise, their confusion and disbelief at discovering she had become a mother. How could she make them understand why she had kept it a secret and the circumstances that had led to such a decision? How would Freya and Greg be able to come to terms with it in light of two years of unproductive infertility treatment? It was all too much – for everyone. She couldn't do it. She would have to put Freya off, making some excuse, sooner rather than later. Opening up her laptop, she composed her response:

Hi Freya. It's good to hear from you and I'm pleased that you're planning to work in the gallery. I'm sure you'll enjoy it. I know you've been keen to get involved for a while.

About a visit to Florida, it might be difficult for me to fit in a trip around Easter with work being so busy at present. I know how keen you are for a family reunion and I do agree that it's long overdue. Maybe later on in the year when hopefully things will have settled down a bit?

Keep in touch.

Lots of love, Ella x

She knew it was cowardly to defer the inevitable, but she really couldn't see any other option. She was caught in a web of deception and emotional turmoil.

Chapter Twenty

Delray Beach

Easter came and went. It was clear that Ella had no plans to visit Florida again any time soon. Contact between the sisters had reverted to brief impersonal messages every few weeks about nothing in particular. Whilst Freya's involvement with the gallery had proven to be a useful distraction and Greg appeared to appreciate her contribution to the administrative side of the business, she still struggled to accept her infertility. For her own sanity, she had tried to push negative thoughts to the back of her mind, accepting that it was never going to happen, and she was now spending a little less time each day imagining life without a child. Inevitably, she still had days filled with deep sadness and feelings of inadequacy, believing that she was letting Greg down, especially when she observed him interacting so naturally with their friends' children. He would make an amazing father, she thought, watching him run along the beach hand in hand with their neighbours' twin seven-year-old boys, accompanied by squeals of laughter as they splashed in the shallow waves. Time and again, she'd tried to convince herself that surrogacy or adoption were still viable options, but something was stopping her from pursuing them. Maybe it was Greg – something told her he was happy the way things were. She had certainly detected a change in him since she had begun working in the gallery. Nowadays, their conversations inevitably revolved around their shared working days and future plans for the gallery; it was as though life had moved on to a new phase – one that did not include children.

☐

"I've been thinking Greg. Maybe I should plan a visit to the UK to catch up with my sister as she clearly has no plans to come over here any time soon. What do you think? Or do you need me in the gallery?"

"I can manage if you want to go over for a week or two. I'll have to stay here though, if that's OK."

"Yes. That's what I had in mind. The months are rolling by and for some reason, I have the feeling that something is up. I'm not sure what it is, but I think I'd like to find out."

"So, are you planning to just turn up then? I'm not sure that's such a good idea, Freya."

"I think I have to. I know what will happen if I tell her I'm thinking of planning a visit. She'll have a raft of excuses and reasons why I shouldn't go. Anyway, Mum and Dad are at home over the summer months, so I can spend some time with them too. Are you sure you don't mind?"

"Not at all. You deserve the break. I can't thank you enough for everything you've done these past few months. The systems you've put in place at the gallery mean that one of us can take time off every now and again. Have you had a look at flights yet?"

Freya felt pleased that Greg was being so supportive but sensed almost an eagerness to get her on the next plane which she found unsettling.

"I've only just thought about it, Greg. I will do though, now I know you don't mind."

That's what she would do – arrange a week with her parents and then pay her sister a surprise visit in Dorset.

West Bay

Life had begun to settle into a routine that worked for both of them. Ella was able to fit in work around Kai's sleeping routines – two long naps each day. By six-thirty, he was settled for the night and was sleeping solidly for twelve hours, giving her plenty of time to dip in and out of small projects and Greg's commission that graced the corner of her apartment, almost completed. Kai, now eight months old, was developing rapidly. Curious and active, he was keen to explore his surroundings, having begun to crawl and pull himself up to stand at every opportunity. He was also showing signs of stronger attachment forming; he babbled and smiled at her constantly, seeking her attention and pulling at her heartstrings. Despite everything, she loved him dearly.

The hardest part now was keeping him a secret. To do so, she had cut herself off from everyone. Daily life consisted of walking around West Bay and Bridport with the stroller, speaking to clients over the phone, and brief online messages to Freya and her parents. She hadn't formed any close friendships locally since her move to the South Coast and regretted the way she had treated Freya these past few months. She knew how hurt she must be by her infrequent, impersonal messages and her reluctance to arrange a further get-together. As for her parents, she used their frequent travel plans as an excuse to avoid meeting up with them, even though she missed them very much. Maybe she would make plans to see them over the next two months, having heard that they would be in the UK for the summer months.

Wandering over to her easel, she felt grateful that Greg had not contacted her directly about the seascape she had been working on for several months. It had been a source of pleasure to her and she was proud of what she had achieved. In brief messages, Freya had enquired on Greg's behalf as to the progress she had made on it, stressing that the clients were happy to wait for it. Ella realised that the time had come to release it, but she couldn't bring herself to contact Greg. There was no doubt about it, Ella was trapped by her guilt and denial. One day she would have to own up to Kai and maybe much more.

Chapter Twenty-One

Delray Beach

Freya's five o'clock flight was on time but she was feeling a little nervous, not about the journey, but whether she was doing the right thing in visiting her sister unannounced. Time would tell. Her BA flight to Heathrow was due to leave in just over an hour, flying across the Atlantic overnight, arriving on the other side of the ocean just after 6.00 am. As she sat patiently in the departure lounge, she couldn't help but reflect on the fact that Greg had seemed almost too enthusiastic about her trip. Perhaps a break would do them both good - an escape from painful conversations and the chance to re-evaluate their future now they knew it would be childless.

Time for boarding: families with young children called first. Watching struggling parents juggle babies, toddlers and strollers, whilst she sat quietly and unencumbered, made her question whether that life would ever have been for her. She had never had to make sacrifices in her relatively uneventful life and had been gifted a life of luxury throughout their marriage. Being a mother would require selflessness, resilience, adaptability and lots of patience – qualities she had never needed to develop in herself fully.

During the flight, between brief naps and a couple of movies, she had plenty of time to think about her impending visit to Dorset. It was destined to go one of two ways: either her sister would be surprised yet delighted to see her after nearly eighteen months and welcome her with open arms, or she would be shocked and unprepared for an impromptu visit and make excuses for not being able to spend time with her. Freya planned to spend a week with her parents first and contact Ella to gauge her mood, without telling her she was in the UK. Her next move would depend on Ella, but either way, she was going to see her and find out what was going on. She had a feeling that something was amiss. Maybe she was ill and preferred to keep it to herself. Or perhaps she was engrossed in a new relationship that was taking up all her time.

It took a while to get through passport control but her suitcase was already waiting for her on the conveyor belt by the time she arrived in the baggage reclaim area. Her parents would hopefully be waiting for her at the arrivals gate as planned, ready to transport her to their house in Bristol. She was excited to see them but hoped they would understand if she closed her eyes for an hour on the journey home. She was feeling tired and ready for a shower after the long flight.

Scanning the expectant faces of people milling around the gates – some excited, some clearly bored with waiting – she suddenly spotted her parents, her mum's face breaking into the widest smile the moment she saw Freya emerging from the throng of weary arrivals.

"Freya, my darling!" she exclaimed, nudging her way through the small crowd that had gathered, her arms outstretched in anticipation of a hug.

"Mum, Dad - I made it," she announced, accepting the embrace and smiling at her dad over her mum's shoulder.

"So lovely to see you, darling. Come on, let me take your case. Let's get on our way unless you want to stop for a coffee or breakfast first," suggested her father, considerate as ever.

"I'm happy to go if that suits you. It's been a long journey and I can't wait to jump in the shower and get changed."

Fifteen minutes later, they were on their way. Sitting in the back, Freya could already feel her eyes beginning to close, despite her mother's incessant, excitable chatter as her father concentrated on the heavy traffic leaving the airport.

"Have you heard from Ella lately?" asked her mother, glancing at Freya in the rearview mirror.

"Er, not much, to be honest. Have you?"

"Not lately. I think she's very busy with work. She always seems preoccupied when I call her. It's such a pity that we didn't manage that trip out to Florida together, isn't it?"

"It is, but never mind, I'm here now and I'm planning to see her next week."

"You are? Oh, that is good to hear! Maybe we can come too."

"Maybe..." responded Freya reluctantly. It was something she was planning to do on her own. There would be time enough over the forthcoming few days to deter her mother from joining her, but she would need to tread carefully to avoid causing offence or suspicion.

Fortunately for Freya, her mother sensed her weariness and left it there, allowing her to close her eyes for the remainder of the journey.

West Bay

As Ella opened the blinds, she smiled to see that the early morning sun had painted the rugged cliffs with a warm, golden hue, casting long shadows across the pebbled beach - the exact scene she had tried to capture on canvas. On this perfect day, the tranquil waters of the English Channel glistened in the sunlight, inviting early risers like herself for a refreshing dip or a stroll along the rugged coastal path. Seagulls called out overhead as they glided effortlessly on the sea breeze. Kai would be awake at any moment, and after breakfast, they would take a trip out around the harbour to watch the fishermen prepare their boats for a day of angling. Today the air would be crisp and invigorating, filled with the scent of saltwater and seaweed - a promising day of beauty and adventure along the Jurassic Coast. Today would be a good day.

"Come on, little man. Let's go and have an adventure." As she strapped Kai into the carrier, she kissed the top of his head, now covered with fluffy blond hair, the undeniable love she felt for her son catching her by surprise. On days like these – sunny, dry weekends before the arrival of holidaymakers - she allowed herself a break from her work and enjoyed venturing out along the harbour and beach, her tiny companion strapped to her chest. Today they would take the coastal path from West Bay to Burton Bradstock over East Cliff, offering stunning views of the Jurassic Coast, passing towering cliffs, secluded coves and unique geological formations. It seemed that every time they took a walk along the well-worn path, there was evidence of the coastline having changed again – the wind, waves and weather having taken their toll on the soft sedimentary rocks. At one time, she felt as though her life was crumbling away too, especially in those early days following the breakdown in her relationship and her move away from Bristol, her home and her family. But now, after the dramatic change in her circumstances, she felt that her life had been shaped and reshaped, just like the dynamic nature of the coastline, offering her more stability than she had before. Kai had given her life meaning; she had served a purpose, in a way that she had never believed possible. Yet the lies, deception and guilt were constantly eroding any flashes of joy and happiness she experienced, knowing that she had something her sister could not have. Something she felt she had stolen from her. Moving forward, she couldn't imagine how she would ever be able to face Freya again. And for that reason, her life with Kai would have to remain a secret for as long as possible.

Chapter Twenty-Two

Bristol

"I'm planning on seeing some old friends on the Dorset coast in the next couple of days, Mum," Freya announced, sitting at her parents' kitchen table, flicking through a magazine without reading a word. Her father was in the garden and her mother was at the kitchen sink, her back to Freya.

"Really? But you're only here for such a short time. Shall we come with you and stay in a hotel nearby? Then we can all visit Ella," she replied, clearly surprised, as she joined her at the large farmhouse table.

"I'll probably only be gone overnight. It's a bit of a reunion, nothing more and then I'll be back. I wasn't planning on staying long."

"Oh, fair enough. But have you been in touch with Ella? I can't seem to get hold of her. Surely it would make sense to try and see her when you're in Dorset?"

"I haven't heard from her lately. She's busy. Anyway, I'm going to Christchurch; it's about 50 miles away from West Bay."

"Does she even know you're here? It does seem odd that we can't get together whilst we're all in the country for once! Do you know, I'm going to try again today and insist she makes time for us."

"Leave it, Mum. She must have her reasons. We don't know what's going on in her life."

"You're too forgiving. You've come all this way and she can't put herself out just for a few days."

"As I said, it doesn't matter. She's busy and she's been through a lot in the last couple of years. It can't have been easy for her to move to a new part of the country on her own." Freya was desperate to appease her mother and change the subject. This was something she wanted to do on her own. She had no plans to contact Ella before her visit; it was going to be a surprise.

West Bay

Ella's day had got off to a shaky start, caused by an unexpected email from Greg. The completed commission had graced the corner of her apartment for a week or two and she had wondered whether it would remain there forever. She had no plans to contact Greg. Freya had been the link between them and she had enquired after its progress on several occasions, but not lately.

Hi Ella.
I hope all is well with you. I was just wondering whether the seascape commission is ready. My clients have been happy to wait for it, knowing that good art can't be rushed, but they have been chasing it up this week. I would have left it for Freya to contact you, being that she's now working part-time at the gallery. However, she's in the UK at the moment, as you will no doubt be aware, so it's down to me to chase it up. When you see her, as I'm sure you will, please can you make arrangements directly with her for its shipping to the US and your fees.
Best wishes, Greg

It wasn't merely the fact that Greg had made direct contact with her that shook her, but the unexpected and perturbing news that Freya was in the UK. How come she hadn't been in touch with her about her visit? Freya's last few messages had mentioned possible ideas for meeting up, yet she felt she had successfully managed to deter her. But how long could Ella bury her head in the sand? She realised her time was probably almost up. Oddly, Freya hadn't been in touch over the past week or two, so maybe she had given up and had no plans to visit her. She wouldn't blame her. Ella had been nothing but distant and uncompromising whenever Freya tried to arrange to see her.

Her head in a spin, she wandered into Kai's nursery where he was taking his morning nap, bathed in a gentle, comforting glow. She could tell he was dreaming as his little fingers clasped the edge of his favourite soft blanket and he let out soft sighs of contentment. She watched transfixed, his tiny chest rising and falling rhythmically, his chubby cheeks glowing with the innocence of slumber.

Bristol

"Bye then. I'll be back tomorrow." Freya felt guilty at sloping off amid a white lie about her destination. Yet this was something she needed to do alone, and she had no idea how the day was going to turn out. In her heart, she felt something was amiss. There must be a reason for Ella's distance this past year and she was determined to find out.

"Drive carefully and let us know when you arrive," responded her father, as her mother stood frowning, clearly annoyed that Freya was going at all, especially without them. "It will take nearly three hours."

"Will do, Dad." She had studied options for the route: Bristol to West Bay was going to take less time than that – it was much closer than Christchurch. She was planning to travel down the M5 to Taunton and take the A-roads down to the coast, calculating she should arrive by mid-morning.

Although she wasn't familiar with West Bay, she believed it to be a small town and assumed it would be easy enough to locate Ella's apartment once there. In the past, when Freya lived in the UK, she loved to visit Lyme Regis, located just ten miles along the coast from West Bay, to walk along the Cobb on a windy day or scrabble amongst the sand for fossils, but that was usually as far as she had ventured along the Dorset coast. Today would be a new adventure and hopefully the end of the mystery surrounding her sister.

West Bay

Ever since reading Greg's email, Ella had felt on edge. She wondered whether she should message her sister in an attempt to find out what her plans were. She even contemplated going away for a couple of days, but realised that running away would only make things worse if that were possible. Surely Freya wouldn't just turn up? No, she would message or phone beforehand. Then she would be able to make some excuse to deter her from visiting.

As Kai took his morning nap, Ella sat at her laptop, planning to complete some outstanding work on her latest project for the local newsletter. Unable to focus, she re-read Greg's email, then wandered over to her seascape. It wouldn't be long before another dramatic rockfall changed the appearance of the cliff that was the focal point of her painting, causing a portion of the towering crag to break away and cascade down to the beach, dislodging smaller debris along the way. The fallen rocks would create a chaotic scene, reshaping the landscape and leaving behind a jumble of boulders and rubble.

Checking on Kai in his cot, still slumbering peacefully, she wandered into the kitchen for a much-needed coffee. Maybe then she would be able to settle back to her work for a short while before Kai woke up, ready to give him her full attention. Just as the kettle approached boiling point, she thought she heard the buzzer indicating someone was at her door. Most likely, it would be a delivery; she was expecting some parcels today. Desperate to avoid the repetition of a noise that might disturb her peaceful son, and keen to take delivery of her packages, she raced to the door.

[]

The journey was familiar to her as far as Lyme Regis, via the motorway and busy A-roads, then she enjoyed passing through the scenic countryside and charming villages along the coastal road towards West Bay, offering breathtaking views of the coastline before reaching the iconic golden, sandstone cliffs she had heard so much about. As she drove slowly around the quaint harbour, bustling with activity, she spotted colourful fishing boats bobbing in the water and fishermen unloading their catch. Reaching the far side of the harbour, she finally spotted Quay West – her sister's residence - offering spectacular views of the stunning cliffs framing the town, the bustling harbour lined with quaint shops and busy cafés, and the blue-green hues of the sea complementing the golden, sandy beach. Freya could see why Ella had settled here in this quintessential English seaside town, with its natural beauty and historic charm. Yet the rugged, scenic coastal experience of

West Bay could not be more different from the tropical, lively vibe of Delray Beach, known for its subtropical climate, sandy shores and vibrant beachfront, its shores lined with palm trees, trendy restaurants and boutiques.

Having parked the car opposite the block of penthouse apartments, she wandered hesitatingly towards her sister's home. Why was she feeling so nervous? Her heart was racing wildly in anticipation of Ella's reaction at seeing her after all these months and for a fleeting moment wondered whether she should message her to warn her of her arrival. No. That would defeat the object of her visit; she wanted to surprise her – in a good way of course. She envisaged Ella squealing with delight at her arrival and then falling into each other's arms filled with the excitement of being reunited. Then, they would open the bottle of champagne Freya had brought to celebrate their reunion and chat for hours, catching up on all their news, stories and secrets.

She held her breath as she pressed the buzzer to the second-floor apartment and placed her overnight bag on the floor, ready to hug her sister when she opened the door. Several seconds elapsed before she pressed again. Perhaps she was busy with work and she was interrupting her train of thought. Or maybe she was out, yet something told her she was not. This time, she felt she could hear footsteps approaching the door. She was at home after all and they were about to be reunited. Taking a deep breath, she stepped back a little, ready to greet her sister.

"F-Freya? Am I imagining things?" exclaimed Ella, leaping backward in shock. Her reaction was not what Freya had envisaged – no smiles, hugs or kisses yet.

"Surprise!" responded Freya, extending her arms in anticipation of an embrace.

"I can't believe it. What are you doing here? Why didn't you let me know you were coming?" So many questions.

"Well, are you going to ask me in?" Freya asked, laughing at her sister's shocked reaction. It was going to be alright, she felt sure. Within minutes, they would be opening that champagne and toasting their reunion. "Then I might be able to answer some of your questions!"

Yet, instead of ushering her inside, Ella froze and reached out to hold onto the door frame, as though to support herself. Of course, it was a shock for her, but Freya was taken aback by her sister's lack of warmth or welcome.

"Er... I'm busy. It's a bit difficult at the moment," Ella mumbled, looking distinctly uncomfortable. "It's not a good time."

"Ella? I've travelled hundreds of miles from the other side of the ocean to see you. Surely you want to see me? What's the matter?"

"You should have phoned," she repeated. "No one just turns up on someone's doorstep. You know I have to work."

Freya couldn't believe her sister's rude response and reluctance to see her. "But it's me, Ella. Your sister. I can sit quietly and wait for you to finish your work. Or if you like, I can come back in an hour or two," she ventured.

Silence fell between them as Ella accepted that she could not turn her sister away, yet she was in no position to welcome her inside. Then, just as she was about to suggest Freya return in an hour, gentle whimpering sounds could be heard emanating from within the apartment. Ella's heart sank at the disastrous timing of the end of Kai's morning nap - most likely disturbed by the arrival of their unwelcome visitor.

"What's that, Ella?" asked Freya puzzled, taking a step towards Ella's front door.

"What? I didn't hear anything," she replied, holding her breath and praying that for now, Kai would settle again and Freya would leave her in peace. But as the silence between them returned, Kai's cries became more animated. He was wide awake and wanted his mother.

"Ella. Let me in. I want to know what's going on," announced Freya impatiently, pushing past her sister into the hallway.

"No! Stop. You can't just walk in. I need to talk to you," she conceded, following Freya into the lounge, accompanied by the increasing demands of her little son.

"It would appear you are wanted," uttered Freya incredulously, flopping down in an armchair in shock, her eyes swimming with tears.

Ella felt sick as she entered the nursery, her little blond-haired baby now kicking his legs in excitement at the appearance of his mother, his arms outstretched as he began to gurgle in delight. *What am I going to say to Freya? What can I do to protect her?* she asked herself as she lifted Kai from his cot, kissing his baby-scented head and holding him tight. It was time to face the music.

Wandering slowly from Kai's nursery to the lounge door, she prayed for the ground to swallow them up. She was not prepared for this moment and had no idea how the next few minutes, hours and days would proceed, as she stood outside the closed door wishing that she could turn back the clock. Not just the last few minutes since she had opened the front door to Freya, but her time in Florida and that fateful New Year's Eve.

"When were you going to tell me? Or were you planning on never seeing me ever again?" asked Freya, shocked to the core by the realisation that her sister was a mother, her tears now cascading down her burning cheeks.

"What could I say, Freya, knowing how much you wanted a baby?"

"Words fail me, Ella. You've been lying to me for all this time. Why couldn't you have said something?"

Choosing her words carefully, she attempted an explanation to her heartbroken, childless sister. "It has been nothing short of a nightmare, Freya. I found out I was pregnant at the exact time you confided in me that you were unlikely to ever conceive. At first, I couldn't believe it was even possible, and I tried to deny it had happened. Then, when it became an unavoidable reality, you were in the middle of your fertility consultations. How could I have told you? It was the cruellest twist of fate."

"So, who's the father? Where is he?" Freya asked bluntly, still reeling from the shock.

Although Ella had anticipated the question, it still took her by surprise. "He's not part of it. He doesn't even know," she responded, shaking her head, hoping and praying that Freya would move on with her interrogation.

"A secret relationship you've kept to yourself? An old flame? A one-night stand? Tell me, Ella." She wasn't going to let it go.

"It's irrelevant, Freya. He's my son and his father doesn't know about him. It's for the best."

"For the best? So, what about in years to come when your son wants to know about his father? What are you going to say to him? Oh, it was just a one-night stand. You weren't planned. You weren't even wanted."

Ella chose not to respond. The situation was too painful and Freya was correct. Nothing about Kai's parentage was right. In truth, it could not be more wrong. She should never have had him, yet she could never have given him up.

"I cannot get my head around it, Ella," Freya continued. "Why didn't you tell us? It's not normal, to have a child and not tell your family. Do your friends know? Does Marcus know?"

"Marcus? No. He has nothing to do with it. My friends? To be honest, I don't have any close friends here in Dorset. I've been too busy juggling everything. It's not easy trying to work and bring up a baby as a single mum."

"Thank you for telling me, as I will never get to find out," responded Freya bitterly.

"I'm sorry. That was thoughtless and insensitive of me." Silence fell between the sisters. After a few painful moments, as though he knew how to break the ice, Kai began to grumble for attention. "I think he's ready for a drink and a snack."

"I'll hold him," uttered Freya quietly, standing up to take him.

"Oh, thank you. But don't worry, I can manage," responded Ella, unable to imagine how she could cope with Freya holding her husband's child.

"I said I'll take him," she repeated, clearly determined to have her way. Ella froze and clutched Kai tightly, dreading the inevitable handing over of her baby to her saddened, betrayed sister. "Pass him to me," she demanded, outstretching her arms.

"His name… It's Kai. It means *the ocean*," Ella explained, gently transferring him into Freya's arms before leaving the room, unable to face seeing her with him. "I'll make us a coffee, shall I?"

But Freya did not reply. It broke Ella's heart to see her son snuggle happily into her sister's chest, his tiny fingers grasping onto her silky blouse, nuzzling into the warmth of her embrace. Leaning heavily on the kitchen worktop, her head hanging in despair, anguish and sorrow washed over Ella in the knowledge that Kai belonged to Freya too. Her heart sank with the weight of the dreadful truth of Kai's birth as she felt her world crumbling inexorably into a pit of yet more lies, betrayal and deception.

☐

"He's gorgeous, Ella," said Freya, gently bouncing Kai on her knee. "Tell me all about him." It appeared that Freya had recovered from the initial shock discovery of her baby nephew. Her tears had dried up and her face was now all smiles as she cuddled and cooed over one very contented baby. There was no denying it, Freya was a natural.

"What do you want to know?" What a ridiculous response. Ella knew exactly what Freya wanted to know, but she needed to play for time. Should she reveal his birth date? It wouldn't take a mathematician to work out when he was conceived. "Well, it was an easy pregnancy and a textbook birth. No complications. He weighed in at 7lb 3oz and has been a dream baby. I've been so fortunate with him."

"When was he born?" asked Freya, coming straight to the point.

"25th September. An autumn baby." There was no point in lying about this; she could see for herself he was around seven or eight months old. Silence fell between them as Freya did the maths. "Shall I take him off you?" continued Ella, hoping to distract Freya from making the inevitable calculation.

"So, he was conceived around Christmas then?" she pursued, continuing to gaze at Kai, with no plans to pass him back to Ella. "Interesting…"

"What's interesting about that?" laughed Ella, desperately trying to make light of the glaring fact that he was conceived around the time she was visiting Freya over last Christmas and New Year.

"Hmm... A virgin birth then? Unless there's something you want to tell me." Freya was making it very difficult indeed for Ella; she had no plans to let her off the hook.

"Oh, Freya! It's not something I'm proud of. That's why I've wanted to keep it to myself. Remember I left Delray a couple of days earlier than planned?"

"Yes... You told me you were going to look at art galleries in Miami."

"I did do that, but I also had a one-night stand with a guy I met in a bar. Too much sun, too much booze - a big mistake."

"Wow! I don't believe it. That you could get pregnant after one time. It doesn't seem fair, does it?"

"It isn't. And I'm not proud of it, Freya. I was so shocked that I couldn't believe it had actually happened, and it was several months before I allowed myself to accept it. By then, all my conversations with you about what you were going through made it impossible for me to tell you what had happened. Life is so unfair, isn't it? There's you, with a seemingly perfect life, desperate for a baby, and then there's me – a single mum dealing with an unplanned pregnancy after a sordid one-night stand. How could I have told you? Put yourself in my shoes. Surely you can see why I tried to deny it and hide it from you? I didn't want to hurt you any more than you were already hurting from months and months of heartbreak and disappointment."

Freya was listening but seemed lost for words as she stared at the beautiful blue-eyed baby nestled comfortably in her lap, his fluffy blond hair framing his cherubic face. He reminded her of Greg. "He doesn't have your dark hair, does he?" she remarked suddenly, gently stroking his soft blond hair. "So, tell me about the mystery man. Your son appears to have inherited his hair colour."

Ella felt her heart constrict at the prospect of telling more lies. But Freya was not going to let it drop. "There's nothing to tell. I can hardly remember him, to be honest. It was merely a moment of madness."

"But where did you meet him? In a gallery? A bar?"

"Freya, please!" she implored, unable to face any more of her persistent questioning that was only going to lead to further fabrications. "I don't want to talk about it. He's irrelevant. I'm never going to see him again."

"Fair enough. I can see I'm not going to get much out of you." An awkward silence fell between them until Kai began to grizzle impatiently, appearing to sense the uncomfortable atmosphere forming. "I think he's had enough of me for now. Is he hungry?"

"I guess so. I'll take him from you. How about you? Would you like some lunch?"

"I was thinking maybe we could go out for lunch – my treat of course. I'd love to try out one of those food shacks I spotted around the harbour. Could we take Kai for a walk in this warm sunshine perhaps?"

"That would be lovely," Ella conceded, releasing a sigh of relief at changing the subject, hoping and praying that her sister's interrogation was at an end for now.

"So, do Mum and Dad know?" continued Freya over lunch.

"What do you think?" retorted Ella abruptly, annoyed by what she deemed to require an irritatingly obvious answer.

"Well, who knows? I'm still reeling from the shock. I just wondered whether they knew and you were all in it together, protecting poor childless Freya from even more heartache."

"Oh, Freya. I'm sorry. I didn't mean to snap at you. No, I just couldn't bring myself to tell Mum and Dad. That's why I've been so distant, from all of you, and why I didn't follow up on your plans for a family get-together. I just felt like I needed to disappear for a while and work out how to tell you all. I suppose I hoped and prayed that things would work out for you and Greg in the end, that your fertility treatment would be successful, and then I could let you know about Kai."

"So, are you going to tell them now? Because I don't think I'm going to be able to keep it to myself when I see them next."

"Of course. I'll tell them now that you know, and I'll try to explain my reasoning, as I have to you, that it was because I wanted to protect you."

"In person? Or are you going to message them?" she added somewhat sarcastically, Ella felt. "How about heading back to Bristol with me, for that long overdue family get-together? Surely, it's about time they saw their grandson - their one-and-only grandchild."

"I don't know," hesitated Ella, filled with dread at the prospect of yet more interrogation and having to respond with a pack of lies to cover up what could potentially destroy the entire family. "Let me think about it."

[ ]

Despite everything, it turned out to be an enjoyable afternoon. The sun continued to shine on them and Kai was content to be out in the fresh air, whilst the sisters chatted amiably over lunch about anything but the circumstances surrounding his birth. Thankfully, for now, Freya appeared to have accepted Ella's story about her one-night stand in Miami, and eventually, after weighing up the pros and cons, Ella had agreed to accompany Freya back to Bristol to see their parents. On one hand, she was dreading it, but on the other, she felt some sense of relief at the prospect of an end to hiding herself away, pretending that Kai didn't exist. They were going to be shocked and hurt at being kept in the dark, but she would try to explain her reasons, as she did to Freya, that the timing had made it impossible to tell them.

"I assume Mum and Dad know what you've been going through, Freya," mentioned Ella, presuming that Freya had shared her problems, at least with their mother. They had always been very close.

"Er... No, as it turns out," responded Freya, looking somewhat sheepish.

"No? Really? You surprise me."

"I don't know why you would be surprised. You haven't told her about Kai."

"I know, but you've always been so close to Mum. You know I've always found it hard to share things with her. She can be rather judgmental, can't she? She made it clear what she thought about

Marcus, and she doesn't understand why I moved down to Dorset."

Freya smiled in acknowledgement. "I suppose I thought it was too big a problem to share long-distance. What could she do? What can anyone do as it turns out? I felt I wouldn't be able to face the prospect of her worrying constantly and checking on progress every month. And I suppose I just hoped that it would work out in the end."

"Is there no chance at all then?"

"I don't think so. The fertility treatment hasn't worked and I've been told that there is virtually no hope of IVF being successful in my case." Freya explained fully the reasons why, leaving Ella understanding that their only hope of ever having a child would be through surrogacy or adoption. Fleetingly, she wondered whether Freya and Greg were now considering these options, but for some reason, felt the overwhelming need to change the subject.

"So, when are Mum and Dad off on their next trip?"

"Soon, I think. They certainly enjoy themselves, don't they?"

"Good for them, I say," concluded Ella, suddenly feeling doubtful that they were going to understand her dilemma.

Chapter Twenty-Three

Bristol

The sisters had driven separately to Bristol, as Freya's time in Dorset had come to an end, and Ella was not planning on a protracted visit. Throughout the journey, she was playing over and over in her mind what she was going to say to her parents, especially now that she knew that Freya had no plans to divulge her infertility issues to her parents. It made matters tricky, especially as she would probably end up in an even more complex web of lies than she was already in.

Pulling up on the drive behind Freya, her heart began to race at the prospect of seeing her parents after such a long time, now with a son they knew nothing about. Before their departure, the sisters had formulated a plan for their arrival to minimise the shock that was likely to follow. Freya, having arrived first, would tell their parents that she had changed her plans at the last minute and dropped in on Ella in West Bay. She would then warn them that Ella was following on behind, due to arrive shortly, and that she had a big surprise for them.

"Surprise? What surprise?" asked her mother somewhat agitated.

"Wait and see!" replied Freya, laughing. "It's a good surprise, believe me." Hearing Ella's car pull onto the drive, she made her parents sit down in the lounge while she went out to meet her.

"Come on. Mum's all wound up, as you can imagine. She's desperate to know what's going on. Is Kai OK?"

"He's fine. He's been asleep most of the journey. Hopefully, he'll be in a good mood now we're here. Well, here goes," murmured Ella, stepping out of the car and releasing Kai, still half asleep, from his car seat in the back. Ambling somewhat reluctantly to the front door, Kai in his mother's arms, and Freya carrying a small selection of toys and his changing bag, both sisters felt a sense of unease as they entered the house, unsure what reaction they were likely to face.

"I'm lost for words," uttered their mother, clearly shocked and struggling to process the fact that she had just found out she was a grandmother. "I just can't understand how, or why, you've kept it all to yourself. Why would you do that? It doesn't make sense."

"I know, Mum. To be honest, I'm not sure what I was thinking. It was such a shock to discover I was pregnant, and if I'm honest, I was a bit ashamed at it being so unplanned."

"So, what were you thinking? That you'd hide him away until he was 18 and then set him free?"

"No, of course not. I just needed to get things straight in my mind. I needed to work out how I was going to bring him up on my own, balancing work and living away from family and friends. I wanted to be in a position to say: here he is and we're doing fine - and that is exactly where we are now."

"Well, he's a wonderful little chap. Congratulations my darling," offered Dad, supportive as ever. "Can you stay for a few days, so we can get to know him a bit?"

"Thank you, Dad. I could stay overnight, but I haven't planned to stay longer this time."

"He's got blond hair," said her mother suddenly, stating the blindingly obvious. It was going to take a while for her to come round to what had been not only a shock, but a disappointment that she hadn't been involved along the way, through Ella's pregnancy and Kai's birth. "He hasn't got that from you. So, who's the father?"

"Mum, leave it," answered Freya abruptly, on Ella's behalf, sensing building tension in the room.

"It's OK, Freya. I don't mind telling Mum the truth," admitted Ella. "I don't know the father. Kai is my child – mine and the product of a one-night stand."

"I see," responded her mother, temporarily silenced by Ella's revelation.

As the day wore on, the mood eventually began to lighten. Ever since their arrival, Freya had been incredibly supportive of her sister and refused to allow their mother to dampen their spirits or pursue a relentless stream of questions. Her father was his usual laid-back self, accepting and enjoying the fact that he was now a proud grandad. It was clear that her mother had struggled to understand why she had been kept in the dark for so long, yet at the same time, was thrilled to meet her grandson, who appeared more than happy to meet her too. Ella and Freya exchanged knowing smiles as their mother took Kai off into the garden purportedly to show him the goldfish in their raised pond and point out hungry sparrows perched on the wooden bird table. Looking through the window, it was heartening to see Kai content in her mother's arms as she snuggled him close, whispering in his ear and stroking his head affectionately. Seeing that he had won her over, Ella hoped that she had been forgiven – for now at least.

Curled up together on the sofa, the sisters were finally enjoying Freya's bottle of champagne, opened amidst a feeling that there was now something to celebrate: they were all reunited; Kai had been introduced to the family and their parents had retired happily to bed.

"Thank you for being so supportive, Freya. I couldn't have coped with today without you."

"It's fine. It was always going to be a shock for Mum, as it was for me, but I think she's got used to the idea now."

"I reckon so. They've bonded already, haven't they?"

"They certainly have and that's no surprise. He's gorgeous, Ella. You're so lucky," added Freya with a tinge of sadness in her voice.

"I am and I know it. I didn't realise it at first because it was such a massive shock. Now I know I've been truly blessed."

"I'm pleased for you, Ella, but it makes me even more sad for myself. I'm just being honest with you. Seeing Kai and spending just a short amount of time with him has made me realise how desperate I am to have a child in my life. Until now, I've always said that if I couldn't have a child using my own eggs or womb, then I wouldn't pursue it further.

But the problem lies with me, Ella; there's nothing wrong with Greg. So now, I think the time has come to stop being so narrow-minded and selfish and consider the other options available to us."

Ella caught her breath as she realised what her sister was implying. She was referring to adoption or surrogacy, yet mentioning Greg's unimpaired ability to father a child led Ella to believe that her first choice would be surrogacy. As a deafening silence fell between them, Freya's distant gaze and furrowed brows indicated that she was deep in thought, triggering in Ella a suffocating sense of panic at what Freya might be about to propose.

Just as Ella was about to change the subject in an attempt to lighten the mood, the uncomfortable silence was interrupted by the ringtone of Freya's mobile phone, causing them both to start.

"Hiya, darling! How are doing? What time is it at home?" asked Freya, clearly excited to be in touch with her husband on the other side of the ocean. An ideal opportunity to slope off to bed, thought Ella, to escape the awkward conversation she felt was sure to follow if they had sat there for much longer. Mouthing 'goodnight' to her sister, she smiled in relief and left the room.

Chapter Twenty-Four

Bristol

After a restless night, Ella was more than ready to head home. Her head had been filled with fear and dread at the prospect of her sister broaching the subject of surrogacy, so she was keen to ensure that her final hour in Bristol was spent in the company of the entire family to avoid it happening. Consequently, the conversation around the breakfast table was mainly superficial, revolving mostly around Kai, who appeared to be enjoying the attention.

"So, how are you managing to cope with work now you've got Kai?" asked her father, helping himself to another cup of coffee.

"At the moment, I tend to work when he sleeps. He takes two long naps during the day and is in bed early evening. It's working out fine, although I'm not taking on as much as I did before. Once his sleep routine changes, I might have to make some changes – perhaps a couple of mornings at nursery."

"And what about your painting? Are you still doing that?" added her mother, helping Kai with his breakfast.

"Not so much. It's mainly graphic design for local companies now."

"What about your seascape?" interjected Freya. "Mum, you should see what she's been working on for Greg. It's brilliant. Which reminds me, Ella, I meant to ask whether it's ready to be shipped."

"I think it is. At last. I know it's taken a while, but it seems that every time I take a walk along the beach, the structure of the cliffs has changed again and it makes me want to keep working on it."

"What do you mean, about the cliffs changing? Surely, it's a gradual process," enquired her father, genuinely puzzled.

"You'd think so, wouldn't you? But the cliffs along the Jurassic Coast are made up of soft, easily erodible rocks, like limestone, shale and clay, so the erosion and weathering are rapid. New formations are constantly emerging while others are disappearing into the sea. Since I began the painting, there have been some huge rockfalls, causing sections to crumble and collapse."

"What a worry. I honestly didn't appreciate it was happening so quickly."

"But the painting, Ella… You'll never be able to keep up with the changes, so I think the time has come to release it to Greg's clients." Freya was right, of course. Ella had been using this argument as a reason to hold onto the painting and avoid contact with Greg. But now the time had come to release it; she would arrange with Freya to get it shipped as soon as possible, as Greg had suggested in his email. The sooner the better, to avoid further communication with him.

"Yes, you're quite right. I'll get it shipped next week. But I'm glad you've seen it and are happy with it – it's the largest commission I've ever undertaken, you know."

"Perhaps it will be the start of something big! I know Greg would like to display your work in the gallery. Maybe you could get in touch with him," Freya suggested, filling Ella with dread at the very idea. She aimed to sever contact with Greg, not to develop an ongoing business relationship.

"What a great opportunity," added her father, enthusiastically. "It sounds like another trip to Florida is on the cards, Ella!"

Ella had no plans to return to Florida. Not now, not ever. Taking Kai into her arms, she wondered whether she would ever be able to face Greg again. For now, she had managed to create a plausible story surrounding Kai's father, but in her heart, she wondered whether it would be possible or ethical to conceal the truth from her son for the rest of his life.

"We'll have to see," murmured Ella without conviction. "Anyway, I think I'd better be making tracks. If I leave now, I'm hoping Kai will fall asleep on the journey."

It took ten minutes or so to gather their few belongings and exchange goodbyes, by which time, Ella was relieved to be heading home, having escaped further tricky conversations with Freya. She had done it; she had finally introduced Kai to her family and somehow managed to explain her way out of what was becoming an increasingly complex web of lies.

PART THREE

Chapter Twenty-Five

Delray Beach

"She has a son and she never told you?" Greg was utterly flabbergasted by Freya's news that her sister was the mother of an eight-month-old baby. Doing the inevitable maths, he felt an additional overwhelming shock at discovering he may have fathered a child. He needed to know more. What had Ella told her family? What did the child look like? Did he look like him? "So, who's the father? Did she tell you?" His head was spinning with questions.

"She said it was a one-night stand," offered Freya, planning to keep the details to herself – not that she knew very much. It was none of his business.

"A one-night stand? Where did she meet him?" He felt the need to know more. His mind flitted back to that fateful New Year's Eve in the dunes – a night he'd tried in vain to forget. Surely, the child must be his.

"I don't know. It doesn't matter, does it?" Freya was keen to put an end to his questions, thinking it odd he was even interested.

"Well, no, but I find it surprising, that's all."

"What? That she had a one-night stand? It doesn't surprise me at all. She's been single for a while now and she's a very attractive woman, as I'm sure you'd agree." Glancing over at her husband, she couldn't help but notice a gentle blush spread across his cheeks before he hastily looked away from her. It was clear that he did agree.

"Do you have a photo of the child?" he continued, steering his questions away from Ella.

"His name is Kai, and of course I have a picture. Do you want to see?" she asked, scrolling through the photos captured on her phone. For some reason, she felt irritated by his interest. She had imagined a very different response from him when she told him about the baby. She had expected sympathy, knowing that it must have been a huge shock for her to discover her sister had given birth in secret. She had expected some consideration for the fact that she had undertaken months of infertility treatment, disappointment and ultimately heartbreak at the realisation that she was never going to become a mother. Pushing her disappointment aside, she slid her mobile phone across the kitchen table for Greg to see a photo of her holding her blond-haired baby nephew.

"Oh! That's a great photo of you," responded Greg, gazing at the photo for several seconds, clearly deep in thought. Perhaps he was reflecting on the fact that his wife had become an aunt but would never be a mother. "And the baby – Kai – he's cute too."

Cute. What a weak adjective to describe him. Little did she know, that Greg was reeling from the shock of seeing what he believed to be a mirror image of himself when he was a baby, with his soft blond hair framing his angelic face, his big blue eyes and cheeky grin. It was as clear as day – Kai was his child. Surely Freya could see it too? But she wouldn't suspect a thing, would she? Why would she, if Ella had offered Freya a version of totally believable events? One that left him out of the frame. He wondered what she had told Freya and how he could find out without raising suspicion. For now, he would let matters lie and change the subject, sensing that Freya was not planning to open up to him.

"I meant to ask you earlier whether you got anywhere with the commission?"

Feeling relieved to be moving on from baby talk, Freya told Greg that she had seen the painting and arranged for it to be shipped, mentioning how impressed she was with Ella's talent and suggesting he pursue his idea of showcasing her work in the gallery. Whilst he seemed relieved that the commission was finally completed, Freya sensed he was distracted by something. His mind was wandering; she could see it in his eyes.

"Is everything OK, Greg?" Freya finally asked, feeling frustrated at his odd behaviour. "You seem preoccupied."

"Yes, yes. I'm fine. Just processing everything. Your news has given me lots to think about."

"Do you mean regarding the gallery?"

"Well, yes. And the baby…"

"The baby?" Freya couldn't imagine what he was about to divulge.

"I do appreciate what a shock it must have been to discover your sister had given birth during the time you've been undergoing fertility treatment. To be honest, I'm amazed at how well you seem to have accepted it. Deep down, are you ok?"

Taken aback by his thoughtful words, her eyes filled with tears. "I don't know, Greg. I thought I was, but now I'm not so sure."

"Talk to me. Tell me what you're thinking. There's no point hiding things from me, after all we've been through this past year."

She wanted to tell him everything: how unfair it was that Ella had conceived after a one-night stand; how she was ashamed of the envy she felt towards her sister who was now the mother to the most perfect, beautiful baby; how she thought that maybe they shouldn't give up on their dreams to become parents after all – not when there were still options open to them. But not tonight. She needed more time to think things through.

West Bay

During the week since Freya's visit, Ella and Kai managed to settle back into comfortable routines with relative ease. In all honesty, she felt as though a huge weight had been lifted from her shoulders now that Kai was no longer a secret. Upon her return to Florida, Freya had messaged Ella at length, sending her the warmest of wishes and offering her full support for the difficult decisions she now knew that Ella had faced during the year. To her relief, there was no mention of Greg in her message, other than to thank her for shipping the seascape. Maybe Ella was worrying needlessly. Now that Freya was back in Florida and busy with the gallery, it seemed probable that she would push thoughts of having a child to the back of her mind again. She certainly hoped so.

It had been a good day. The fine weather was encouraging visitors back to West Bay for the start of the summer season and the kiosks around the harbour were bustling with activity once more. That afternoon, Ella and Kai had wandered leisurely along the jetty, taking in the invigorating scent of saltwater and the cries of seagulls soaring overhead, the waves below crashing against the shore with rhythmic intensity, creating a soothing soundtrack to their stroll. With every step, Ella filled her lungs with the fresh, salty air, rejuvenating her spirit as she enjoyed the views of the towering cliffs, their stratified layers telling their ancient stories. Once home, fed and bathed, Kai was more than ready to settle down for the night, leaving Ella free to pour herself a glass of chilled white wine and relax in her favourite chair to watch the sunset painting the sky with vibrant shades of orange, pink and crimson.

For the first time in ages, she felt truly content – relieved that Kai was no longer a secret and that Freya appeared to have forgiven her. She was also glad to be rid of the commission that had graced the corner of her apartment for months; it had been a daily reminder of her dalliance with Greg. For the rest of her life, however, she would have to learn to live with her guilt. Thankfully the oceanic distance between the sisters would mean that their paths would seldom cross.

Feeling relaxed in the warmth of the early evening, she felt her eyelids begin to droop as her mind drifted to happy thoughts of forthcoming summer days on the beach with Kai. Everything was going to be alright, she felt, allowing herself to give in to her weariness.

Suddenly, after what could not have been more than a matter of minutes, she was awoken by the abrupt notification ping of an incoming email. Tempted to ignore it, she found she could not settle and decided to refill her empty wine glass and spend a few minutes with her laptop. After all, she had all night to relax.

Opening up her email inbox, she was shocked to discover the sender was Greg. What could he possibly want? Perhaps it was a courtesy message about the commission or even a suggestion of putting more business her way. There was only one way to find out.

Hi

I'm not sure that an email is the right way to contact you about this, but I don't think I have much choice, do I? So here goes.

Freya told me that you have had a son since you came to visit us.

Congratulations. The only thing is, I've done the maths and I've seen his photo. And I'm no detective, but I can tell he's mine. Am I right, Ella? If I am, I deserve to know the truth.

I look forward to hearing from you,
Greg

Ella must have stared at the screen, reading and re-reading its contents for several minutes, shocked to the core. For some reason, it hadn't even occurred to her that Greg might make the connection. Surely, Freya would have recounted Ella's story to Greg about her one-night stand in Miami at the end of her trip to Florida? And after the way she had behaved on New Year's Eve, it was not beyond the realms of possibility that it had happened again, with someone else. Yet, there was no denying that her son bore a strong resemblance to her blond-haired, blue-eyed brother-in-law. So, what did he want and what would he do with the truth?

She needed to take time to think before replying. Her gut reaction was to send an immediate response denying his involvement and sticking to her one-night stand story. Yet, that would perpetuate the lies that she was struggling to live with. She tried to imagine how he might be feeling right now. He must be shocked, disbelieving, and unsure of how to proceed, especially in the light of his infidelity. Perhaps he was filled with a sudden sense of duty and responsibility, and a need to provide for his child. Or did he fear judgment from others and the impact it would have on his life? Maybe he, like Ella, needed time to reflect on his actions leading to the situation before deciding how to proceed.

[]

It took several days for her to compose a reply:

Dear Greg
Apologies for the delay in responding to your email, but I needed time to think it through.

Kai was born as the result of a one-night stand, just as Freya told you. But as you suspected from the striking resemblance, it happened on New Year's Eve, not in Miami as I led Freya to believe. I wanted to protect Freya – and your marriage. Surely you see why I lied to her? And why I kept Kai's birth a secret. I was so ashamed about what we had done and incredibly guilty that it resulted in me having a child whilst Freya was undergoing her fertility investigation.

Every day, I struggle to live with the guilt and I don't want to ruin Freya's life by her finding out what happened between us. It was a stupid moment of madness, nothing more. Not enough to ruin your marriage, surely?

There, you have it. The truth. What you do with it is up to you, but please, Greg, think carefully about your next move. You and Freya have each other – this might destroy what you have.

Regards, Ella.

Checking and editing her words many times before pressing 'send', she hoped and prayed that Greg would weigh everything up before pressing what she believed would be a 'self-destruct' button. She wondered whether he would respond to her email, letting her know of his decision or asking further questions of her about his son. Only time would tell.

Chapter Twenty-Six

Delray Beach

"I've been thinking, Greg," announced Freya, snapping him out of his reverie. "Maybe we should give serious consideration to surrogacy. What do you think?"

"Where's this suddenly come from? You've always given me every reason under the sun why that isn't an option for you. I thought we'd made a final decision about having a child."

"You mean about not having a child," she responded curtly.

"You know what I mean. I thought you were happy working in the gallery. That's what it was all about – to help you move on."

"Do you seriously think that working a few hours every now and again in the gallery is enough to stop me thinking about becoming a mother? You have to be joking."

"No, of course not. But we've been through this so many times, Freya. You've always said you only wanted a child if you could carry it yourself. And that isn't ever going to happen."

"Wow, Greg. What's happened to you? Why are you being so defeatist?"

"It's not me. I'm only going on what you've always said. I truly believed we were moving on from all this."

"All this? Is that what you call it?" Freya's eyes began to fill with tears of frustration. She had changed her mind. Wasn't it obvious that meeting her sister's baby had given her food for thought? Surrogacy was still an option for them, and an incredibly viable one, having discovered that her sister had already given birth to the most perfect, healthy baby.

"I'm sorry, my darling," responded Greg, mortified at seeing his wife so upset. He had been flippant and thoughtless in his handling of the topic that was clearly still at the forefront of his wife's mind. "I can see we need to sit down and talk about this again. Let's plan to do that this evening. I was just about to head off to the gallery."

Feeling relieved and reassured, Freya agreed and decided to spend her day at home researching – for the millionth time – the implications, possibilities and legalities involved in surrogacy.

[]

Surrogacy *is an arrangement, often supported by a legal agreement, whereby a woman agrees to* delivery/labour *on behalf of another couple or person, who will become the child's parent(s) after birth. People may seek a surrogacy arrangement when a couple or single woman does not wish to carry a pregnancy themselves, when pregnancy is medically impossible, when* pregnancy risks *are dangerous for the intended mother, or when a single man or a* male same-sex couple *wishes to have a child.*

Freya knew the definition off by heart; she was the woman in that paragraph for whom pregnancy was medically impossible. She knew the options too. For her, it would have to be a traditional surrogacy arrangement whereby Greg's sperm would be used to fertilise the surrogate's egg. Reading on, insemination could be through natural or artificial means. In other words, it could be through sex. At least surrogacy would lead to their child being genetically related to Greg. Then there were the legal implications to consider: Freya would need to go through an adoption process to have legal parental rights. But this wouldn't deter her - it was still an option for them to discuss seriously. They could have a child after all, and she now knew who she intended to ask to act as the surrogate.

[]

He was late. The table was set, dinner was ready and the wine was chilled. Glancing at the clock, Freya was determined to keep her frustration to herself; she didn't want to create a poor atmosphere the moment he eventually walked through the door. Yet she was annoyed; he knew she would be waiting for him this evening. He had promised

Freya that they would discuss her latest thoughts about having a child of their own, so she had spent all day, and many others before, researching final options for them. She was ready for him.

Wandering outside to sit on the edge of the pool with a chilled glass of Sauvignon, she waited patiently for the sound of his car sweeping onto their drive. Finally, just as she was about to refill her glass, she heard him arrive.

"Hi, darling! Sorry I'm late," he called out as soon as he made his entrance.

Without responding, Freya strolled into the kitchen to meet him, a warm smile painted on her face in an attempt to welcome him home after his busy day.

"You wouldn't believe it. Just as I was about to lock up, three customers walked in. I couldn't turn them away," he explained, hoping to be forgiven.

"It's fine, although we should probably make a start on dinner."

"Of course. No worries. Let me pour some wine."

During the next half hour or so, whilst enjoying his favourite appetiser of conch fritters with aioli, they chatted amiably about the gallery. Freya was keen to leave her important contribution to the conversation until the evening was well underway, ideally managing to maintain Greg's high spirits with a constant flow of wine. Eventually, the moment arrived.

"Remember what we started talking about this morning?" she began, smiling as she stroked his hand affectionately. "Well, I've been giving it a lot more thought. I've come to accept that surrogacy is a serious option for us, Greg."

Even though Greg was expecting to hear this, his heart skipped a beat as he thought about his baby son living on the other side of the ocean. In all honesty, he'd thought of little else all day and had re-read Ella's email so many times, that her words were ingrained in his memory. After weighing up all the options, he had come to a decision: there was no way he could tell Freya about Kai. Ella was right, it would destroy everything. For now, he would keep it to himself and listen to what Freya had to say. "What's brought about your change of heart?"

he asked gently.

"Well, I'm sure you've guessed. Since my trip to the UK, all I've thought about is having a baby. Seeing Ella with Kai has made me understand what we're missing. You would love him, Greg."

"I'm sure I would," he managed to utter, feeling his heart begin to race wildly at the mention of Ella and Kai. This was going to be a challenging conversation, there was no doubt about it.

"So, I've come up with an idea…" At this, Greg felt the need to fetch himself another drink – something stronger – anticipating with dread what he was about to hear.

"An idea? Sounds ominous."

"A great idea, as it turns out. I can't believe we haven't considered it before!" she continued excitedly. "It's an obvious solution."

"I'm not sure what you're about to suggest. I can't imagine what's going through your mind." What he meant was that he was dreading what she was about to suggest and feared what was undoubtedly going through her mind. Yet he sensed it was important to listen, appear to go along with her plans and avoid creating any suspicion. "I'm all ears," he added attempting to lighten the mood.

"Ella. We'll ask Ella." That was it – no further elaboration offered or required, it appeared.

"Ella?"

"As I said. It's obvious. Ella has managed to give birth to a healthy baby boy and sailed through both the pregnancy and labour. And she is family, so we can trust her. She can be our surrogate – her egg, your sperm. She can have a baby for us, Greg! It's a perfect solution.

If only it were, thought Greg. He would need to choose his words carefully if he were to give the impression that he was prepared to consider it as a viable option for them. "Surrogacy is a huge decision, Freya. It would take a lot of careful consideration, not to mention professional advice, guidance and support."

"I know, but I just have a feeling that Ella would want to help us."

"What about the emotional, legal and medical implications? It's so complex."

"Don't be so negative! We should at least think about it."

"I'm not being negative. I'm being serious and practical. I haven't said no, have I?"

"It is an option, Greg. We could ask her though, couldn't we?"

"As I said, let's give it careful thought before asking her," suggested Greg, playing for time. "Don't go rushing into anything."

"So, you're not ruling it out then?" confirmed Freya, feeling a sense of relief.

"I'm not ruling it out, but I want us to think it through carefully."

Nodding in agreement, Freya felt that their discussion had gone as well as could be expected. What she was suggesting was huge, and was bound to have repercussions for all of them in one way or another. She tried to imagine Ella's reaction to her idea. Would she be willing and supportive, honoured to be asked to help her sister fulfil her dream? She was bound to have mixed feelings; perhaps both a willingness to help and apprehension about the physical and emotional challenges of surrogacy. Freya was fully aware of the reservations she might have about the impact on her own life and future plans, or the potential emotional complexities of carrying a child for them. There was, of course, one other possibility: she might simply decline to help.

Chapter Twenty-Seven

West Bay

An entire week had elapsed since emailing Greg with the news that he had fathered a child, leaving Ella feeling constantly on tenterhooks. She was surprised that there had been no word from him and checked her junk mail regularly just in case she'd missed an email from him. Nothing. In the absence of a response, she could only imagine what was going through his mind. He was bound to be shocked to the core, especially after a year of facing Freya's fertility treatment. In all probability, he would be experiencing guilt and regret for the night that led to Kai's conception, particularly considering the familial relationship involved. And what about feelings of responsibility and obligation? Would he want to support or care for his child in any way or would he choose to deny his involvement? And then there was Freya and the impact of the revelation on their marriage and family bonds to consider. The complex mix of emotions he was bound to be experiencing was going to require careful reflection, communication, and decision-making, and it was going to take time. For her part, she hoped and prayed he would opt to focus on Freya and the preservation of his marriage. She couldn't deny that what happened between them was immoral, but it had been meaningless, and certainly not worth destroying everything for. Surely he could see that.

Delray Beach

A whole week had elapsed since Freya had raised the subject of surrogacy with Greg. Since then, he had been unusually subdued and pensive. Instead of worrying about his reticence, she took it as a positive sign that he was giving the matter serious thought. After all, he hadn't dismissed the idea; he had asked for time. The more Freya thought about it, the more the idea appealed to her and she hoped that

Greg would feel the same way in time. It crossed her mind to approach Ella now, before broaching the subject again with Greg, then at least she would know whether it was a serious option. Yes, that's what she would do today; she would speak to Ella while Greg was at the gallery.

Greg had thought about nothing else since his conversation with Freya last week. The answer to her question about whether surrogacy was an option for them was simple: no, never. The wider issue of asking Ella whether she would consider being their surrogate was what was playing on his mind. He had already fathered a child with her. How could either of them possibly enter into discussions about surrogacy with their complex background of betrayal and deception? It was unthinkable. Part of him hoped that he would never have to lay eyes on Ella again – then there was at least a chance of escaping from the ever-present cloud of guilt that hung over him. Yet part of him was desperate to see her again, this time as the mother of his child.

After days of deliberation and several sleepless nights, he had finally arrived at a decision: he needed to see his son. He'd planned how to make it possible; he would leave Freya in charge of the gallery whilst he took a trip to the UK, under the pretext of visiting art collections at various coastal locations. As for Ella, he had no plans to forewarn her of his visit.

Chapter Twenty-Eight

West Bay

It wasn't an email from Greg that eventually solved the mystery of his lack of contact, but a phone call from Freya, exactly a week after breaking the news.

"Hi! How are you?" Freya began. "I thought I'd give you a call rather than messaging."

"It's great to hear from you. I'm fine, thank you," Ella replied trying hard to maintain a calm, natural tone, despite her racing heart in the face of what she feared might be about to follow.

"And Kai? How's he doing?"

"He's doing well too. Growing fast and into everything now he's more mobile."

"How exciting, though. You must send me some more photos."

"I will. He's got six teeth now, so it's changed his appearance a bit."

"Is he still sleeping well?" Freya seemed genuinely interested to know.

"Still going through the night, so I can't complain."

"You're very lucky. So lucky."

"I am," responded Ella, realising that Freya was referring to being a mother, not merely having a child who slept through the night. "So how about you? What's your news?"

Taking a deep breath, Freya had decided to come right out with it; there was no point in prevaricating. "Well, that's the reason I wanted to speak to you, Ella. Since visiting you, I've come to realise that I have to pursue my dream of having a child of my own. I could see for myself what joy Kai has brought you, how he's given you a real sense of purpose and new direction in your life. Something that I feel I lack in my own life."

"It hasn't been easy, Freya. And some days are really tough," she explained in an attempt to steer her away from the path down which she was evidently heading.

"I can imagine. Especially being on your own."

"Too true. Sometimes, weirdly, I feel lonelier than I did before. I suppose it's the overwhelming responsibility of being a parent and not having anyone here to turn to when I'm having a bad day."

"That makes sense."

"Anyway, enough about me. Tell me about the gallery."

"I want to talk to you about something important, Ella," replied Freya, an ominous silence forming between them as she prepared herself to ask her question, whilst Ella held her breath, knowing what was to follow. "Don't answer straight away. Just hear me out. As I said, we seem to have come full circle and, now that we know my fertility treatment has failed, we realise that we still want to pursue having a baby of our own. Only one option remains, and that is surrogacy." She paused, and the silence on the other end of the line told her that Ella knew what was coming. "Greg and I want to ask you to be our surrogate. We both want you to know that we've given it a great deal of thought and understand that what we're asking is huge. We will respect your decision and promise you that it won't affect our relationship."

"What about adoption?" asked Ella, clutching at straws.

"That is an option, but it's not for us. We've looked into it. But for you to carry our child, knowing that Greg was the natural father, would be halfway to fulfilling our dreams, Ella. We understand what we are asking is huge, as are the medical procedures, legal considerations and emotional aspects that it would entail. But I promise that we will be there for you every step of the way. Please, Ella, please think about it."

How was she expected to reply to a request so huge, when her sister's dreams depended on her? She would somehow need to deliver her response with empathy and understanding, recognising the emotions involved. She must express gratitude for being considered for such an important role, acknowledging the trust and confidence she had placed in her. In refusing, she would need to explain her decision clearly and respectfully, offering love and support in other ways. Without a doubt, she needed time to compose her response. "I will give it some thought, Freya, but what you are asking has come as something of a shock. I'm going to need time to process it."

"Of course, I completely understand. Thank you for at least considering it. I love you so much, Ella, and for you to be my baby's natural mother has got to be the closest I will ever get to achieving my dream. Shall we speak in a few days when you've had time to think about it?"

"Yes. I'll be in touch before the weekend," she responded quietly, desperately trying to contain a whole range of emotions bottled up inside her.

The moment the call was ended, Ella made her way quietly into Kai's nursery. Standing over his cot in the comforting glow of his night light, she gazed tenderly at her son, marvelling at the innocence of his peaceful slumber, in the painful knowledge that he was exactly what her sister was asking for.

Delray Beach

"So, when are you planning to go?" asked Freya, somewhat surprised by his sudden announcement that he planned to take a trip to the UK.

"At the weekend. I was thinking maybe Saturday. I'll keep the weekend free to get over the travelling and then visit galleries from Monday. I've been making calls all day today."

"Sounds great," responded Freya flatly, thinking the whole idea was a little random. He had never done this sort of thing before. In this day and age of the World Wide Web, the need to travel to source artwork was unnecessary.

"Are you sure you're happy to run the gallery for the week?"

"Of course I am. I'm perfectly capable."

"Well, I know that. I meant, do you need me to do a handover or anything?"

"I'll be fine."

"So, what's the problem? You don't seem too happy."

"It's not your trip that's bothering me. Or the gallery. It's the fact that we talked about asking Ella to be our surrogate and you haven't mentioned a word about it since. It was over a week ago."

"Believe me, I've thought about little else, Freya. To be honest with you, I'm still thinking about it. I do have deep reservations though."

"I see. Do you want to share those with me now? Or do you want to wait till you get back?" To be truthful, Freya was happy to give him more time whilst she waited to hear from Ella. Hopefully, by the time he returned from his trip to the UK, she would have had word from Ella that she was happy to proceed.

"Give me the week, my love. It's a huge decision, and let's face it, I'm going to have plenty of thinking time over the next week, especially on those long-haul flights!"

"Fair enough. So where are these galleries? Are you doing the south coast?"

"I think that's my best bet. I'll probably head from London down to Brighton and travel west."

"Probably? I thought you had it all planned out."

"Roughly speaking. I want to see as much of the south coast as I can whilst I'm there. In my mind, I have this idea of portraying the English coastline as being the antithesis of our Floridian coast in terms of geography and culture, yet linked by climate change across the ocean."

"I like that. So, do you plan to visit West Bay?" asked Freya tentatively.

"Er... Probably no need. I know Ella's work and that part of the coast pretty well. I'll be focussing on other areas. I'd like to see Lulworth Cove for starters."

"I've seen some amazing pictures of it, with its horseshoe shaped formations. But if you're that close to Ella, you might as well pay her a visit." The fact that Greg was thinking of visiting the Jurassic Coast filled her with hope that he might make the effort to see her sister. She truly believed that once he saw Ella with Kai, Greg would realise that the answer to her question was yes: Ella would make the perfect surrogate mother to their child.

West Bay

Ella had no idea how she was going to respond to Freya's request, but she needed to do something about it sooner rather than later. She had promised Freya she would think about it and let her have her decision before the weekend, but she was going to need a few more days. A blunt refusal was not appropriate; she would need to explain her reasons, but where to begin? Having given birth, she now knew first-hand that maternal feeling of instant bonding and unconditional love. She was certain she would not be able to carry a child for nine months and then hand it over to someone else, even to her poor, desperate sister. Then there was the whole guilt around Kai's conception weighing her down; she was sure Freya would never want to see her again if she knew what had happened that night. Her plan had always been to create a distance between them so that she would never need to know. Cowardly and dishonest perhaps, but surely kinder in the long run?

The other option was to agree to do it. If it hadn't been for her one-night stand with Greg, would she have ever considered it as a possibility? She certainly felt empathy towards her sister and a desire to see her happy, and she understood that being able to offer a genetic connection to the baby would maintain a biological link with the family. Part of her even felt she owed it to her sister; perhaps it was the price she must pay for her sins.

The one thing she was certain of was that she needed more time to compose her response.

Chapter Twenty-Nine

West Bay

The harbour was bustling with activity as Ella rehearsed her carefully prepared response to Freya's request inside her head. Kai, happy to be pushed along in his stroller, was enjoying the sound of seagulls overhead and the sweet and savoury aromas wafting from the busy food kiosks. The holiday season was now well underway, with locals and visitors exploring the waterfront shops, enjoying boat trips, and strolling along the pebbly shoreline, hunting for fossils.

Stopping at her favourite coffee stall overlooking the picturesque harbour, Ella scooped Kai out of his stroller, bouncing him playfully on her lap as she waited for her cappuccino to arrive. Entertained by the colourful bobbing boats and hungry seagulls on the lookout for scraps, Kai babbled happily, distracting Ella from the anguish that had overwhelmed her for the past few days. Later today, taking account of the five-hour time difference between the UK and Florida, Ella planned to let Freya know that she had come to a decision.

"Hello Ella," came a deep male voice from behind her, taking her by surprise. Yet before she had the chance to turn around with Kai on her lap, the mystery person had taken the seat opposite her. No words could express her shock at discovering his identity.

"Greg? What on earth are you doing here?" She felt her heart racing as Kai began to snuggle closer into her for comfort and protection from the stranger.

"Sorry if I've startled you, but I was in the area."

"In the area? What are you talking about? Why didn't you tell me you were visiting?"

"So many questions! I'm here on business so I thought I would visit you whilst I'm over and get to know my son…" His eyes were fixed on Kai as he allowed his words to sink in.

"How did you know where to find me?" she asked, tightening her hold on Kai.

"Well, it wasn't exactly difficult. I was walking around the harbour looking for your condo and there you were. I spotted you straight away."

"My apartment, not condo," she corrected, not knowing what else to say, still reeling from a state of shock and disbelief.

"So, this is Kai," he ventured, smiling warmly. "We meet at last."

"Does Freya know you're here?" she asked, ignoring his hint for an introduction. "She didn't mention anything about a visit from you when I last spoke to her."

"You've spoken to her recently?" Now it was Greg's turn to be surprised. Freya hadn't mentioned being in recent contact with her sister; he assumed Freya was waiting for him to follow up on their conversation before speaking to her.

"Yes. About a week ago."

As the timing coincided with the initial discussion they'd had, it led Greg to wonder whether she had already told Ella what was on her mind. No doubt he would get to find out in the next hour or two.

"She didn't tell me that you'd spoken to each other."

"I don't expect you tell her everything either," added Ella pointedly, causing Greg to raise an eyebrow in response, understanding her meaning.

"In answer to your question about why I'm over here, is that I'm visiting coastal galleries and it so happens I found myself here on your Jurassic coast. It made sense to drop by."

"Hmm... Any other reason?"

"I think you know. Let's end the pretence."

"I'll order you a coffee and we can talk," suggested Ella, grappling to make sense of the situation.

"Then can we go back to your apartment so that I can meet my son properly?"

My son. It sounded so wrong. Kai was her son, not his. She didn't want Greg to have anything to do with him. But here he was and she knew she could not deny him the opportunity to meet Kai. So much for her plan to contact Freya later.

"Yes," she answered simply, unsure how else she could respond to what was a reasonable request.

After coffee and a chat about the gallery, they made their way leisurely across the harbour toward Freya's apartment. As they approached her front door, Ella suddenly felt overwhelmed by a mix of emotions, mostly nervousness and apprehension, but also a sense of pride in introducing her baby and an unexpected element of connection and bonding between them.

"Shall I take him?" offered Greg as she struggled to find her keys whilst balancing Kai on her hip.

"Er… ok," she conceded, somewhat reluctantly. "He might cry though. He's not used to strangers."

Greg chose not to respond; he did not plan to be a stranger for long. "Come here, little man," he cooed, holding out two strong, welcoming arms. Miraculously, Kai went to him without a fuss and allowed Greg to carry him into the lounge whilst Ella dealt with the stroller and then made her way to the kitchen to give the two of them a few minutes alone to meet each other properly.

Why was he here? It made no sense to arrive without warning her. Yet she would never have allowed him to visit her if he had asked. How did she feel about him? There was an undeniable connection between them, brought about by the uncanny resemblance between father and son with their matching twinkly blue eyes and blonde curls. Then there was a resurgence of unbearable guilt. Surely Greg felt it too? The fact that the two of them were together again, having betrayed her sister, felt wrong on every level.

"He's a fine little fella," announced Greg as Ella returned to the lounge with mugs of tea and a plate of chocolate biscuits.

"He certainly is. I'm very lucky."

"You are. So, tell me all about him," asked Greg, balancing Kai on his lap whilst attempting to entertain him with a wooden rattle and a furry rabbit.

"What do you want to know?"

"Tell me everything, right from the beginning, from the moment you discovered you were pregnant."

"I'm not sure you want to know all that."

"Believe me, I do, Ella."

"Fair enough. But first, I need to tell you how shocked I was. To this day, I can hardly believe it was possible. For the first few months, I didn't even realise I was pregnant and then I tried to deny it. I felt so guilty and saddened knowing what Freya was going through."

"What we were both going through," he corrected her. "Months of sadness and disappointment; the stress and frustration of failed fertility treatments; mutual feelings of blame and inadequacy; painful conversations, the list goes on…"

"I can only imagine. It seems so unfair, doesn't it?"

"Carry on. Tell me about his birth." Over tea and biscuits, with Kai playing happily at their feet on his playmat, Ella described the pregnancy and birth, sparing him some details, but making it clear that she had coped admirably and was enjoying life as a single mum.

"Well, I can see what a good mother you are. It can't have been easy for you to manage all on your own."

"Thank you. It's been possible because he's an easy baby. The hardest part has been keeping him a secret. Can you understand why I decided to do that? I thought it was the kindest thing to do, for everyone's sake."

"I get it, but things are different now."

"What do you mean? What's different?" she asked anxiously, wondering what was on his mind.

"What's different is that I've discovered that I am a father, at the very time that my wife is asking me to consider surrogacy as an option for saving our childless marriage."

His direct, honest statement drove her to silence, whilst conflicting voices swirled randomly around her mind as she struggled to find a coherent response.

"Oh, Greg. I'm so sorry. If I could turn the clock back, everything would be different."

"You mean there would be no Kai."

"No Kai. No guilt. No dilemma," she stated bluntly. "What we did was wrong. Does Freya know?"

"Of course not. There's no need. How could she process that, especially with everything she's been through the past year."

"How do you live with yourself? I know how much I struggle with it and I don't have to face her every day like you do."

"I can assure you, it isn't easy. But we were drunk and it was a one-off. It's never happened before and it certainly won't happen again."

Once again, his honesty cut through her like a knife. Even though she knew it had been meaningless, she felt cheapened by his declaration.

"So why are you here then?" she asked, genuinely bemused.

"As I said, I wanted to see my son. I wanted to know if I would feel anything to lay my eyes on my own flesh and blood."

"And do you?"

Silence fell between them at the enormity of her question, allowing Ella time to study Greg as he leaned low to offer Kai a toy that had fallen out of his reach. Observing his warm, tender smile and twinkling eyes brimming with tears, she already knew his answer.

Delray Beach

Freya was missing Greg; it didn't make sense as she was used to him working long days in the gallery. Yet the evenings were long and, as in the song lyrics, the bed was too big without him. She missed curling up against his strong, athletic body that more than often than not led to sex these days – no longer desperate attempts at procreation, but pure physical lust reflecting the genuine desire they still held for each other after several years of marriage. Since his departure, they had only exchanged a few messages during that time, mainly updates on Greg's whereabouts. Freya reassured him that the gallery was ticking over smoothly and there was nothing significant to report. Greg's news was that he was making his way along the Dorset coastline, briefly describing the relaxed, beachy atmosphere of the galleries with their paintings, sculptures and photographs capturing the beauty and diversity of the dramatic coastal landscapes, so different from their own.

Freya had no plans to mention Ella again whilst he was away, sensing his need to get away from the challenging discussions they'd engaged in just before he left. It was not something that could be continued merely over brief messages. In all honesty, she welcomed a short break from the topic herself, especially following her recent conversation with Ella. They all needed a little more time. Then upon his return, she hoped, their prayers would finally be answered.

In the morning, Freya made her way to the gallery extra early to avoid the build-up of traffic on Atlantic Avenue. Plus, she'd been awake half the night, clock-watching, thinking about Ella and the surrogacy. Sleeping lightly in between her wakefulness, she found herself stuck in the oddest of dreams; it had unnerved her. In her dream, she was waiting at the arrivals gate for Greg to return home after spending a year in the UK. She'd been waiting for hours and eventually, the airport was completely deserted apart from her. Just as she was about to give up and go home without him, she spotted him in the distance making his way to the gates, all alone it appeared. As he got closer, she could just about make out that he was carrying something – a parcel or holdall perhaps? Eventually, as he walked through the gates, it became clear what was in his arms. It was a child. A blond-haired, blue-eyed boy in the image of Greg himself.

What did the dream mean? Hopefully, it was a sign that he was going to come home keen to pursue her plan for Ella to act as their surrogate. The child in the dream looked just like Kai. She supposed it was obvious that he would, as she thought about Kai constantly, looking at his photo regularly as she dreamed of one day becoming a mother herself. She decided to take it as a good sign that everything would work out for them.

As soon as she entered the gallery, she opened the shutters, switched on the coffee machine and logged onto the office laptop to check incoming emails. Despite a poor night's sleep, she was eager to busy herself with office admin this morning. She had a full hour before opening.

After responding to a few incoming emails, she then set about organising and decluttering the inbox by unsubscribing from various mailing lists and moving messages into new folders, archiving and deleting old mail. Once finished, she poured herself another coffee and returned to the laptop to review her work; it was so much better. Greg would be pleased. Before moving on to her next plan for the day, she decided to test out the automatic email sorting feature she'd created based on senders, subjects and keywords, by typing in Ella's name. Sure enough, the search displayed several emails containing her name in the subject line or body, plus emails addressed to her and received from her. Scrolling through the list, she decided to archive the mail relating to her seascape commission now that it had been successfully shipped to its purchasers. Whilst in the process of scanning the entire contents of the search, her eyes were suddenly drawn to an untitled email to Ella from Greg:

Hi

I'm not sure that an email is the right way to contact you about this, but I don't think I have much choice, do I? So here goes.

Freya told me that you have had a son since you came to visit us. Congratulations. The only thing is, I've done the maths and I've seen his photo. And I'm no detective, but I can tell he's mine. Am I right, Ella? If I am, I deserve to know the truth.

I look forward to hearing from you,
Greg

Feeling sick and disorientated, Freya was unable to process the contents of what she was reading and re-reading. The shock was so intense and overwhelming that she was overcome by a sudden, paralysing feeling of disbelief that left her physically and mentally stunned. Struggling for breath, her heart racing uncontrollably, she knew she must be dreaming or trapped in the worst nightmare ever because what she thought she had read was impossible. Utterly impossible. Yet those unbelievable words jumped off the screen like daggers stabbing her violently in the heart: *I can tell he's mine.*

Eventually, after what must have been several minutes but felt like many hours, Freya staggered to the bathroom to succumb to the physical shock of the news. Resting her pounding head on the cool marble tiles next to the sink, she wondered whether she had the strength to return to her desk. After splashing her face with cold water in an attempt to revive herself, she returned somewhat reluctantly to the gallery, ensuring the 'Closed' sign on the door was firmly in place - she had no plans to open up or face the public today – and sat heavily back at her desk planning to absorb the contents of the email and decide how best to deal with it.

But first, she needed to work out how, when and where it had happened. How was it even possible that something had happened between them? She had been with Ella the entire time during her visit, hadn't she? And Greg? When had he been alone with her? Just once, she remembered. That day he had taken her to the gallery. Yes, they were gone a while and she recalled wondering at the time whether they had spent the entire day at the gallery, yet there were no signs that anything more had happened. Surely she would have noticed a change in Ella's behaviour if something had happened between them? But she hadn't. Nothing had seemed amiss. She and Ella had enjoyed a happy day together before she left for Miami, she recalled, and everything seemed normal. Or had it? Ella had been keen to cut short her stay with them to visit Miami's galleries, where she supposedly had that one-night stand. It had seemed a little odd at the time, but also plausible. Perhaps it had all been a pack of lies. At some point during her stay, she had slept with her husband and decided, most likely out of sheer guilt, to beat a hasty retreat back to the UK.

As for Greg, she was lost for words. Her beloved husband. How could he possibly have slept with her sister? She couldn't imagine anything more unlikely. Yes, he'd been unusually helpful during Ella's stay – collecting her from the airport and taking time away from the gallery to be with them over the festivities. And he'd been sociable and reasonably welcoming towards her, but Freya assumed it was due to their shared interest in the world of art and his plan to commission her for the gallery. She hadn't observed anything more going on between them in the very short space of time they had been in each other's company. What was she missing? There must have been an opportunity sometime during her stay if Greg was to be believed. But why would he lie about something so significant?

Returning to the search facility, Freya began to frantically work her way through every email associated with Ella's name, particularly around the time of the one she had just read. Aware that deleted emails were filtered out of results, it became clear that any other personal correspondence between Greg and Ella must have been removed. Only this one incriminating message had managed to slip through the net. There must have been more. Perhaps there was a way of retrieving deleted emails, she wondered, desperate to explore every avenue of finding out more. Checking the 'Deleted Items' folder, it became clear that any items had been permanently removed. It was empty.

Feeling sickened and exhausted by the shock, Freya closed the laptop and walked out of the gallery into the warm breeze, locking the door behind her.

Chapter Thirty

West Bay

"So, what do you think?" asked Greg. "As soon as I get home, I'm going to have to have the conversation with Freya. I've kept her waiting for my response, but that time's nearly up."

Ella was dumbfounded. She assumed Freya had contacted her about her surrogacy plans behind Greg's back to gauge her response before asking him about it. Ella's response was unchanged from the moment Freya had suggested it: it was a definite no. But now, face to face with the father of her child, she felt lost for words. Spending the afternoon with Greg had been something of a surreal experience. On the one hand, it had been wonderful to see her son interacting so happily with his natural father. But on the other, and firmly in the forefront of her mind, was the devastating betrayal of her sibling relationship, compounded by the fact that it had resulted in the one thing that her sister wanted more than anything else in the world. "Oh, Greg," she finally began, her head in her hands. "What can I say?"

"Would you do it for us?" asked Greg bluntly.

After a few moments of gathering her thoughts and attempting to compose herself, Ella began to formulate her response, quietly and calmly. "When Freya asked me, my initial response was a resolute no. Nine months of pregnancy is tough enough, but the thought of giving the baby up at birth is another thing altogether. Unimaginable, to be honest. Yet, I've thought of very little else since she asked me. After a while, I started to wonder whether I owed it to Freya; a chance to try to make right a huge wrong. I'm permanently burdened by intense feelings of guilt and betrayal, reminded constantly by the presence of my perfect son. Perhaps, in time, I would learn to forgive myself if I were able to offer her the gift of her own child." Pausing to maintain her composure, she glanced at Greg to gauge his reaction. His eyes had misted over and he remained silent, intent of hearing her out. She continued, glancing at her son playing happily with his toys. "Seeing you today, Greg, has thrown me into further confusion. I thought I wouldn't have to see you ever again and then the memory of what happened between us would fade in time. But now you know about Kai, and I can see how much you've enjoyed meeting him, I'm unsure what the future holds for us. All of us. I can't imagine this will be the last time you see him, can you?"

"No," he replied simply, clearly deep in thought.

"But how can that happen without Freya finding out? Are you planning to tell her?"

"I just don't know. Like you, I couldn't get over what happened between us. I've been wracked with guilt. And you might not believe me, but it's never happened before and it will never happen again. I love Freya so much and I can't bear the thought of risking losing her. But then I ask myself, how could she ever forgive me? You're her sister for Christ's sake! What the hell were we thinking? And then there's Kai. Can you imagine what would happen if she found out?" He was becoming deeply agitated with himself and the impossible situation they were both facing.

"I don't think she should know the truth. It would be too painful. That's the only reason I can think of for lying to her. A protective mechanism, if you like. How would you feel about concealing the truth about Kai from Freya?"

He paused to consider his response. Ella was right; Freya could not be expected to accept the circumstances of Kai's birth. It would finish them. Yet could he go along with Ella's proposal of denying his involvement? He knew for sure that he would want to be part of his son's life to some extent in the future. "So, what are you suggesting then?"

"Accept being his uncle rather than his father. If you were to do that, I would undertake to visit you each year or make you welcome here, so that you could see Kai regularly. And I'll get better at keeping in touch with Freya, sending photos and updates on Kai's progress. Please, Greg, think about it. I think it's a way of saving your marriage."

"Hmm… I don't know. Maybe it's a possibility, if you promise what you're suggesting."

"The choice is that, or to tell Freya the truth, at the risk, or almost certainty, that you would destroy your marriage and cut off ties permanently with me and Kai."

"Is that a threat?"

"No! It's the reality, Greg. There's nothing between you and me, other than we both happen to be Kai's parents by some fluke of nature. I'm suggesting that if we ignored that fact, you would get to see Kai regularly in the context of family visits, which would not happen if you were no longer with Freya."

"I understand," he responded, having calmed down a little following her clarification. "But the question still remains: would you act as a surrogate for us?"

"I've come round to thinking I might agree to it," she replied somewhat vaguely. "But there's so much to consider. I would need to have an open and honest conversation with both of you about the implications and potential challenges involved. And we'd have to explore all aspects of the decision and consider what's best for all of us."

"I understand. It could be really complex. There must be all sorts of legal loopholes, not to mention the practicalities of arranging it."

"Especially as we live an ocean apart…" she added, gazing out to sea, wondering what on earth she was about to commit to.

Delray Beach

Greg would be wondering what was going on. Freya had not been able to bring herself to message him over the past couple of days for fear of what she might say. She needed thinking time and he would be back at the weekend. He had messaged her, but she hadn't responded. In the meantime, her head was full of what she'd like to say to him, but she needed to gather her thoughts properly. She wasn't sleeping and she'd lost her appetite. Her main preoccupation was running over every aspect of Ella's visit, desperately trying to work out what she'd missed. She recalled leaving the pair of them together late one night. She had gone to bed and she seemed to remember they planned to watch a movie together. In fact, she now remembered Ella telling her that they had watched 'The Holiday'. It was coming back to her now. Then there was New Year's Eve, but they had all drunk too much that night and she could hardly remember how they managed to get home. Other than those two evenings, and that day at the gallery, Freya had been constantly by her sister's side. It would be interesting to hear Greg's version of events.

Thinking ahead to the weekend, she tried to envisage how she would manage his return. Would she – could she – pretend nothing was amiss? Or would she greet him with an onslaught of accusations the moment she laid eyes on him? She was veering towards saying nothing, biding her time and seeing how much he was prepared to divulge. It would take a monumental effort on her part to pretend that everything was normal between them, but she was prepared to give it a try. She still wanted that follow-up discussion he had promised her on his return about Ella being their surrogate. His response to that particular question would now be somewhat intriguing.

And what about Ella? How was she going to handle her complex feelings towards her cheating, lying bitch of a sister? She was filled with such a range of intense and conflicting emotions towards her. Deep hurt and anger had smashed to smithereens the trust and loyalty she had expected from both of them. It was the ultimate betrayal and she had no means of comprehending how either of them could do this to her. As for her marriage, the loss of trust was in danger of destroying it forever, leaving her feeling profoundly sad and grieving. As for the future of her relationship with her sister, she was experiencing such disbelief and shock at her betrayal that she wondered how she would ever be able to rebuild their relationship. As for the surrogacy, how could she ask her now, even if it were her only chance of having a child?

Chapter Thirty-One

West Bay

Two days had gone by in a blur since Greg's visit and it felt as though she had done nothing but go over and over every aspect of their conversation and its implications. Some things were clearer now that she had seen him, and others were more confusing than before. To her huge relief, what was now crystal clear was that she had no feelings towards Greg whatsoever. Yes, she found him attractive, but nothing more. In her opinion, he was essentially a good man with an unremarkable personality, who had made one stupid, drunken blunder, and didn't deserve to spend the rest of his life paying for it. Yet he possibly might have to. That would depend on how her plan unfolded.

Her main focus was Freya. She couldn't bear to think of the hurt and anger she would undoubtedly feel in the face of her betrayal and subsequent lies. She was desperate to protect her and her marriage, and as she had told Greg, maybe the only way to pay for her sins was to offer to be her surrogate. A huge price to pay, but it was the one thing that would fulfil her sister's dreams and hopefully lead her to forgiveness should she ever discover what had happened between Greg and herself.

Arranging surrogacy between sisters residing in two different countries was bound to be a complex process for legal, logistical and practical considerations. They were bound to need legal advice from professionals experienced in international surrogacy laws if they were to understand the legal requirements and regulations governing surrogacy in both the UK and USA, covering the rights, responsibilities and expectations of all parties involved. Then there would be medical evaluations, screenings and psychological assessments, before working out the logistical protocols of the surrogacy itself, followed by the prenatal and postpartum care and support for Ella and the baby. She wondered whether people ever bypassed all these complications and just made their own arrangements. She would need to research the legalities and simplify arrangements where possible if it were to work.

For now, she would leave matters in Greg's hands, wait for him to put it to Freya and take it from there. The hard part was over - agreeing to something she hoped she would not come to regret.

Delray Beach

After two days of deliberation and silence, Freya eventually messaged Greg to let him know she would collect him from Miami airport on Saturday morning, enquiring briefly whether he was enjoying his trip. He had responded immediately and equally concisely, confirming that his visit had been successful and – to her relief - that he was happy to travel back to Delray by train. The prospect of the stressful, busy journey from the airport had always filled her with dread, but never more so than now, as she wondered whether she would be able to withhold her thoughts and emotions upon seeing Greg on his return. Interestingly, there had been no word from Ella during his visit to the UK, despite her promise to come back to her with a decision on the surrogacy, suggesting that he may not have even visited her. Yet now, after everything that had gone before, she could no longer trust either of them.

☐

Saturday morning. He was due back before midday. For some reason, she decided to take extra care over her appearance and ensure that the house was perfect for his return – perhaps to remind him what he was potentially about to give up. Looking closely at herself in the mirror, she could see faint traces of dark shadows under her eyes, evidence of several sleepless nights and a constant headache. And having eaten virtually nothing for days through loss of appetite, her dress felt looser from dropping off a few pounds from her already svelte figure. Making her way down the spiral staircase, she reflected on how hard it had been to function these past few days in the face of her dreadful discovery. During that time, she had attempted to process a wide range of emotions whilst attempting to make decisions about the future of her relationship with Greg and her sister, particularly about whether to confront them about her discovery.

Glancing at the kitchen clock, she estimated he was due to land within the hour and would probably be home around midday. It would give her time to rehearse the words that had been running through her head for the past few days. The initial shock of the discovery had now begun to morph into anger and only time would tell how she would vent it once face to face with her weak, cheating husband.

☐

Greg had offered to make his own way home from the station. Attempting to relax by the pool, Freya closed her tired eyes to relieve the tension that had built up across her forehead like a tight elastic band. Filled with dread at the prospect of him walking through the door, she envisaged how she was likely to react to his return. Ordinarily, she would be excited to see him and bombard him with questions about his trip, hugging and kissing him before he had chance to get through the door. She would pour him a beer and suggest he take a shower whilst preparing something for him to eat. Today was likely to be very different, but she was determined to maintain composure and strength.

Twenty minutes or so later, waking her abruptly from the light sleep she had succumbed to, she heard the familiar open and shut of the front door. Immediately, she felt her heart begin to race in anticipation of facing Greg.

"I'm back!" he called out, stating the obvious. "Where's my girl?" She didn't move from her lounger, but waited for him to find her by the pool.

"Hi," she responded neutrally, allowing him to take her into his arms. "I've just woken up."

"How are you? What's the news?" he asked, smiling broadly, clearly happy to be home.

"I'm fine, thanks," she lied. "Why don't you go and sort yourself out while I prepare some lunch? You must be exhausted."

"Let's have a drink and a chat first. I've missed you."

Without responding, Freya handed him a chilled beer. She wished he would go upstairs to shower and unpack; she needed more time to process everything. She suddenly felt confused and unprepared for whatever lay ahead. Sitting down at the kitchen table, she decided to take things slowly and calmly, rather than rushing into something she might regret. "So, how was it?"

"Good. Really good," he responded briefly.

"Good? Was it worth going all that way?"

"I know you think I could have sourced pieces online, but honestly, Freya, seeing the English coastline for myself was so valuable. It's absolutely stunning, isn't it? Especially the Jurassic coast. All that natural beauty and diverse landscapes, those rugged cliffs and sandy beaches... It's fantastic, and so different to what we have here."

"Did you get to see Lulworth Cove?"

"I did. It's spectacular – especially Durdle Door, the limestone arch. You get amazing views of the surrounding cliffs and coastline. It's very busy though."

"And did you head along the coast to West Bay?" ventured Freya, holding her breath in anticipation of his response.

"Briefly," he replied, beginning to look a little agitated by her interrogation. Several seconds of silence fell awkwardly between them. "Actually, I think I might have a shower and sort myself out now, my love, if that's ok."

"Sure," responded Freya, unsurprised at the timing of his exit. She had no plans to stop him; in fact, she needed a break from the conversation to give herself time to process the fact that he had visited West Bay – something he had failed to mention in his brief messages.

So much for showering and unpacking. Two hours later, there was no sign of him. Tiptoeing into their bedroom, Freya's thoughts proved correct: he had fallen asleep. His suitcase lay open and empty, and the laundry basket was full. He had half-closed the shutters and lay peacefully on their bed, showered and naked. There was no denying it, he was a gorgeous, sexy human being. No wonder she hadn't been able to keep him for herself. But her sister? It was so wrong, and utterly unforgiveable. What were they thinking and why hadn't they thought about her? Sinking to the floor, she hung her head and let the tears flow freely – something she had not allowed to happen until now.

After what must have been ten minutes or so, she dried her tears and left Greg to sleep off his jet-lag. He was going to be asleep for a while. She was so confused. Would she ever be able to forgive him? Despite everything, she still loved him and couldn't imagine life without him. Yet it would always be there in the background: that knowledge that he had slept with her sister; that he had fathered a child – Ella's child – something she was unable to do for him. Not only that, but now, there was no way she could ask Ella to act as their surrogate. How could she? She despised her and what she had done.

Chapter Thirty-Two

West Bay

Since Greg's visit, Ella had been unable to think straight. She felt as though she was disintegrating like the crumbling East Cliff, trying desperately to stay strong despite the constant threat of landslides and rockfalls. Her recent mental and physical strength had been severely eroded by conflicting emotions, guilt and insecurity stemming from her conversation with Greg and the fact that she had not been in contact with Freya. By now, Greg would surely have spoken to Freya about his trip, including his visit to West Bay. She felt certain that he would have told Freya that he had seen her and that they had discussed the surrogacy, culminating in Ella agreeing to do it for them. By now, she would have expected Freya to have contacted her, keen to set the wheels in motion. But as the days ticked by, she began to wonder what was going on between them – all three of them. So many elements of their relationship were shrouded in secrecy and lies: only Ella and Greg knew the truth about Kai and what had happened between them; Greg was unaware that Freya had discussed her surrogacy plans with Ella, and that she had deceived him for more than a year before beginning fertility investigations. Now she was left wondering where she stood and what would happen next. Agreeing to act as their surrogate had been an incredibly difficult decision to arrive at, and it wouldn't take much for her to change her mind. With each passing day, she felt worn down by the complex mix of emotional, physical, ethical and legal considerations that it would undoubtedly entail.

Delray Beach

"I was only in West Bay for an hour or two. I wanted to see East Cliff, being as it was the subject of the commission."

"Hmm… so that was all you did? You didn't visit Ella?"

"I thought about it, but it didn't really work out. It was a flying visit and I didn't think it was right to just turn up unannounced."

To Freya, his response felt odd and unconvincing, yet he was adamant that he hadn't seen her. Surely, he would have wanted to see his son. With a heavy heart, she felt sure he was concealing the truth – something that seemed to becoming second nature to him. Now he had left her with no choice but to take a different approach. "You said you were going to think about asking Ella to be a surrogate for us. Have you given it any more thought whilst you've been away?"

Freya watched her husband closely as the colour drained from his complexion, his facial muscles tensing and twitching whilst he composed his response.

"I have. I'm happy for you to ask her," he answered bluntly.

"That's all you have to say? Surely you want to discuss it with me."

"We already have. You told me before I went away that it's what you want."

"Well, yes, but surely you want to discuss the implications with me?"

"It's going to take a lot of research and planning, but it's our only option. If it's what you want, then I'll agree to it."

"But is it what you want? Do you want a child as much as I do?"

"You know I do."

"I thought you did, but now I'm not so sure. I wonder whether it's something I want much more than you do."

"I don't know why you're suddenly saying that. Nothing's changed."

Everything had changed. Absolutely everything. He was a cheater, a liar and already a father, and she felt sure that his lies were growing. He must have visited Ella and Kai – in fact, that was probably the main reason for his trip to the UK. Under normal circumstances, she could have asked Ella, but she now felt there was no point; they were all entangled in a complex web of lies.

West Bay

As the days continued to roll by, with no word from Freya, she came to a decision: she would contact her. The silence between them was eating away at her; she wondered whether something had happened. Despite everything, she needed to know that her sister was alright. She would message her in the first instance and try to find out what was going on.

Hi Freya,
Just checking everything is OK. You asked me to come back to you when I'd had time to give your idea serious thought. I think I've come to a decision. Give me a ring, to suit you.
Love Ella x

Her index finger hovering over the 'send' button, she re-read her short message to check its content and tone, wondering how long it would be before she received Freya's response and hoping it would be soon. She needed an end to all this uncertainty and speculation.

Within the hour, she heard the ping of a notification, sooner than she had anticipated. Taking a deep breath, she opened it up, unsure what to expect.

We need to talk.

Four words. Yet they held so much meaning. Ella was right; something had happened. Her brief response indicated that she was in no mood for small talk, and the absence of a greeting or sign-off kiss suggested that Freya was not happy with her for some reason. What had happened since Greg's return? There was only one way to find out.

Delray Beach

"Hi Freya. How are things?" she ventured, feeling nervous.

"Hi," she returned somewhat abruptly, followed by an awkward silence for the next few seconds.

"I said I'd come back to you with a decision."

"You did." Freya wasn't making this easy for her.

"Well, I've thought about little else since you asked me, and I think

I've made my mind up."

"I'll be interested to hear what you've got to say," said Freya, her voice tinged with an iciness that indicated to Ella that something was seriously amiss.

"Is everything ok, Freya? I'm sensing it's not."

"Really?"

"Please talk to me. Tell me what's wrong." Ella's mind began to spin trying to imagine what might have happened to upset her.

"Answer me this first. Did Greg visit you last week?"

No more lies. She would tell her the truth. "He did – very briefly. He didn't tell you?"

"Interestingly, no, he did not. I wonder why?"

The conversation was going from bad to worse and Ella regretted her decision to contact her sister. She should have waited for Freya to make the first move – or Greg. She had blundered her way into a situation she was not fully prepared for. "Really? As I said, it was just a quick, chance meeting. He literally bumped into me around the harbour." At least there was some truth in that claim.

Freya waited to see what else she was prepared to reveal and allowed silence to fall between them for several tense seconds. Nothing more was forthcoming. "Did he meet Kai?" she continued, probing deeper.

"Yes. As I said, around the harbour. We were taking a walk."

"That was a stroke of luck, then," she added sarcastically.

"Oh, Freya. I do find it hard to talk about Kai, knowing what you've been going through. And you've taken me by surprise asking me about Greg's visit to West Bay. I would have thought he would have said something to you."

"You would think he would want to tell me he'd met his son, wouldn't you?" The intense shock of Freya's words cut into her like knives, paralysing her, immobilising both her mind and body. Unable to process her sister's rhetorical question or respond coherently, Ella ended the call.

Pouring herself a large glass of wine, Freya wandered outside to process what she had just learned. Greg had lied to her again. He had visited her sister and met his son. She now needed to work out how to deal with the situation, weighing up what she could afford to lose and what she should endeavour to save. If she had not read that email, she would be none the wiser, satisfied that Kai was the product of a one-night stand with an anonymous stranger. She would have believed Greg when he told her he'd had insufficient time in West Bay to visit Ella. But she had read the email stating that he had slept with her sister and was likely to be the father of her child. Then he had lied to her about visiting his son – he had done so to protect her.

If she had not read the email, her feelings towards Greg would be unaltered, her love for him as strong as ever. If only she could turn back the clock: she would never have allowed Ella to visit them and she would not have discovered that email. Then maybe, they would have been able to pursue surrogacy with Ella. As things stood, her marriage was in tatters, smashed to pieces by a web of lies, betrayal and deception; her relationship with her sister was damaged beyond repair, and her only chance of becoming a mother was no longer an option.

Were there any circumstances in which she could forgive and forget? She thought not. What they had done to her was despicable and totally inexcusable. Was it a one-off, or had they continued their relationship during his visit to the UK? Is that why he went? She had always thought it was odd. If it weren't for Kai, perhaps they would have been able to make a fresh start, separated by thousands of miles of ocean. Yet, the fact remained that Kai did exist. He was her husband's son and he would always want him in his life.

Chapter Thirty-Three

Delray Beach

Greg would be back from the gallery within the hour and she was ready for him. There was no dinner awaiting him this evening. She had no appetite and neither would he once he heard what she had to say. Since speaking to Ella, Freya had thought of nothing else. She was ready to confront Greg with what she had discovered and she was hoping he was prepared to be honest with her. She was fed up with his lies.

Sitting at the kitchen table, sipping a large glass of Sauvignon, she stared at the front door, glancing away only briefly to check on the time displayed on the large wall clock. Another long day at the gallery, another late night for Greg. It was becoming a habit. He had picked up on her poor mood since his return home from the UK and was no doubt wondering what had happened during his absence to cause it. His cowardly means of dealing with it had been to keep out of her way, keeping conversation to a bare minimum, but Freya's patience had run out, especially now she had the facts.

It was just as well she hadn't prepared dinner for them; Greg didn't return within the hour or the next. During that time, she had polished off the bottle of wine and her head was beginning to spin, having had nothing to eat. He had left her with no choice but to message him: *Where are you? I need to speak to you.*

Where was he? In some bar hiding away, unable to face her, no doubt. He must have realised his time was up. He hadn't bothered to respond to her message either, although she could see he had read it from the two blue ticks. If he thought she would give up waiting and go to bed, he was much mistaken. She would wait up all night if that was what it was going to take.

It was almost midnight when he eventually walked through the door. Freya was still waiting for him.

"You're still up," he said, stating the blindingly obvious and sitting himself down opposite her at the kitchen table.

"Where have you been?" asked Freya, feeling nervous and tearful now that he was back. She wasn't looking forward to this conversation any more than he was. She just wanted to turn the clock back so that none of this would be necessary. It was clear that Greg had been sitting in some bar all evening, now a little worse for wear judging by his tired eyes and slightly reddened complexion. The thought that he had driven home under the influence of alcohol infuriated her. What was he thinking? Part of her wanted to scream and shout at him, but she wondered what she would achieve in doing so. He would probably get up and leave her sitting there, stewing in her anger.

"I'm sorry I didn't come home earlier. I needed some thinking time."

"I bet you did," replied Freya, leaving him in no doubt that she knew everything. "I'm waiting…"

"It's late, Freya. Can it wait until the morning?"

"You know it can't."

Dropping his head into his hands, he sighed deeply, resigned to the fact that his time was up. "So, what do you want to know?" he ventured after a long, painful pause in their exchange.

"I want to know the truth – about everything." Freya wasn't sure how she was managing to keep her cool, when part of her felt like screaming and shouting abuse at him for all that he had done to her. Perhaps she realised he would be more forthcoming if she managed to keep calm.

"I did see Ella," he began. "I don't know why I told you that I hadn't."

"I know you saw her. She told me. The question is, why did you keep it from me?" His answer to this would determine how far he was prepared to go with his version of the truth.

"I don't know. I suppose I thought you would think it a bit odd." Little did he understand, it was odder that he had kept it to himself. He clearly had something to hide, and Freya knew exactly what that was.

"So, tell me about your visit to see Ella and her son." *Her son. His son.* How much was he prepared to divulge? Would anything he said correspond with Ella's version?

"It was honestly by chance. I was in West Bay taking a good look at the harbour, wandering around looking at the art stalls and food kiosks, when I suddenly spotted Ella."

"And Kai."

"Yes, and Kai. She was sitting at a table on the harbour wall and Kai was in his stroller. I must admit, I was really surprised to see them."

"Were you planning on visiting her at her apartment? Had you contacted her beforehand?" she continued, somehow maintaining her calm.

"I've had no contact with her and it crossed my mind that I could knock on her door whilst I was there. My main focus was seeing the cliffs at West Bay, being as they were the subject of the commission."

Part of his version rang true as it matched Ella's: they had bumped into each other by chance. Yet, if he really were Kai's father, surely the visit was pre-planned? What she knew for sure from reading the email was that Greg had slept with Ella. He had assumed the child was his, and so had she. Yet Freya hadn't heard from Ella that he actually was; she had ended the call abruptly before responding to her suggestion that he was the father. Maybe she had this part of the story wrong. Perhaps Ella really did have a one-night stand in Miami and therefore didn't know for sure who was Kai's father. Unlikely, but possible. Perhaps she was clutching at straws.

"What did you think of Kai? Does he still look the image of you?" Freya watched Greg's expression intently as he took his time to respond. His eyes had softened but he glanced away from her and began to fidget nervously.

"He's great. I don't see why you say he looks like me though. He's just a baby and I'm a grown man," he replied, attempting to distract her with a touch of humour.

"You know what I mean. He has your colouring, your eyes and features."

"So, what are you suggesting?" For the first time, Greg appeared rattled by her interrogation.

"I'm not sure. I wonder whether there is something else you need to tell me. I did say I wanted the truth – the whole truth."

"And I've told you the truth. I saw Ella. I should have told you before and, to be honest, I don't know why I didn't."

"I know exactly why you didn't tell me." Freya was determined to get a confession from him one way or another.

"What are you on about?" Beginning to lose his patience and maybe his composure, he stood up to pour himself a glass of water.

"You have feelings for Ella," she declared whilst his back was turned. She didn't want to see his face in case it revealed that it was true.

Turning around slowly, his eyes ablaze with fury, it was clear that his patience was at an end, or that he had been found out. "You what?"

"You heard me. I think you have feelings for my sister and you went to see her because you wanted to continue something you started when she was here."

"Wow! That is crazy," he responded, laughing incredulously. "I hardly know her. I could count the times I've seen her on one hand!"

"And how about the times you have slept with her?" Her question floored him. It wiped the smirk off his face as it drained of colour, his trembling hand moving nervously towards his glass of water as he attempted to compose his response.

"This is bloody ridiculous. You've been drinking."

"Yes, I have. God, I've needed a drink to get through all this. I'm sick of your lies." She really was. Enough was enough. She was unable to maintain her composure any longer. "Just tell me the truth!" she screamed, standing up to confront him once and for all. Taken aback by her sudden change in demeanour, he turned towards the door preparing to walk away. "Don't you dare! You're staying right here until you've told me what happened. Come on, Greg. Surely, after everything we've been through, you owe it to me." Angry tears began to course down her flushed cheeks.

As he turned back towards her, Freya noticed that his tired, bloodshot eyes were also brimming with tears. Inhaling deeply, she braced herself for his confession. "Sit down. Let's sit down," he suggested nervously.

For what seemed like an eternity, they sat in painful silence whilst Freya waited edgily for Greg's confession, twiddling her fingers and fidgeting anxiously on the uncomfortable bar stool. "I'm waiting," she uttered at last, drying the last of her tears.

"Oh, Freya. I can't believe we're even having this conversation. There is nothing going on between us. I've seen Ella just once since she visited and we've only been in contact about that sodding commission."

"But that isn't the truth, is it?"

"It is!" he yelled impatiently.

"It isn't. You slept with Ella. I know, so there's no point trying to deny it." There it was: the truth at last. Now everything was bound to unravel: their marriage; the trust that had always existed between them; her relationship with Ella; her last-ditch plans for a baby. Silence. Agonising silence that spoke a thousand words. Yet she wanted answers, an explanation. "Say something! I can't bear it any longer."

"I don't know what to say, Freya." She had never seen him so sad. Perversely, it broke her heart. She wanted to hold him and say it didn't matter, making it all go away, so that they could be happy again. But it was too big a crime. What they had done to her breached every unwritten rule. She could never forgive him, or her. "Tell me what you know," he finally uttered, his head in his hands.

"That's not how this is going work, Greg. You are going to tell me what happened between you and Ella. No more lies. You owe it to me."

After a lengthy silence, he began his confession, his voice tentative and full of emotion, of regret. "It was New Year's Eve. We were all so drunk. It was back here – you had gone to bed, we wandered down the beach. And then it happened. Just that once. I promise you, Freya. It meant absolutely nothing. Nothing at all. I have no feelings towards your sister whatsoever and I am filled with so much guilt and regret that it's eating away at me. The only thing that matters is you."

She believed him. As he looked into her eyes, there was no doubt that this was the truth. She believed him when he said that Ella meant nothing to him and she believed him when he said he cared about her above all else. Actions speak louder than words, so they say, and his actions always told her that he loved her deeply. Could she forgive him? It wasn't that simple: there was Kai to factor into this sorry story.

"And Kai? He changes everything," she added eventually, having given his confession time to sink in.

"Kai? How does he change things? I've explained that it was a meaningless one-off, never-to-be-repeated mistake, that I will regret for the whole of my life. Please believe me, Freya. I love you so much."

"He's your son, Greg. That's how he changes things."

"My son. After a one-night stand. That doesn't happen, Freya."

"It does happen and it has happened. He is your son. Nothing could be more obvious. I'm no mathematician, but the dates line up. And look at him – he's your image."

"But Ella told you she met up with someone in Miami. I bet that wasn't a one-off."

"She didn't. She was covering up for you. Don't take me for a fool, Greg."

"But...but..."

"Stop it, Greg. Stop treating me like a fool. Admit it and then we can try to make sense of this whole ugly situation."

"But Ella has agreed to be our surrogate. She will give us our own baby. Isn't that enough of an apology? Can't we take her up on that?"

"Ha! You must think I'm bloody stupid or have no feelings. She has given birth to your son and now you think she's going to do it all over again and hand the baby over to us. I don't think so somehow. You already have a son. I don't. I never will. And I would never want a child that has anything to do with her. What were you two planning, or have you already done it? Another shag, another child – only this time, to hand it over."

"I can't talk to you when you're in this mood."

"In this mood? Are you joking? I have just discovered that my cheating, lying husband had sex with my whore of a sister and then miraculously managed to produce a perfect baby boy after one shag. As if I believe that! You have the one thing I wanted more than anything else in the world and you've managed to ruin everything we had in the process. I will never want to see my sister again and I can't imagine how we're going to recover from what you've done. And you tell me that I'm in a mood. That's rich, Greg. Absolutely fucking rich." She had lost it. Her breathing had become intense and rapid; her heart was racing wildly, threatening to burst out of her chest and her head had begun to spin, making her feel confused and irrational. The emotions that had been running high for so long had finally bubbled to the surface. Staggering from the bar stool, she made her way to the staircase, blinded by tears, to escape from the collapse of everything she had always believed in.

Chapter Thirty-Four

West Bay

Ella was bemused and unsettled by the lack of communication from either Freya or Greg. Something must have happened. The last she had heard from her sister was that phone call more than a week ago, when Freya had implied that she knew everything that had happened between them, including the fact that Kai was Greg's son. In shock, she had ended the call abruptly; she needed time to process everything. And in the meantime, Greg had agreed to stick to her version of events, for the sake of his marriage. So, what had gone wrong? Surely Greg would have let her know if something significant had happened between them since his return home.

Feeling concerned, she toyed with the idea of calling Freya. Maybe then she would have more idea where she stood and whether Freya had believed Greg's story or still believed Kai to be his son. Surely Greg had withheld the truth from her; it was the kindest option after all. Then they would be able to move on and focus on the future, pursuing their dream of having a child in the knowledge that Ella had agreed to act as their surrogate.

The other option was to contact Greg, but she knew there would be risks in doing so. She did not want to add fuel to the fire if Freya suspected there had been anything going on between them. But in the absence of hearing from either of them, she was left feeling bewildered and confused, unable to concentrate on her work or give Kai her full attention. It felt as though everything had become a struggle. Her freelance contract with the local gallery appeared to be drying up and just lately she'd been in no state of mind to pursue other avenues. With the holiday season ahead, she was considering trying to sell prints of her work from one of the stalls around the harbour, but that would only generate a small amount of revenue. In the meantime, she had the funds from the lucrative commission to fall back on, at least for the next few months.

As for Kai, it was not so easy to juggle work and childcare anymore. His daytime naps were now shorter and less frequent, leaving her little opportunity during the day to work whilst he slept. When he was awake, Ella needed eyes in the back of her head now that he was crawling and pulling himself up to stand at every opportunity, grabbing objects and generally being more demanding for her attention. As a result, she was exhausted at the end of the day and in no mood to start on her work. In recent weeks, she had begun to feel somewhat unsettled and isolated; she realised the time had come to do something about it. It was no longer enough to while away the hours wandering around West Bay with Kai in the stroller. They both needed company and more structure in their week now that Kai was becoming socially aware and beginning to develop a sense of independence and adventure.

Delray Beach

Freya had never been more unhappy. She hadn't spoken to Greg for almost a week. They had become expert at avoiding each other: Greg left the house early each morning and spent long days at the gallery, returning late in the evening by which time Freya had gone to bed. During the day, Freya typically dragged herself out of bed by mid-morning and made her way to her favourite poolside lounger with a coffee and a book, her mind fully occupied, incapable of focusing on reading. For the remainder of the day, she would swap coffee for wine and maybe take a dip in the pool.

Today, however, the Florida skies were full of foreboding. Distinctive bands of thick, dark cloud patterns amid reddening hues were moving ominously in from the horizon, obscuring the sky and reducing visibility. Winds were picking up, becoming gusty and erratic, and there was an uncomfortable heaviness in the air - a significant change in atmospheric pressure.

The hurricane season was upon them: the atmospheric and oceanic conditions were coming together as they often did at this time of the year – warm ocean temperature and moist, unstable air, forming and strengthening the threat of tropical cyclones. They had been fortunate over the past few years, escaping most threats of approaching hurricanes, but this time the forecast was grim with warnings of strong winds, heavy rainfall, storm surges and even tornadoes. Their home, being situated in the heart of the hurricane zone along the Atlantic coast, was considered to be highly susceptible to experiencing significant impacts from hurricanes should they head their way. Today, they were being warned to remain vigilant and prepare for potential threats, including making evacuation plans, to ensure their safety.

Listening intently to the televised advice from the National Hurricane Center and regular updates from local news stations, she realised that Greg needed to be informed and involved. Hiding away in the gallery might protect him from her wrath but it would impact his awareness of the outside world and its weather. She needed help in protecting their home and it was apparent they needed to act quickly, and together . She had no choice but to break their silence.

"Freya. Hi. Are you ok?" He sounded surprised, but happy to hear from her.

"Have you heard the news?" She wasn't in the mood for small talk.

"What news?"

"The weather. There's a hurricane heading our way and we've been told to evacuate our home."

"Seriously? I hadn't heard, although I haven't been logged onto a news channel today. What are they suggesting? And are you ok?"

"I'm fine," she responded abruptly, then proceeded to paraphrase what was displayed on the TV screen. "An Evacuation Order has been issued. Apparently, we need to pack a 'go bag' with essential items such as clothing, medications, important documents, non-perishable food, water, supplies and such. But most importantly, we need to secure our home by boarding up the windows, securing loose outdoor items and turning off utilities. We need to act promptly and follow the evacuation route suggested to a safe location."

"I'm on my way." She sensed urgency and slight panic in his voice.

"I'll make a start on packing up."

"Love you," he added before ending the call. Why did he have to say that? This had nothing to do with their relationship which had gradually been disintegrating in a turbulent storm of its own these past days. Her unresolved grievances and a deep-seated resentment towards him remained deep within her. Being forced to unite in the face of a weather phenomenon was not the end of their problems; it was merely the start. Yet they could no longer hide away from each other, ignoring the oppressive atmosphere and heavy, dark clouds that had been gathering ominously over their doomed relationship.

Chapter Thirty-Five

Delray Beach

Having lived in the hurricane zone for several years, they knew what they needed to do to secure their home, even though they had never needed to actually evacuate their property before. But this time, the hurricane forecast and evacuation orders by local authorities deemed it necessary for them to leave. Putting on a united front, they had packed essential items together – clothing, toiletries, essential documentation, credit cards – and set about securing their property. It was fitted with storm shutters to minimise potential hurricane damage, and together they brought inside their outdoor furniture and garden ornaments, turned off utilities and locked all doors and windows securely. Everyone in their zone - all along the coast and extending three miles inland - had been instructed to adhere to the evacuation orders promptly to move to a safe location outside the hurricane's path.

The general evacuation route designated by the local authority was for residents to travel northward away from the hurricane's path on either Interstate 95 – the major north-south highway running along the eastern coast – or the Florida Turnpike, running parallel to I-95 and offering an alternative route. The A1A State Road – the scenic coastal highway running along the Atlantic Ocean – was deemed out of bounds due to the hurricane's trajectory. Freya and Greg planned to take the I-95 Northbound and merge onto the Turnpike towards Orlando. Ordinarily, under normal traffic conditions, the 200-mile journey would take three to four hours, but today, they could expect a longer, congested journey, as they made their way to safety with everyone else.

The increasing tension ahead of the impending storm was palpable, with media outlets providing continuous updates on the storm's progress, urging residents to stay vigilant as they made their way to evacuation routes. To ensure safety and minimise hazardous conditions, closures of schools, businesses, government offices and public transportation services had been announced, and emergency shelters had been made available for those who were unable to evacuate. As the storm drew nearer, the atmosphere was becoming increasingly eerie, with darkening skies, gusty winds and sporadic rainfall, the air heavy with anticipation and the sound of howling winds intensifying as they made their final preparations.

"Well, I think that's everything," announced Greg, his hands on his hips as though this were an everyday occurrence. "Are you ready?"

The impending hurricane had forced them together and they had no choice but to unite to safeguard their home and follow instructions to get themselves to safety. Heading inland, they had managed to book into one of Orlando's hurricane-resistant resorts along with thousands of other evacuees from the high-risk coastal zones of South Florida.

"I'm ready," she replied, experiencing a complex range of emotions. The obvious anxiety and stress of having to leave their home and the uncertainty of what they might return to once the storm had passed were exacerbated by the tension and discomfort of having to deal with being forced together after a week of avoiding each other.

In silence, they locked the front door and began their long journey north, music playing loud enough to drown out any prospect of a conversation.

West Bay

It was featured on the Six o'clock News. The weather forecast showed the current position of the hurricane and its predicted path, outlining the expected direction it would move over the coming hours and days. It appeared to be approaching Florida from the southeast tracking north-westward along the eastern coast, moving across the warm waters of the Atlantic Ocean, threatening devastating winds, heavy rainfall and catastrophic storm surges, with expected landfall in Miami-Dade County and neighbouring coastal areas. Evacuation orders had been issued to residents in those areas and footage showed queues of traffic heading north. There was no doubt about it, Freya and Greg would be amongst those crowds, making their way to safety.

Ella tried to imagine the anxiety and fear they must be experiencing in having to leave their beautiful beachfront property, plus the uncertainty of what they might return to once the storm had passed, especially in the light of recent events. As she hadn't heard from Freya since their aborted conversation over a week ago, she could only assume that they were both travelling to safety, forced together through necessity, and was left wondering how things were between them after everything that had happened. She desperately wanted to hear that they were alright and prayed that they would escape harm from the storm, yet she wondered how was she going to find out.

Later that evening, she received a telephone call that answered some of her questions. "Hi, Mum. How are you?"

"All's good here. How about you?"

"Fine thanks, but I'm concerned about that hurricane heading to South Florida."

"Haven't you heard from Freya? They've had to pack up and leave."

"I haven't heard anything lately, but I expect they've been in a panic to get organised. Where have they gone?"

"They're heading up to Orlando with all the crowds. Have you seen it on the news? Apparently, the big hotels and resorts around there are all hurricane proof."

"Let's hope they are. Orlando seems to be a safe bet then being much further north and inland."

"I was hoping you'd heard from Freya and you might be able to throw some light on what's going on. She wasn't herself when I spoke to her the other day. I've got a feeling something has happened."

"Really? Like what?" Ella ventured, dreading what her mother was about to reveal.

"Well, I don't know. I have a feeling it's something to do with Greg. She was very short with me when I asked after him."

"I don't know, Mum. Try not to worry about it. I'm sure they've been under tremendous pressure with all this going on. It must be absolutely dreadful thinking you could lose your home."

"Hmm...of course. I've just got a feeling there's more going on."

"Well, let's hope not. Just keep me posted if you hear anything else from Freya. I'll be relieved to hear they've arrived safely and then hopefully that the storm has missed Delray so they can go home again."

"Will do. Before I go, how's Kai?"

"He's doing really well, thanks Mum. It's getting harder to juggle work now that he's growing up though. He's sleeping less and is into everything. Anyway, when are you next off?" she asked, keen to change the subject away from herself.

"We're cruising out of Southampton in a couple of weeks – a tour around the UK."

"I like the sound of that." During the rest of the conversation, Ella heard all about the ports of call in detail and where they were heading off after the cruise. It was good to speak to her Mum; she made her feel closer to Freya again.

Chapter Thirty-Six

Orlando, Florida

Their tense journey to safety was filled mainly with painful, prolonged silences, giving them plenty of time to reflect not only on their evacuation from their beloved home but the fragile state of their marriage. Their limited conversation focused purely on journey-related topics, with neither of them daring to broach the subject that had torn them apart. Now was not the time.

"We should be there within the hour if the traffic keeps flowing at this rate," said Greg, glancing across at Freya, whose eyes were fixed firmly on the lanes of cars through her passenger window.

They were heading for Rosen Shingle Creek on Universal Boulevard – a large luxurious resort offering a central location, expansive grounds and extensive amenities - apparently designed to withstand Florida's weather conditions. In normal circumstances, this would have been something to look forward to with its choice of pools, spa, tennis courts and walking trails, and its 18-hole golf course for Greg. They had stayed there before, in happier times. Yet today, Freya was filled with dread at the prospect of spending a few days here; the hurricane had forced them together. There was so much that needed to be said, on both sides. How Freya wanted to scream and shout at Greg and distance herself from him until she was able to understand what had happened. And how Greg wanted to sit Freya down and calmly explain how he had made the biggest mistake of his life, begging her for forgiveness. He wanted everything to be back to the way it was before. Then they could ask Ella for the child they dreamed of.

West Bay

Ella's eyes were glued to the World weather forecast. The hurricane still appeared to be heading for the coast of Southeast Florida; it would be only a matter of hours before the extent of its severity became known. There had been no news of Freya and Greg from her parents, other than a brief message to confirm they had arrived safely in Orlando. She was desperate to know more – not just about the storm, but what was going on between them. Forced together in the face of adversity, it seemed inevitable that some difficult conversations lay ahead. If she had the opportunity, she knew exactly what she would want to say to Freya. She would tell her that Greg was nothing more than a brother-in-law to her and that what had happened was merely a moment of drunken madness – nothing more. She wanted to beg her for forgiveness and ask her for the opportunity to make amends; she would give them the child they dreamed of.

Orlando

According to the latest update, there was every possibility that the eye of the storm might miss them:

Hurricane Rafael, a Category 3 storm, is on course to make landfall near Miami on Wednesday at approximately 3.00pm, bringing maximum sustained winds of 120 mph, a central pressure of 950 millibars and a storm surge of up to 10 feet in some coastal areas. The hurricane is likely to cause widespread power outages, leaving residents without electricity, with the possibility of coastal flooding and damage to beachfront properties. Roads are likely to become impassable due to fallen trees and debris. Emergency shelters have been set up across the state. The National Weather Service predicts that the hurricane will move northward across Florida and into Georgia.

Although the forecasted trajectory of the storm appeared to have changed, with landfall now likely to be south of Delray Beach, there was still a significant risk of high winds and heavy rainfall, with damage to structures, trees and power lines expected along the coastal areas to the north and south of Miami.

"It looks as though it might miss us," remarked Greg, still desperately attempting to break the silence that remained between them. He was deeply concerned about Freya; she had barely uttered a word since they had left their home. Professing to have no appetite, she looked pale and drawn, and was either asleep, reading, or out somewhere wandering around the extensive hotel grounds. In many ways, he wished she would lash out at him and tell him exactly what was going on in her mind. Then he might get the opportunity to explain to her what had happened and beg her forgiveness. He wanted to promise her the future she dreamed of, back in their perfect home with the prospect of their own child. But she was having none of it.

"I'm going for a swim," she replied, ignoring his hurricane update.

"I'll come with you."

"I'd rather go on my own," she replied, turning her back on him.

"Fair enough, but Freya, we need to talk at some point."

"Not yet. I've got some thinking to do." She had opened the door, clearly desperate to make her exit.

"Can we talk when you get back then? Please, Freya."

"Maybe." The door closed behind her.

☐

As she headed for the large, freeform tropical pool, she spotted an empty cabana surrounded by lush landscaping and palm trees – the perfect place to escape for a while. She had toyed with the idea of visiting the lap pool again. Swimming offered her a brief respite from all the stress and worries as she powered through the water, concentrating instead on engaging her body in rhythmic movements and controlled breathing. It helped to calm her mind and body, offering a fleeting sense of peace and well-being. But today she felt drained of energy and opted instead for a relaxing hideaway.

In a day or two, they would be able to head home if the weather reports were to be believed, so she needed to give serious and rational thought to what she was going to do next. Her head and heart ached heavily with all the hurt. Greg was beside himself with worry and was trying his utmost to appease her, but she wasn't prepared to give him the opportunity. She couldn't work out what she wanted to happen;

nothing made sense any more. Part of her felt like disappearing for a while and hoping it would all go away. Yet in stronger moments, she realised that the better option would be to deal with her feelings. She needed an opportunity to vent her anger to Greg and Ella, otherwise it would fester for ever. Then maybe she would be able to move on, whatever that entailed. Did she want to throw everything away? Her marriage and her chance of a family? Or did she have it in her to forgive and forget? Maybe in time it might be possible. And then what about a baby? Did Ella really mean it? Could it ever work out? So many questions raced through her mind. Perhaps Greg was right: they did need to have a conversation, sooner rather than later.

"Good swim?" asked Greg the moment she walked through the door. She'd been gone all afternoon and he hoped and prayed that she was in the mood to talk.

"I just sat by the pool, thinking," she responded, hinting that she might be.

"Is now a good time to talk, or do you have plans?"

"I'm going to shower and then maybe we could get a drink."

"That sounds good," responded Greg, overcome by a sense of relief. Although he had rehearsed his explanation, apology and tentative plans for their future over and over in his head, he knew that he needed to be guided by Freya, remaining calm and level-headed whilst listening to everything she had to say and accepting all the blame. This felt like his one and only chance to save their marriage.

To Greg, it felt like an eternity, but after what must have been about half an hour, Freya emerged from the bedroom of their suite. Beautiful, fragile Freya. He loved her desperately and it broke his heart that he had hurt her so badly. Somehow, he had to put things right between them.

"Let's go," she announced, walking towards the door without giving Greg the chance to comment on her appearance.

As they made their way to the pool bar, they walked a good arm's length apart from each other and spoke only briefly about the hurricane, opting to sit at a quiet table on the edge of the water away from other guests.

"A glass of wine?" he asked tentatively.

"That's fine."

"And then it's over to you…"

"All I want to know, is why?" she responded sadly, her eyes glistening with tears.

"The simple answer is alcohol and opportunity."

"Wow! There must have been plenty of other occasions if that's all it took."

"Freya, I promise you, it was the one and only time I have ever cheated on you, and if I could turn the clock back, it would never have happened. There is and has never been anything at all between Ella and me. It was the most stupid mistake I have ever made and it meant absolutely nothing to either of us."

"But it happened…" she whispered, as the tears began to flow down her pale cheeks.

"I know. But you have to believe me when I say that it should never have happened and I regret it every second of every day."

"But it's not that simple, is it?"

"What do you mean?"

"Because there's Kai, of course. You have a son. And I don't. Not just that though. He's going to be a permanent reminder of everything that's wrong between us for the rest of our lives."

"It doesn't have to be that way, Freya."

"But it will be! You will always want to have Kai in your life. And I completely understand that. He's your biological son."

"Even if I did, Freya, he lives so far away. I have to accept that I can only ever be an occasional parent to Kai."

"So, how does Ella feel about that?"

"She doesn't want me in her life any more than you do. She regrets what happened every bit as much as I do. If I never saw her or Kai again, it would suit her."

"Doesn't she want you to support Kai financially?"

"She wants nothing from me. All she wants is for everything to be ok between us – you and me."

Freya believed him. He meant every word; she could see it in his eyes. He was devastated by what had happened and full of regret. Taking a sip of chilled white wine, she gazed across the pool, her head spinning with his words and her thoughts about what he had said. She needed time to take it all in.

"All I want, Freya, is to turn back the clock. I want us to go home to whatever's left of our house after the storm had passed, and start all over again. I promise you, I will do anything and everything to make you happy."

Could she forgive him? In time, she might be able to see a way forward. But what about their future - the one that she dreamed of? The one that involved having a child. That desire remained as strong as ever, but how could she accept Ella's offer after all that had happened between them?

"There's a lot to think about. You need to give me more time."

"I will give you all the time in the world, Freya. Believe me when I tell you how much I love you and want to make amends. I'll do whatever it takes." After days of separation and hostility, Greg dared to reach over to her hand that rested on the edge of the table and placed his gently over hers. She did not withdraw from his touch but allowed its genuine warmth and affection to melt her frozen heart.

"Let's get something to eat," she suggested, feeling a hint of appetite for the first time in ages.

As the evening wore on, and the wine continued to flow, Freya knew she wanted life to return to normal just as much as Greg did. In time, she believed she would be able to forgive Greg for the sake of their marriage, but she was less sure about her feelings towards Ella. That decision would be much harder. Somehow, her betrayal felt worse, due to the lies and deception she had maintained for so long. And judging by the way she felt, she could no longer imagine taking her up on the offer of surrogacy. For that to happen, they would need to be completely intertwined in each other's lives for months to make the necessary arrangements. As things stood, their relationship was in tatters; she could not imagine how they would ever be able to restore it to the way it was, not that they had ever been particularly close.

Opening the door to their suite, an awkwardness formed between them as they moved to opposite sides of the room towards the two separate queen beds that they had been occupying since their arrival.

"Do you fancy a nightcap from the mini-bar?" suggested Greg tentatively, hoping he had not misjudged the mood.

"Go on then," she replied unexpectedly, half-smiling for the first time in ages.

"It's been a good night, hasn't it?"

"A step in the right direction, I'd say. A start."

"Thank you, Freya. Thank you for listening and giving me a chance to explain. Let's look forward to getting home and starting over again."

"Come here," she murmured, her eyes glistening. "Forget about that drink. I don't need one."

"Are you sure?"

"About a drink? Yes. About you coming over here? Yes." She meant it. She wanted to hold him again. She wanted him back.

Chapter Thirty-Seven

West Bay

According to the latest world weather reports, Hurricane Rafael had been less severe than originally feared. As it made its way towards land, it had weakened and been downgraded to a tropical storm, bringing with it heavy rain, flash flooding and strong winds all along the coastal regions around Miami. The news bulletin showed footage of the damage caused to trees, power lines and structures by strong gusts of wind, leading to power outages and some property damage to beachfront properties, but it seemed that the eye of the storm had missed Delray Beach, meaning that Freya and Greg would be able to return safely to their home in the coming days.

Unsurprisingly, Ella hadn't heard a word from her sister, although her mother had been in regular contact to let her know that they were staying in a resort in Orlando and report what she had heard on the news about the hurricane's path. She was relieved to learn that the storm had missed them, but she still felt perturbed by the lack of communication between them and was undecided as to what she should do about it. She wondered whether she should compose a carefully-worded letter of apology to Freya, offering some sort of explanation for what happened and asking for forgiveness. It might open the door to a conversation between them, when she would then restate her offer to act as a surrogate.

Over the past couple of days, Ella had been feeling under the weather, probably due to the stress of everything that was constantly racing around in her mind. Her head was pounding and she was exhausted through lack of sleep, making it incredibly difficult to deal with even Kai's basic needs. She had resorted to taking painkillers at regular intervals throughout the day, but they were hardly touching her headache, and she had lost her appetite.

This morning, she felt worse. Much worse. She had woken very early from a night of broken sleep and disturbing nightmares, to a stabbing pain across her forehead; she had somehow managed to stagger out of bed just in time to give in to the nausea that had been affecting her appetite for the past few days. Feeling weak and confused, she felt a slight tingling and numbness beginning to affect her hands and feet. Something was seriously wrong with her.

Kai was still asleep; she needed to work out how she was going to deal with him once he was awake but she didn't have much time – maybe an hour if she was lucky. She needed help. Urgently. But who could she ask? There was the couple in the flat next door, but she couldn't recall their names. She had a vague recollection of seeing the young woman recently. They had chatted and exchanged numbers, she thought. What was her name? Why couldn't she remember? It was only the other day.

Making her way cautiously to the kitchen, she managed to locate her phone on the end of the work surface and sat down heavily at the kitchen table, her head spinning and her vision blurring. She had to focus. She needed to call for help – not just for herself, but for Kai. Eventually, she was able to open up her contacts and managed to press one randomly. After several rings, the call was answered with an abrupt "Hello."

"Hello. Hi," she uttered, struggling to hold the phone to her ear.

"Ella? Is that you? Are you ok? It's really early, you know," came the response. The voice was female and a little abrupt.

"Who is it? Sorry. I... don't feel... well."

"It's Amelia from the magazine. What's the matter, Ella?"

Amelia. Why had she phoned her? "I'm not well...I don't know...what to do."

"Do you want me to come over? Do you need an ambulance?"

"I...I'm not...sure..."

"I'm coming over now. I'll be with you as soon as I can."

After what seemed like an eternity, but was in fact only fifteen minutes, there was a knock at the door. Holding her head with one hand and grabbing furniture for support across the room with the other, Ella was able to open the door just in time to fall into her friend's arms.

"Oh my goodness, Ella. Let's get you to the sofa. I'm going to call an ambulance."

"My baby… my boy…" Ella managed to utter as she collapsed onto the cushions.

"It's ok, Ella. Just lie there while I make the call."

"My baby…" she repeated, desperately trying to make some sort of sense to her confused, scared friend, who was now speaking to someone on the end of the phone.

Suddenly, there was a cry from the nursery. Kai had woken, disturbed by the raised voices and commotion, causing Ella to remove her hand from her pounding head.

"I'll go. You sit there and wait. Don't move. An ambulance is on its way."

Ambulance? What was happening to her? She felt as though she was having an outer-body experience with no understanding of what was going on. A strange woman was holding a crying child in the room. The child's arms were outstretched towards her whilst the woman held him tightly, jiggling him up and down and telling him gently to shush. The stabbing pains in her head were now unbearable, seemingly worsened by the light that was now pouring into the room. She squeezed her eyes shut and held her head in her hands which felt heavy and tingly. She just wanted it all to stop.

The emergency medical team arrived quickly, unbeknown to Ella, who was drifting in and out of consciousness. They acted swiftly to assess, stabilise and rapidly transport her to the hospital, checking her breathing, circulation, and administering drugs throughout the journey.

Amelia, having explained that Ella had contacted her for help, was more than happy to take on the role of the designated emergency caregiver for Kai whilst his mother received medical attention, until such time as closer family or friends could be contacted to assist. She planned to stay in Ella's apartment and attempt to contact her parents in the first instance, realising how little she knew about Ella's close friends and family.

"Oh, hello. This is Ella's friend, Amelia. Sorry to contact you out of the blue, but I'm afraid I have some concerning news about your daughter."

"Amelia? Ella? What's happened?" responded Ella's mother, shocked and confused. She had never heard of Amelia before.

"I'm sorry to tell you, but Ella has been rushed to hospital this morning with head pains. She's been taken to Dorset County Hospital in Dorchester for an initial evaluation. She contacted me, probably because I live close by in Bridport. We both work on the local magazine."

"What about Kai? What's happened to him?" she asked in panic, struggling to take in the news and wanting to ask a million questions all at once.

"I have Kai. He's fine. I'm happy to stay here at Ella's apartment until family or close friends are able to take over."

"We'll be there as soon as we can. We live in Bristol so it's going to be a few hours, but we'll be with you by early afternoon at the latest."

"Don't rush. I'm happy to look after Kai. My husband is at home to take care of my own children, so please don't worry about him."

"But what about Ella? Do you know what's happened?"

"I honestly don't know any details, but they managed to stabilise her before they took her off to hospital. It seems that she had a severe headache that was making her ill and confused. If I hear anything more, I'll let you know straight away."

"Thank you so much, Amelia. We're so grateful. We'll be with you as soon as we possibly can."

"No worries. See you later."

By the time her parents arrived in West Bay, Ella had been transferred to a specialist neurosurgical unit at University Hospital Southampton, the main referral centre for complex neurological cases from Dorset.

The urgent medical attention Ella had received, involving emergency stabilisation, a CT scan and medical intervention, revealed that she had experienced a serious brain bleed – an intracranial haemorrhage. The severity of the bleed and its likely long-term effects were as yet unknown – only time would tell. For now, she was stable and in recovery. It could have been much worse.

Chapter Thirty-Eight

Delray Beach

Other than some missing roof shingles and a couple of minor leaks from detached gutters and downspouts, they had escaped the brunt of the storm. A few fallen branches from palm trees were strewn across the pool and small amounts of beach debris had been washed up onto the property from the storm surge. It would not take long to clean up and restore the property to its former glory.

As they worked alongside each other on the clean-up operation, it felt almost like the old days again, their troubles behind them. Ironically, the storm had forced them together and given them both the time and opportunity to face up to what had happened. Painful as it had been, Freya was prepared to give Greg another chance. As for Ella, that was going to take more time and she wasn't ready to have that conversation yet.

"Your phone's ringing, Freya," called Greg from the kitchen. "Do you want me to bring it out to you?"

"Can you answer it for me? I'll be there in a sec," she answered from the veranda, pulling off her protective gloves and kicking off her shoes. As she made her way into the kitchen, she was bemused by the shocked expression on Greg's face as he handed over the phone. "It's your Mum." She had clearly already told him her news.

"Mum? Hi. Everything ok?"

"Oh, Freya. You haven't heard, have you? It's Ella. She's in hospital."

"In hospital? What's happened?"

"It's serious," she managed before bursting into tears.

"Mum... tell me what's happened!"

"She's had a brain bleed, Freya. I'm so worried about her."

Listening intently whilst struggling to take in the shocking news, her mother went on to describe in detail what had happened, according to Ella's friend, Amelia, who had thankfully come to her rescue. She was relieved to hear that her condition was described as stable, but greatly concerned to hear that the after-effects and prognosis were as yet unknown.

"What about Kai?"

"Well, he's with us for now. He's happy enough, but I've no idea what's going to happen. It might be months before Ella's capable of looking after a child. We just don't know."

There was no point in trying to predict the future. Freya needed to speak to Greg urgently. "Mum, I need to talk to Greg about what we can do to help. Keep me posted, won't you?"

"Of course I will, darling. Speak soon."

As she placed the phone down, her eyes met Greg's as they faced each other across the kitchen table. "What are we going to do?" she asked.

"What were you thinking?" He needed to hear what she had to say before making his own suggestion.

"You're Kai's father. You need to take care of him until Ella's well again."

"It might be weeks or months though…"

"It might be years or for ever," continued Freya. "Who knows what the future holds for Ella?"

"I just don't know what to say. We can't just up-sticks and move over to the UK. What about the gallery? Our home?"

"How about he comes to stay here, with us?"

"Ella's not going to want that, is she? Be realistic, Freya."

"I am. She's seriously ill, Greg. From what Mum's told me, it's going to take a long time to get over what's happened, and that's if she's able to make a full recovery. As soon as she's better, or allowed to travel, she can come here too."

"You really mean it, don't you?"

"We have no choice. You're Kai's legal guardian and Ella is my sister. It's what we have to do."

Chapter Thirty-Nine

University Hospital Southampton

Ella had been transferred to UHS to be cared for by a team of specialists for patients with neurological conditions, for close monitoring and tracking of her neurological status, intracranial pressure and other critical indicators of potential long-term damage caused by the bleed. Thankfully, initial indications were encouraging: she was in a stable condition, with little evidence of serious complications. Regular neurological assessments were being conducted to monitor for changes in consciousness, movements, speech and other key functions, and further tests and CT scans were due to be undertaken to determine the cause and extent of the bleed. Depending on the outcome over the critical next few days, a programme of rehabilitation would begin aimed at recovering any lost functions.

Understandably, visitor access was restricted to ensure Ella received focused medical care and to maintain a calm environment for her. Once she was conscious and considered stable, her parents were allowed to visit briefly under strict instructions to avoid tiring her. However, she was exhausted and disorientated, drifting in and out of sleep, unable to communicate verbally at this early stage. Only when her mother mentioned Kai, did her eyes flicker in response, indicating there was some recognition of their presence. It was shocking to see their daughter lying there, wired up to so many monitoring and medical devices. The consultant had explained to them that continuous cardiac and blood pressure monitoring was essential as high or fluctuating blood pressure could exacerbate a brain bleed, but assured them that she was responding well to medication.

In the meantime, for as long as it took, they needed to care for their grandson. Somehow, they would manage.

Delray Beach

"We've booked the flights already," explained Freya to her mother having phoned for an update on Ella's condition.

"Really? When? That's wonderful. You're both coming? What about the gallery?" So many questions.

"Yes, Mum. We're both coming on Saturday and the gallery will just have to close for a week or two. Some things are more important, aren't they?"

"I'll get the spare room ready then."

"No need, Mum. Greg's found us an Airbnb in Clifton."

"Why have you done that? You know you can stay with us. We're dying to see you."

"We need some space if we're going to be helping out with Kai."

"What do you mean? He's fine with us."

"We want to help, Mum. I mean we want to look after Kai." Freya had no plans to divulge anything more at this stage about their plans or the reason for their deeper involvement. That would have to wait and it was not going to be an easy conversation.

Over the past few days and some heated discussions, they had come to a decision. They would spend a couple of weeks in the UK, helping out with Kai and visiting Ella, aiming to return to Florida with Kai until such time that Ella could join them, hopefully persuading her that it was the best place for her rehabilitation. Greg had taken some persuading to go along with her plan. Did this mean he would have to divulge his true relationship with Kai or could he continue to support the family in his role as 'uncle'?

"You don't need to say anything. I don't think my parents can take much more at the moment. I'm her sister and we're in a position to help the family."

"I don't know why you think Ella is going to let us bring her son back here with us. She's not going to agree to it."

"She doesn't have much choice, does she? Surely Kai needs to be with his father if he can't be with his mother? Don't you think it's your right to have him?"

"I haven't earned any rights, Freya. Ella made it clear that my involvement in Kai's life is not required. She didn't want any of this. She suggested that I take on the role of his uncle rather than his father, because she was desperate to save our marriage and her relationship with you. She meant it when she offered to be a surrogate for us, you know. She was desperate to make things right."

"But it hasn't turned out that way, has it? I know what happened and I know that Kai is your son. You should take care of him, Greg. And Ella needs to let you. She can join us in Florida for as long as she likes once she's feeling better."

"What if she can't? No one knows whether she has incurred any lasting damage. Maybe she'll need looking after herself."

"We'll cross that bridge when we come to it. Our priority is Kai."

Southampton

In the days that followed, Ella was suffering from severe fatigue and a persistent headache. Still bed-bound, she felt nauseous and dizzy much of the time, and was undeniably confused and disorientated, unable to concentrate or remember what had happened. Her body felt weak all over and she had no idea whether she was going to be left with any long-term damage. It was obvious that she was facing a period of rehabilitation, whatever that might entail.

Her parents had visited earlier and had worn her out by talking at her incessantly, or so it felt. She had tried to listen but felt herself drifting in and out of sleep; her medication was powerful and her concentration levels were hugely diminished by her pounding head pains. She was so confused. Where was she? She was aware she was in hospital but not that she was in Southampton. Why did they keep talking about a child? She had no idea.

Unbeknown to Ella, brain imaging and a series of neurological examinations had revealed the location of her bleed had affected the hippocampus and temporal lobes - the areas playing a significant role in memory formation and retrieval. It seemed that she was suffering from retrograde amnesia – the loss of pre-existing memories – causing her to forget significant parts of her past, including knowledge of important personal relationships.

Bristol

"We'll head down to Southampton first thing in the morning," announced Freya. They had arrived late morning, following an overnight flight from Miami and a tiring drive from Heathrow in the rush-hour traffic. "How's she doing?"

"She's making good progress, I think. She seems more responsive than she was a few days ago," offered her mother optimistically.

"She's exhausted and confused," added her father. "I'm not sure how much she takes in when you talk to her."

"She's doing well, but you're right, she doesn't seem to want to hear about Kai."

"That's odd," said Freya, wondering why this might be. Surely, he must be her main concern. "Perhaps she's blocking him out at the moment because she knows she's not in a position to look after him."

"Maybe, but it's strange. It's almost as though she doesn't know who he is anymore."

"Have you taken him in to see her?" asked Greg.

"No. It's no place for a baby," responded Mum, glancing at her watch.

"When will we get to see him?" asked Freya, aware that Kai must be coming to the end of his regular midday nap.

"Any time now!" she laughed, hearing mumblings on the baby monitor. "I'll go and fetch him."

Greg and Freya exchanged knowing glances. This was the moment they had been waiting for: Greg was about to be reunited with his child and Freya would be there to witness it. It felt surreal but oddly wonderful.

"Here he is! Do you want to take him?" she suggested, holding him out towards Freya. He was utterly perfect and wonderful; her heart filled with instant love at the sight of him.

"You take him, Greg," murmured Freya, holding her breath in

anticipation, her arms dangling resolutely by her sides.

"Hello, little man," whispered Greg, taking his son into his strong, protective arms. "How are you doing?"

"Look at you two with your matching blond curls!" announced Mum, failing to understand the significance of her words. Father and son, reunited. They were perfect together; they were meant to be.

En route to Southampton, they had the opportunity to talk things through. The plan was to take Kai to their accommodation in Clifton upon their return to Bristol, having asked Ella for her blessing. They had tentatively discussed their longer-term plans with Freya's parents, who seemed to accept that it made good sense for Kai to have a holiday with his aunt and uncle, while they focused on taking care of Ella once she was discharged from hospital.

Everything hinged on Ella. How would she cope with seeing them after what had happened between them? She could only imagine what Greg must be feeling; he must be dreading it.

Southampton

"How is she doing?" asked Freya, having introduced herself as Ella's sister to the consultant, Mr Jackson, who was keen to speak to them about her condition.

"She's making good progress, but we're still to determine the longer-term effects. Early signs indicate that there has been some damage to the part of her brain that's responsible for memory. You might find that Ella is unable to remember events, experiences, or even people from her past. The type of amnesia she has usually involves facts rather than skills, and her most recent memories are likely to be affected rather than her oldest ones, possibly those from the year or two before the incident."

"Will her memory return?" asked Freya, shocked to discover the potential extent of damage caused by the bleed.

"It's possible. There is every chance that she will experience a temporary loss, but there is a slight chance of it being permanent or progressive. We won't know immediately."

"Can a temporary memory loss be treated?" She had so many questions running through her mind.

"Well, there are no known effective medications for what is known as retrograde amnesia. The priority will be treating the cause of the amnesia. Ella will be seen by the occupational therapist to help her replace lost memories in the first instance. Then it will be important for family and friends to support her by providing emotional support and engaging her in activities which can improve memory and cognitive functions."

"I understand. We will help her in any way we can," said Freya, realising how important their support was going to be over the next few weeks or months. "We're mainly concerned about her ability to care for her young son. He's just a baby."

"I see. Are you in a position to support her? It's likely to be a few months at least until she's ready to look after a child, although much will depend on her progress over the coming days."

"We are," uttered Greg, taking Freya by the hand, as the consultant led them to Ella's bedside.

"How are you doing?" asked Freya gently, placing her hand gently over Ella's. Seeing her sister lying in a hospital bed, wired up to monitors and attached to drips, she realised that she had to draw a line under the recent past events that had nearly torn them all apart.

"I'm not sure," she uttered, smiling weakly. "It's good to see you both. Thank you for coming." There was recognition of who they were and the fact that they were there as a couple. "I'm tired most of the time, so forgive me if I drift off. How are you?"

"We're good, thanks," offered Greg. "We wanted to make sure you are ok, and to offer our help with Kai." Freya was pleased that he had come straight to the point; she had been wondering how to broach the subject.

"Kai? I'm sorry. What do you mean?" Her eyes gave away her confusion and almost panic at the realisation that her cognitive ability was impaired.

"Your son, Ella. Kai is your baby boy," explained Freya gently, perturbed to see that Ella's reaction to this revelation was to close her eyes.

As silence fell between them, Greg and Freya exchanged knowing glances, then focused again on Ella who appeared to have either fallen asleep or shut her eyes to withdraw from the conversation. Was it possible that the recent memories Mr Jackson spoke of, wiped out by Ella's amnesia, included Kai and the circumstances of his birth?

"Ella..." whispered Freya eventually, stroking her hand, "Are you awake?"

After several seconds, she opened her eyes, which began to fill with tears. "I'm sorry. It's early days, I suppose. I can't remember what happened."

"Don't worry about it at the moment. You're doing well and we're here to help."

"Thank you, Freya." That short sentence answered the question Freya was dying to know the answer to: did she know who she was? Her recollection of older memories, including people, appeared to be intact; it was the recent ones that were missing.

"Ella, you have a little boy and we want to help look after him until you're better."

"I don't understand," she uttered, closing her eyes once more.

From Ella's response, it was evident that their visit had come to an end. They would need to speak to Mr Jackson again for his advice on what to do about Kai. It was complicated; they weren't going to be able to simply take him back to the States without legal considerations. Without Greg being named as Kai's biological father on his birth certificate, he had no parental responsibility, and Ella was evidently in no state to give consent to allow them to take her child out of the country. It was most likely the courts would need to determine what arrangements were best for Kai's care and stability during his mother's rehabilitation. Greg would need to seek a court order.

Chapter Forty

Southampton

Over the next few days, Ella began to show encouraging signs of recovery and was clearly over the acute phase of her episode. Her headache was much improved and she was generally more alert and aware. Other than memory loss of recent events, she appeared to have escaped any other physical, cognitive, or speech impairments and was therefore assessed as being fit enough for discharge on the basis that she was medically stable and that post-hospital care was in place in the form of family support. She would require rehabilitation time with outpatient therapy and follow-up care from medical professionals to support her with the recovery of her memory loss. It could have been so much worse.

In the meantime, plans were put in place for Kai to accompany Freya and Greg back to the States. Following consultation with the medical team and conversations with her family, Ella finally accepted that she must have given birth to a child and gave her permission for Kai to be cared for by her sister, involving a visit abroad, thus avoiding the need for a court order. Their departure date was dependent on how quickly his passport application was processed through the fast-track service – likely to be within one week rather than the usual three.

In an attempt to restore Ella's memory surrounding the circumstances of Kai's birth, her parents had been advised to use photos to introduce her gently to the fact that she had a son and allow her time to process the information. Once home and reintroduced to her son, she was likely to need opportunities to bond with her son without pressure to gently encourage memory recall. However, it would all take time.

"Our priority is to allow Ella time to rehabilitate before being expected to care for her son," explained Mr Jackson. "She needs time to stabilise physically, cognitively and emotionally. A person suffering from memory loss is likely to feel overwhelmed by the demands of childcare and ideally, Ella would benefit from a break from them to give herself time to heal. Initially, she is likely to have difficulty remembering critical information, which could impact on the child. I strongly recommend family stepping in to support her child and aid her in her recovery. Our goal is to ensure Ella's well-being and her son's safety and care."

"We were planning to take Kai home to Florida with us for a few weeks if it can be arranged, and if Ella agrees of course," explained Freya. "Then, we are hoping she will be able to join us just as soon as she can."

"When will she be able to fly?" asked Greg, appreciating the potential risks of air travel, such as changes in cabin pressure, reduced oxygen levels and the logistics of medical care during a long-haul flight.

"Specific timing will depend on several factors. Ella is going to require a period of recovery and observation, but in theory, as long as she continues to make good progress and is fully stable, it might be possible in a few weeks."

Bristol

Just a few days after Ella's discharge from the hospital, Kai's passport arrived, meaning that the time had come for Freya and Greg to think about going home. Meanwhile, Ella continued to make good progress, and other than struggling with extreme tiredness and repeated mild headaches, she was coping reasonably well with daily routines. Following Mr Jackson's advice, Kai stayed with them in their accommodation to ease Ella gently back to the idea of being a mother. That part of her rehabilitation was not going so well, with Ella showing not just a lack of recognition but a reluctance to interact with her son.

"Morning! How are you doing today?" asked Freya, balancing Kai on her hip as she entered the room.

"Hi. Pretty well, I think," Ella responded flatly, hardly glancing at Kai.

"Do you want to take him?" asked Freya tentatively, sensing her reluctance.

"I think he's happiest on the floor. Let's find him some toys to play with. So, when are you off?"

"Tomorrow, if that's ok with you. It's no problem to change the flight if you'd rather us hang around for a bit longer."

"No, no. I think the peace and quiet will do me some good. I'm so grateful to you both. I just hope in time I'll be back to where I was before all this happened. To be honest, I can't imagine being a mother, either in the past or the future. I know it sounds dreadful, but I just can't face it at the moment, the way I'm feeling. I'm sorry."

"Don't apologise. You just need more time. It will be fine, don't worry. You've been through such a trauma. It's no wonder you're feeling like that. In a few weeks, when you've had the chance to rebuild your strength, you can come out and join us. I'm sure you'll start to feel the way you did before."

"I'm not so sure," she uttered, tears building up in her eyes.

Seeing Ella so altered by what had happened, Freya somehow managed to shelve all her negative feelings towards her sister. There was no point dwelling on what had gone on between Greg and Ella anymore. Her priority was Kai. In just a matter of days, Freya had fallen head over heels in love with him and could think of nothing more important than taking care of him for however long she was allowed. Despite the upheaval of what had happened to his mother and having to be cared for initially by his grandparents and now his aunt and uncle – or rather, father – Kai seemed remarkably unaffected. They had bonded well; he was eating heartily, playing contentedly and sleeping peacefully through the night. The hardest part of each day was taking him to see Ella, who seemed reluctant to interact with him and unable to accept that he had anything to do with her. Instinctively, Kai kept a distance from her too, preferring the distraction of his toys or attention from Freya, Greg or his grandparents. Freya could not wait to take him home.

Chapter Forty-One

Delray Beach

The first few days back home were busy ones, buying essential baby equipment and settling into new routines. Greg returned to the gallery but managed to get home each day in time for Kai's bath and bedtime. Freya was immersed in looking after Kai and loving every minute; it was everything she dreamed it would be. No more endless empty hours of time-wasting, wandering around shopping malls and drinking coffee with acquaintances, talking about nothing in particular. Suddenly, her life had meaning. She loved every minute of the day spent with Kai, teaching him new words, singing and reading to him, playing for hours with stimulating and educational toys or just splashing around in the pool. Her patience was limitless and her love unconditional. As the days rolled by, Freya couldn't bear to imagine what life would be like without him.

"Have you heard from Ella today?" asked Greg after Freya had recounted every moment of her day with Kai, from what he had eaten for breakfast to which book he had enjoyed that evening.

"I hear from her every day," responded Freya, the smile vanishing from her lips and the lights disappearing from her eyes at the mention of her name.

"I know. I mean, how was she today? Do you think there's any change?"

"She seems to be doing well. I think she's becoming more confident to try things out. Apparently, she went shopping with Mum for an hour today."

"Did she mention Kai?"

"She didn't, but she never does. It's odd, isn't it? I don't really understand what's going on."

"It's as though she doesn't really believe Kai is her son."

"I know. If I mention him, she changes the subject. Today, I asked her if she'd given any thought to when she wanted to come out, but she said she thought a long-haul flight would be too much for her."

"Well, I can understand that. It's a big deal even if you're in good health, let alone having just experienced a brain bleed."

"We're fine though, aren't we?" asked Freya, her question loaded with deeper meaning.

"Of course we are, but it won't be like this forever, will it?"

"Why not?"

"I don't need to spell it out, surely?"

"Ella doesn't want Kai anymore, does she? He can stay with us. We can look after him."

"Don't kid yourself, Freya. Ella's getting stronger every day. It won't be long before she's fully recovered and her memory is restored. She'll remember being a mum and will want Kai back."

"And she'll remember who his father is, won't she?" Freya couldn't help herself. Greg chose not to reply and turned away.

Bristol

"You have a visitor, Ella." Her father had woken her from an afternoon nap, leaving her feeling confused and disorientated. Blinking and shuffling into an upright position on the sofa, she attempted to focus on the person standing in the doorway to the lounge. Her eyes must be deceiving her, or she was still half-asleep and caught up in a dream.

"Hi, Ella. How are you doing?"

"Marcus..."

"I heard what had happened and wanted to check you're ok."

"I'm... I'm fine, thanks," she uttered, trying to make sense of the situation. "This is a surprise."

"A good one, I hope." How could a visit from her cheating ex-partner be a good surprise, she wondered. "I've brought you some flowers and chocolate – your favourites." Bright yellow roses and a block of the expensive dark chocolate they used to enjoy together.

"Thank you. Do you want to sit down, or are you just popping by?"

"I'm here to see you, to catch up on all your news." Ella's memory of everything relating to Marcus was undamaged. She remembered enjoying absolutely everything about her ten-year relationship with him apart from his painful betrayal and the break-up that brought it all abruptly to an end. She had not been able to forgive him or be prepared to give him a second chance.

"How's Maria?" asked Ella.

"Maria? Oh, you haven't heard then. She went off with the company director and they're living in Dubai now. We weren't together for very long. It was a big mistake."

"Really? So, what went wrong?"

"I shouldn't ever have been with her. You knew that, didn't you? I was stupid. I don't think a day has gone by when I haven't regretted throwing away what we had. We were good, weren't we?"

Ella was lost for words and chose not to reply. He was right though. They were good together and if it hadn't been for his immaturity and obsession to be seen as 'one of the lads', they would probably still be together, maybe with a family of their own. But he had thrown it all away. By moving away to Dorset, she had deliberately lost touch with him and all their friends and had never tried to find out what had happened to him, or Maria. Her coping mechanism had been to cut them both out of her life completely.

Aiming to break the silence, Marcus decided to change the subject and engage Ella in some sort of conversation. "Are you still working in graphic design?"

"Before this happened, I was doing some freelance work for a magazine and some local galleries in Dorset. I'm hoping to get back to it as soon as I can."

"When do you think you'll be able to do that?"

"I'm not too sure. I'm feeling stronger every day, but a little cautious about being on my own."

"I can fully appreciate that."

Before the conversation could develop further, Ella's mother entered the lounge with a tray of tea and biscuits.

"It's good to see you, Marcus," she said, somewhat insincerely. She had never forgiven him for cheating on her daughter. "How is life treating you?"

"Not so bad, thank you. My main focus is my work these days."

"How's Maria?" she asked, no holds barred.

"I don't really know, to be honest. We're not in touch."

"Oh, I see," she answered abruptly, not seeing at all.

"I'm here to find out how Ella is doing. I had heard she was in Bristol."

"Well, it's just as well you came now before she goes."

"Mum, I can speak for myself! I'm perfectly capable, you know," interrupted Ella, irritated by her mother's interference.

"Do you mean you're going back to Dorset soon?" asked Marcus, a little confused.

"I'm in no rush," replied Ella, keen to change the subject.

"She's taking a holiday first – in Florida – to spend some time with her son."

Her announcement had a freeze-frame effect on the room, capturing Marcus with a shocked open-mouthed expression; her mother with her eyes glinting mischievously and Ella's blank expression, revealing nothing whatsoever.

"Florida?" Marcus uttered eventually, breaking the uncomfortable silence.

"That's the plan when I'm up to it," explained Ella.

"I see. To spend time with your son?"

"That's right. My son, Kai. He's nearly one."

"I didn't know about him," mumbled Marcus awkwardly, as Ella's mother stood up to allow them to continue their conversation in private. "Are you with his father?"

"No. I'm not."

"So, forgive me for asking, but why is your son in Florida?"

"He's with my sister. She's taking care of him until I'm better. The plan seems to be that I'm to take an extended holiday with them until I'm ready to take over being a mum again."

"You must miss him dreadfully."

"Just between us, I don't. I have no maternal feelings whatsoever. It turns out that my recent memories have been wiped away by what happened, and that includes Kai and the circumstances of his birth. In a perfect world, I would hope to get better soon and return to my apartment in Dorset where I could take up my work and rebuild my strength and my life. I don't see how a small child can fit into that plan."

"Surely your memory will improve and you'll want to be reunited with your son in time."

"I don't think so. I can't imagine suddenly finding the strength or confidence to bring up a child on my own, especially after what has happened to me."

"What about his father? Can't he help out?"

"As I told you, I can't remember anything about how he came into the world. It's a mystery. Maybe that's a good thing."

The conversation continued for a while, the familiarity between them offering Ella some comfort amid all the recent confusion and loss of control.

"Can I see you again?" asked Marcus tentatively.

"Do you want to?"

"I do, Ella. If I can help in any way, as an old friend, I'd love to."

And with that, he left, making Ella feel hopeful for the first time in ages.

Chapter Forty-Two

Delray Beach

Days turned into weeks, with no prospect of Ella visiting them and reclaiming her son. Their daily conversations had become shorter with Ella becoming more distant and seemingly less interested to hear the regular updates on Kai's progress.

"He's taken his first steps, Ella," reported Freya excitedly. "I'll send you a video."

"That's good," replied Ella, with about as much interest as hearing that she'd just finished reading a good book.

"Any more thoughts about coming out to Florida?"

"I'm not sure. I'm planning to go home in the next week or two. Mum and Dad cancelled a cruise to look after me, but I think they're ready to book up their next trip. I don't think they've been at home for such a long spell in ages. I'll be fine at home now, so long as I take it easy."

"How are the headaches?"

"More or less cleared up now. I get tired but I'm definitely feeling stronger every day. I just want to get back to some normality now."

"I can imagine. So, what about Marcus?" Ella had told Freya all about his surprise visit a few weeks ago. "Have you heard anything more from him?"

"As it turns out, I have. He's been to see me every week. In fact, several times a week."

"Really?"

"Yes. It might seem strange, but it feels good to have him back in my life, especially after everything that's happened lately. I realise how much I've missed him."

"I'm pleased for you. It's reassuring to think he's there to keep an eye on you. But what's going to happen when you go back to Dorset?"

"He's taking a week off work and plans to join me in West Bay."

"That's great, Ella. I'd be worried to think of you on your own. It's early days."

"Not really. I'm feeling so much better now and just want to get home and back to normal. I'm looking forward to getting back to the coast and painting again."

"And what about Kai?" Freya knew she had to broach the subject, even though she dreaded Ella's response, fearing that her time with him was about to come to an end.

"I'm not ready yet, Freya," replied Ella. "Is it wrong of me?"

"No!" cried Freya, desperate to reassure her. "You need to take time to build your strength. He's absolutely fine with us."

"I know he is. Thank you both for what you're doing for him, for me. What's worrying me though, is that I might need more time than I first thought."

"Take as much time as you need, Ella. Don't put yourself under any pressure. Kai is happy and so are we. Take one day at a time and maybe aim to join us for a holiday in a few weeks if you're ready."

"I will. I'm so grateful to you."

Once their conversation was at an end, Freya joined Greg and Kai in the pool where they'd been playing happily together for the past half hour, splashing and laughing together in the late afternoon sunshine. For the next few weeks at least, it seemed they were going to be able to continue playing happy families without the threat of Ella joining them. She couldn't imagine it all coming to an end. Over the past few weeks, the bonds between the three of them had continued to develop and strengthen. Freya's confidence to care for Kai was growing by the day and Greg was as happy and fulfilled as she had ever seen him. They were a family at last and it was everything that she had ever dreamed of.

West Bay

As soon as the call ended, Ella dropped her head into her hands – not because it ached, but because it was full of confusion and anxiety. She was no closer to recalling any memories relating to Kai and the circumstances of his birth than she was several weeks ago, and she had absolutely no desire to travel to Florida, either for a holiday or to be reunited with the son she had been separated from, both physically and emotionally. Her overriding desire in these early days of her recuperation was simply to rest. She was enjoying being back in West Bay, filling each day effortlessly with hours of reading, painting or strolling around the harbour, taking in the sea air and coastal views. Her overriding fear was having to face up to the fact that she had apparently given birth to a child who was currently living miles across the Atlantic Ocean, and the expectation and pressure for her to be reunited with him, sooner rather than later.

Her life was beginning to take shape again with regular weekend visits from Marcus being a particular highlight. He was due to arrive within the next hour or two and she was looking forward to his company after spending the midweek days alone, painting and taking gentle exercise strolling around West Bay's harbour. He would turn up with flowers and treats, then offer to fetch fish and chips or take her out to her favourite restaurant across the river. They would spend the evening chatting and reminiscing, and he would eventually retreat to the spare bedroom, having discussed plans for the weekend. Ella reflected on her new, revived relationship with her ex. He made her happy – happier than she had been in a long time – and it felt as though they had been able to pick up almost from where they left off before he cheated on her. Back to the good old days of shared interests, a perfectly synched sense of humour and loads of warmth and affection. Ella appreciated his kindness and sensitivity towards her; he understood she needed time and space to recover her lost memories, and knew to avoid certain topics, but would be ready to support her when the need arose.

"How are you doing?" asked Marcus, kissing her chastely on the cheek, before removing his coat and shoes.

"Really well. Good journey?"

"That's good to hear. Yep. No problem on the roads this evening.

Just a bit of traffic build-up through Chideock."

"Come on in. Can I get you a drink?"

"A tea would be great. Then, I was thinking, shall we go out for dinner tonight?"

"I'd love that."

"That's good, because I've made a reservation at Rise."

Her favourite. Just a stroll away around the harbour and across the river. What a perfect way to spend a Friday evening.

After an hour of relaxing and chatting over a cup of tea, they prepared to go out. Ella looked closely at her reflection in the bathroom mirror. She was looking better than she had in a long while. Colour had returned to her complexion and her eyes were bright with renewed health and happiness. Her healthy diet and avoidance of alcohol were clearly impacting on her general wellbeing.

"You look great, Ella," commented Marcus as she emerged from her bedroom, having changed into her favourite emerald green dress that seemed to enhance her features.

"Thank you. You don't look bad yourself," she replied, laughing affectionately. "Come on. Let's go now and take a walk first. It's a lovely evening – cool, but clear skies."

As they walked along the waterfront, Marcus took Ella's hand into his own. She did not resist as they chatted non-stop about the week's events and looked back at the cliffs from the end of the jetty.

"It's been more stable lately," remarked Ella, nodding in the direction of East Cliff. "No recent rockslides."

"Why's that, do you think?"

"It's probably the raising of the beach. All that shingle that you can see. It's reduced sea damage and slowed down erosion." That's exactly how she felt herself, that Marcus was there to protect her from any harm. She was feeling stronger and more stable than she had for a long time, bolstered by the support Marcus was offering her just by being in her company, both physically and mentally.

Over their dinner of seared scallops, followed by mussels in a Thai broth, they conversed with ease as they looked over the moonlit mouth of the river.

"I'm not sure how I would have coped without you, Marcus," confessed Ella. "I'm so grateful to you, you know."

"I wasn't sure whether you would let me back into your life after making such a mess of our relationship. I'm so sorry that I did that to you, to us. I was such a fool."

"Maybe the time has come to move on and put it behind us. I know there are things that I need to face up to, but I'm not sure I can do it on my own."

"Do you want to talk about it?" Marcus sensed that the time was right. He had no plans to push her, but wanted to give her the opportunity whenever she felt the time was right.

"I'm not sure," she hesitated, glancing away from him, her eyes settling on the water's edge.

"That's fine. No rush." He would say no more and leave it to her to make the next move. "Another drink?"

"I want to talk about it, Marcus, but I honestly don't know what to say," she replied, ignoring his question. "I'll try to explain, but it probably won't make much sense."

"Take your time. It might help to talk."

After several seconds of silence, Ella took a deep breath and began to release the words that had been prepared and stored in her mind for the past week or two. "It feels as though a chunk of my life has been erased – possibly a year. I can remember how and why we ended our relationship and my decision to move to West Bay, and I can recall spending most of my time here painting and being involved in freelance work. The next thing I remember is what has happened since falling ill – my family gathering around me, my sister and brother-in-law visiting me from Florida and you coming back into my life."

"Is there anything else you can remember," added Marcus, gently prompting her to mention the elephant in the room.

"You mean my son, don't you?"

"I do."

"I honestly can't recall how he came to be in the world. I can't describe to you how it feels to see his nursery and toys in the apartment. It hardly makes sense. How is it possible that something so major could have happened to me, that I just can't remember? And what makes it worse, Marcus, is that it scares me. I don't want it to be true. I've never wanted to be a mother, so how did it happen? And who the hell is the father?"

"Someone must know. You would have confided in Freya, wouldn't you? Have you asked her?"

"I don't want to know. I don't want to be a mother and I just want it all to go away so I can live my life here, simply and unencumbered. That sounds so wrong, doesn't it?"

"Far from it. You've been through a massive upheaval. It was always going to take time to restore your memory, that's if it ever does return. But what about Kai? Is your sister happy to continue to look after him until such time as you're ready to see him?"

"That's where I'm so lucky. Kai is really happy with my sister and brother-in-law. They've always wanted a family, but aren't able to have children. That information was something else that had been erased from my memory, but Freya tells me she had undergone fertility treatment prior to me becoming ill and was hoping to find a surrogate."

"And now she has your child…" Greg's words struck her hard, but that was the harsh reality. Her childless sister had become a mother as a direct result of her life-altering illness. How much more did she want to know? And looking ahead to the future, what did she want to happen? These were the questions that remained unanswered but ever-present in her troubled mind.

"Do you want to visit your sister and find out more? I could come with you. Maybe your memory would return if you spent an extended time with your son. And, I'm sure you've thought this yourself, but you could ask Freya what she knows about Kai's father."

"I'll think about it, but I'm not sure it's what I want right now."

For the remainder of their evening, they spoke of other things and wandered back to Ella's apartment hand in hand, both sensing a shift in their relationship. It had been a special night, enhanced by good food, honest exchanges and a starlit sky.

"Thank you for tonight, Marcus. It's been perfect."

"I'd agree. It was really good."

"Well, time for bed, I think," announced Ella, easing herself onto her feet from the comfort of the sofa cushions they had been sharing.

"I guess so. It's late. Goodnight, Ella."

Smiling, Ella chose not to reply and stretched out her hand in his direction instead.

Without another word, Marcus stood and allowed himself to be led into her bedroom.

PART FOUR

Chapter Forty-Three

Delray Beach

Freya had never felt happier as she prepared their Thanksgiving meal of roast turkey, stuffing and pumpkin pie, to be shared with their neighbours, and followed by games on the beach in the afternoon. Thinking about what Thanksgiving meant to her, Freya reflected on the personal gratitude she felt for the events of the past few months. Kai was everything to her; the love she felt for him was complete and unconditional. As for her relationship with Greg, it had never felt stronger. Having Kai in his life had brought about several positive changes in him, such as a healthier work-life balance and deeper emotional satisfaction leading to a stronger sense of purpose and direction in his life. Additionally, the shared responsibility of raising a child had deepened mutual respect and collaboration between them, and given them both a greater appreciation for life's simple pleasures.

"Have you heard from Ella lately?" asked Greg as he poured them a glass of celebratory champagne.

"She's gone a bit quiet lately, to be honest. I spoke to her last week."

"Did she ask after Kai?"

"No. It's odd, isn't it? To think she gave birth to this wonderful little human being and she doesn't even know or seem to care."

"I'm sure she cares, Freya, it's just that she's unable to process what happened in those months before she fell ill. Don't be too hard on her. She's been through such a lot."

"I'm not being hard. I'm just wondering how long we have before it all comes to an end. It's going break my heart, Greg, if she takes him away from us."

"We have to prepare ourselves for that. You know we do. He's her son."

"But he's also your son, Greg."

It always came back to that. And she was right. He was Kai's father and maybe there was a conversation to be had with Ella, whenever the time was right.

West Bay

The end of November leading into the start of December was not the best time of the year to enjoy West Bay. The tourists had long gone and there would be only a half-hearted attempt at acknowledging the onset of the festive season. The weather was grim and the days short. The highlight of Ella's week was Friday night, when she clock-watched until Marcus arrived around six o'clock, always armed with flowers and treats. This evening, he was laden with seasonal goodies – a poinsettia, a Jo Malone fig-scented candle and Ella's favourite cherry liqueurs.

"You spoil me!" she exclaimed, throwing her arms around his neck before he had hardly had chance to get through the door.

"You're worth it, I suppose," he joked, keen to rid himself of his parcels so he could concentrate on embracing and kissing Ella, who he had missed beyond words during the week.

Their relationship had gone from strength to strength since the night she'd invited him into her bedroom. The magic was still there between them, perhaps more so. He loved and appreciated her more than he had ever done and was not prepared to risk losing her again. He wondered what the future for them might look like. His work was based in Bristol but there was a possibility of hybrid-working should their relationship progress to him moving in with her one day. Yet, he was not sure about West Bay. Much as he liked the little town and the surrounding areas, there was little opportunity for him outside of the city in his line of work. Yet perhaps he was looking too far ahead and was jumping to conclusions. It was a conversation they had yet to have.

"Any plans for Christmas?" he asked, expecting her to say she might visit her parents and spend some time with him in Bristol.

"Ah, that's something I was going to discuss with you, a bit later on."

"That sounds cryptic. Do you want to tell me now?"

"Ok. I was wondering whether I might take that trip to Florida. It's been two years since I was last there."

"Really?" Marcus was somewhat taken aback by her suggestion, mainly because it was so unexpected, but also because he wondered what her motives might be. "What's brought this on?"

"Well, it's what everyone seems to expect of me. A reunion with my son, I mean."

"Are you sure you're up to the journey? A long-haul flight is going to be tough, especially after what you've been through."

"That's why I want you to come with me."

"I see…" responded Marcus, attempting to process his thoughts.

"Come with me. You're right about it being too much for me on my own, but I think the time is right. Maybe returning at Christmas might trigger some of those lost memories. You never know."

Marcus had no hesitation in agreeing to support Ella, but secretly wondered how the experience might impact on her in the long run. There was every chance of her returning to the UK with her son, and that was something that would change everything. Yet it was bound to happen sooner rather than later; she was going to have to face her forgotten past at some point.

Delray Beach

"Stop worrying, Freya. It was bound to happen before long," offered Greg, equally perturbed to hear that Ella was planning a visit to Florida for the festive season. For him, it brought back painful memories of the night he wished he could erase from his past. He regretted his betrayal of course, yet the fact remained that it had resulted in his wonderful son and that was something that he could not ignore.

"What if she takes him back with her? I don't think I could bear it."

"Let's cross that bridge when we come to it. It might not come to that."

"But it might!" retorted Freya, bursting into tears. Thankfully, Kai was fast asleep having had a wonderful day with his little friends at the Mommy and Me class in the morning and exploring the outdoors at the Tinkergarten during the afternoon.

"There's nothing we can do to stop her coming, Freya. We knew it was going to happen at some point."

"She wants to bring Marcus," added Freya. "How do you feel about that?"

"I see no problem. In fact, it's better him than your parents accompanying her, surely?"

"I guess you're right. It sounds as though things are going well with Marcus. They must be, if she's planning on bringing him with her."

"So, it's decided then. Ella and Marcus are joining us for Christmas. I'll get back to her."

West Bay

The prospect of spending Christmas in Florida was beginning to appeal to Marcus. He'd had enough of the relentless buildup to the holiday season: the constant drone of festive tunes on the radio, annoying adverts, cheap decorations and the crush of panic shoppers in stores. He hadn't been to Florida since he was a child and was looking forward to some winter sunshine and spending some quality time with Ella. Of course, he had reservations about Ella meeting up with her son after months of separation and her reluctance to even talk about him. He had no idea what the outcome of their visit might be due to Ella's reticence on the subject, and that was a little unnerving.

Meanwhile, Ella was experiencing mixed feelings about her decision to spend Christmas in Florida. She was looking forward to spending extended quality time with Marcus, but at the same time, nervous at the prospect of the long journey and even more anxious about seeing her son for the first time in ages. She had no recollection of her trip to Florida two years ago, as it fell into the lost portion of her memory. Maybe a return trip would trigger something inside her. It was something she needed to do; something she needed to discover once and for all.

"Are you taking gifts, Ella?" asked Marcus, noticing she was deep in thought.

"Er… er… What did you say?" she responded, snapped abruptly from her train of thought.

"Presents. Are we taking them over or shall we go shopping when we get there? You've been before. What's best?"

"Let's take a few bits. Nothing much. But Marcus, remember I have very little recollection about my previous visit. Actually, scrap that. I have no recollection whatsoever."

"Maybe take something for Kai," suggested Marcus, as much to gauge her reaction to her son's name as anything else.

"I think I will," she replied quietly, closing down the conversation.

Chapter Forty-Four

Delray Beach

"I feel nervous," admitted Freya, glancing at the clock. Greg had offered to collect their guests from the airport and he was due to leave within the hour.

"Don't be. I'm sure they are more nervous than you are. It's a huge deal for Ella after everything she's gone through."

"And what about you? How do you feel about everything? What if her memory comes back and she remembers what happened between you?" It was rare for Freya to refer to the incident that nearly tore them apart two years before.

"Let's take things one step at a time. The chances are that those particular memories have been wiped forever."

"Let's hope so – for your sake."

Greg had not let on, but he was feeling anxious about seeing Ella again, and desperately worried about her taking Kai from them. Since joining their family, their life had seemed perfect, but he realised there was unfinished business and that he was about to find out how the story would end.

[ ]

He spotted them walking towards the arrivals gate, hand in hand. They made a good couple – they always had done. He had been surprised and saddened to hear it had all gone wrong at the time, but pleased and not really surprised that they had managed to establish a reunion recently.

"Welcome to Florida!" cried Greg enthusiastically as their weary figures approached him.

"Hi!" they returned in unison, relieved to have spotted Greg amongst the crowds. After warm hugs and the usual welcome pleasantries, they made their way to Greg's car in the multi-storey carpark, and before long, they were on the busy highway, heading towards Delray Beach, Freya and baby Kai.

Hearing Greg's car pull up on the driveway, Freya glanced over at Kai who was sitting happily in his highchair, her heart filled with love for him. As much as she was looking forward to seeing her sister, she was terrified by the prospect of Ella wanting to take Kai home with her. And there was every chance she would – surely that was the main purpose of her visit, to be reunited with him now that she had begun to recover her strength, and quite possibly her memories.

"Hi!" called out Greg, announcing their arrival. Scooping Kai out of his highchair, she felt her heart begin to race wildly in anticipation of greeting their visitors. The moment had arrived and she was dreading it as she walked into the entrance hall to welcome them, Kai balanced happily on her hip.

"Ella, Marcus – you made it! Good journey?" she managed, forcing a smile, and stretching out her free arm in their general direction.

"It was, thank you, and the queues at immigration weren't too bad either," replied Ella, barely looking at Kai, who was showing no obvious signs of recognition of his mother, as they all wandered into the kitchen together. "How are you?"

"We're fine, aren't we?" said Freya, looking directly at Kai as he clung tightly to her like a baby koala. "Let's get you something to drink."

Whilst Freya and Greg busied themselves preparing drinks and snacks, Kai was returned to his highchair in the absence of any immediate offers to take him. Eventually, Ella moved to sit closer and began to speak softly to him. Freya could not bring herself to watch the scene unfolding and wandered outside to give them some privacy and an opportunity for bonding time.

Later that evening, once Kai was in bed, settled down by Greg, the four of them sat around the pool chatting.

"How is Kai doing?" asked Marcus, his direct question bringing their easy conversation to an abrupt stop.

"He's doing really well," responded Freya nervously, wondering what to say and what they wanted to hear. "We keep busy, you know, with activities and outings. There's plenty going on around here for babies and toddlers."

"And he loves the water," added Greg, sensing Freya's discomfort. "He'd be in the pool all day if he could! And he adores spending time on the beach too."

"Thank you," uttered Ella quietly. "You've been amazing." It was the first acknowledgement of the fact that he belonged to her.

"We've loved every minute," continued Greg, sensing his wife freeze in fear of what was to come next.

"I don't know what would have happened if it hadn't been for you."

"Well, we're here for you. Now and for as long as it takes."

"Thank you," repeated Ella. "It might take a while."

Over the next few days, it became clear that Ella was no closer to bonding with her son. Her interactions with him were minimal and awkward, resulting in her asking Freya if she minded continuing with her routines with him for the time being, such as feeding, bathing and putting him to bed.

"If you're sure," responded Freya. "Just let me know when you want to take over."

"I'm not sure I ever will, Ella," she replied, her eyes filling with tears. "What's the matter with me? I don't understand how it's even possible for him to be my son. He's like a stranger to me. A lovely one, don't get me wrong, but not connected to me in any way other than through you."

"I'm sure things will change," said Freya, hoping and praying that they would not. "It's early days. Just enjoy being here, all together, and try to look forward to the festivities over the next few days. We have a few things planned. Nothing grand, just a couple of small gatherings for Christmas and the New Year with a few friends and neighbours if that's ok."

"Sounds perfect. Thank you, Freya," replied Ella, wiping her eyes and attempting a smile. For the first time, at the mention of festivities, she experienced a flashback to her previous visit to Florida. She recalled seeing the huge Christmas tree in the centre of Delray and had a vague recollection of sitting in a beach bar with sand between her toes.

Chapter Forty-Five

Delray Beach

"Happy Christmas!" they cried out in unison, toasting the occasion with a chink of champagne glasses. "Cheers!"

Ella tried to recall this day two years ago, when she had stood in this very kitchen. Her memories were blurred and confused by having Marcus by her side and Kai in Greg's arms. Two people who were not present when she was last here. Two people who had brought new dimensions to her life in recent months. One whom she was considering spending her life with once more, and the other threatening to rock her second chance at happiness. She felt no connection whatsoever to Kai. Of course, she marvelled at his very existence, but only inasmuch as him being a perfect little human being now belonging to Greg and Freya, who were the epitome of perfect parents to him. She could make a great auntie, but nothing more. She hadn't been able to speak to anyone about her feelings, not even Marcus, but surely her actions spoke louder than words. She had tried to play with him and hold him, but it just didn't feel right; there was simply no natural connection between them.

"So, the plan for today…" began Freya excitedly, sipping her champagne before continuing. "We've got the neighbours popping round for drinks mid-morning, followed by a late lunch and then we thought about heading onto the beach in the afternoon for a swim and games. How does that sound?"

"Sounds wonderful," replied Ella, in awe of her seemingly perfect sister with her beautiful home and adoring husband. The only thing that Freya's life lacked was a child. Yet that was the one thing that she could give her.

If only she could restore something of her lost memories about the circumstances of Kai's birth – maybe it would explain the distance she was feeling. She had thought about asking Freya what she knew, but decided to wait for the memories to return of their own accord, as and when the time was right.

The day turned out to be every bit as perfect as it sounded, with friends and neighbours popping round with gifts and seasonal cheer; a sumptuous feast of roast turkey with all the trimmings, followed by a wander onto the beach to walk off the excesses.

As soon as they stepped onto the soft white sands at the end of Freya's beachfront property, Ella was struck hard by a sudden shocking memory of walking along that same stretch two years before. It had been late at night. She had been in the company of a man and it had been late, really late, the bright white stars illuminating the ocean.

"Are you ok, Ella?" asked Marcus, slipping his hand into hers.

"I'm fine, but let's sit down here and let them wander on ahead."

Settling on the powdery white sand, on the edge of the dunes, they sat in silence as they watched the golden sun cast a warm glow over the turquoise water, the rhythmic sound of waves crashing gently against the shore, palm trees swaying gently in the breeze providing intermittent patches of shade.

"It's coming back to me," she murmured quietly under her breath. Marcus glanced over at her, unsure whether to respond, or allow her time to recover her memories. After a long pause, she began again. "It happened here. I'm sure it did."

"Are you sure? Do you want to talk about it? Does Freya know what happened? Maybe you confided in her at the time," he suggested.

"I'm sure she knows everything, but oddly, I don't want to hear it from her. I want the memories to resurface naturally, when they're ready to be recovered."

"And Kai? How do you feel about him now?"

"Oh, Marcus. It's best not to ask."

"What do you mean?"

"Well, it feels wrong to admit that I feel nothing. Nothing at all."

"It doesn't seem that way. You're great with him."

"Don't get me wrong, I think he's utterly amazing and wonderful, but I don't have a maternal bone in my body. I love to see him with Freya and Greg and can't wait for them to take him off me. They make the perfect family, don't they?"

"So, what are you saying?"

"I'm not ready to become his mother, if that is what is expected of me. I need more time."

After an hour or two on the beach, they wandered back to relax around the pool whilst Freya put Kai to bed. Ella chose to settle quietly in the shade pretending to read a book, but her mind was elsewhere, as partial memories slowly began to return to her like an old film reel flickering into life in her mind. Fleeting images and familiar scents.

"Fast asleep," announced Freya, returning to her sunbed. "He went out like a light tonight. It's been a good day, hasn't it?"

"A great day," answered Marcus.

"So, for tonight's entertainment..." she continued, "we usually have a film and snacks. How does that suit everyone?"

"Sounds good to me," replied Marcus again, Greg suddenly glancing over at Ella as though to seek her reaction.

"What's everyone's festive favourite?" asked Freya enthusiastically, still in her perfect hosting mode. With no suggestions forthcoming, she continued, "Come on. Otherwise, we'll end up with Greg's choice and I don't think I can face it another year running!"

The Holiday. Ella knew it was his favourite. If her memory served her right, it was the film she had watched with him one evening during her stay. Blurred images of the scene began to resurface and sharpen into focus: Freya leaving them alone; Greg asking her to sit with him on the sofa; feelings of forbidden attraction to her brother-in-law. *Please be wrong,* she thought, holding her breath as she waited to hear his response.

"Have you got *Love Actually*?" asked Marcus, interrupting her train of thought. Now she wouldn't get to find out if her memory served her correctly.

"Absolutely. That's a good choice. So, it's either that or *The Holiday* - Greg's choice obviously. Vote now!"

Instead of responding to Freya's attempt to plan the evening entertainment, Greg glanced over at Ella again, an odd, unreadable expression on his face, and returned to the house.

Chapter Forty-Six

Delray Beach

Since movie night on Christmas Day, it felt as though there had been a noticeable shift in relationships, mainly due to Greg absenting himself from the planned outings and gatherings between Christmas and New Year. Everything was left to Freya to organise – the cooking, dealing with Kai and generally entertaining everyone – yet she seemed happy and in her element. Ella and Marcus tried their best to entertain Kai in an attempt to help out whenever they could, but they were both as hopeless as each other at understanding even his basic needs. It was obvious that some important conversations were needed to clarify the way forward. As things stood, Ella and Marcus were planning to return to the UK very early in the New Year. Marcus needed to return to work but Ella's plans remained undecided. Freya had made it clear that Ella was welcome to stay with them for as long as she liked, and Ella was aware that she was expected to come to a decision about Kai. She hadn't been able to discuss her plans with Marcus, mainly because she was so confused and unsure what to do for the best. In her heart, she knew exactly what she wanted to do. She was desperate to go home with Marcus and rebuild her life and hopefully her relationship with him, ideally one day returning to something that resembled what she had enjoyed before. She was keen to resume her art and return to work herself now that she was feeling so much stronger. However, there were expectations hanging over her: that she would either stay in Florida and continue her convalescence, or return to the UK taking Kai with her. How on earth would Freya and Greg react if she told them she needed more time? Time to recuperate at home, without her son. To complicate matters further, flashbacks of her fortnight's stay in Florida two years before had continued to occupy her mind. She had worked it all out and, in many ways, it made her feel better about what she desperately wanted to do. She wanted Kai to live with Freya and Greg. They could offer him absolutely everything here in their beautiful home in Florida; he would want for nothing. And most importantly, he would be loved in a way that she didn't feel capable of herself anymore. The time had come to talk to her sister.

"Morning Freya, morning little Kai," said Ella in as friendly a tone as she could manage with the prospect of some painful home truths about to be discussed. "Has Greg gone to the gallery?"

"He has. Can't keep away! And what's Marcus up to this morning? I notice the car's gone." Freya had allowed them the use of her car during their stay.

"He's headed off to the Sawgrass in search of some bargains. He's planning on getting some designer labels at bargain prices to take back with him."

"Good for him! So, it's just the three of us this morning. What would you like to do? Do you fancy a morning on the beach?"

Ella had no plans to beat about the bush. She wanted to get this over with. "I wanted to talk to you first, and then maybe we could take Kai out."

"Ok… Sure," uttered Freya, filled with dread at hearing the words that were sure to break her heart.

"I need to tell you, Freya, that I've had some memory recall. It's exactly what my consultant thought would happen if I put myself in the environment where my memory blocks occurred." Freya's eyes had already misted over in anticipation of what she thought she was about to hear. "I've remembered what happened. It was a one-night stand in Miami just before I returned to the UK. I think I told you at the time, didn't I?"

"That's what you told me," replied Freya honestly, holding her breath in anticipation of what would follow.

"I didn't know Kai's father. It was a big mistake. A huge one," she continued sadly. "What would you think of me if I told you I just can't find it within me to bond with Kai? It's as though something has changed since I was ill. He's a wonderful little boy, but I feel so disconnected from him. Do you think that's dreadful?"

"No, not at all, Ella. I'm sure that's a normal reaction after what you've been through. So, what are you proposing?"

"Here comes the tricky bit…" began Ella. Freya felt butterflies in her stomach and palpitations in her heart as she held her breath in anticipation of what was to follow. "I'm not ready to take Kai home, Freya. I need more time."

"Stay as long as you like!" interjected Freya, desperate to hold onto Kai for as long as possible.

Ella chuckled gently before continuing. "You've been so kind to me, Freya. To all of us. But I need to get home. I'm strong enough now and I think I've had enough time to come to some decisions, especially now my memory has begun to return. What would you say if I asked you to look after Kai for me?"

Freya couldn't believe what she was hearing. Surely, she must be mistaken. She truly thought that her time with Kai was close to its end. "Oh Ella, surely you know what I would say? Nothing would make me happier than to look after Kai for you, for as long as it takes. He has become everything to me. I love him so much; he is my world."

"And Greg feels the same way?"

"He feels exactly the same. Our lives have been transformed by having Kai in it, especially after all the heartbreak we've been through on our unsuccessful fertility journey."

"Would you consider adopting him?" There, the question was out. She held her breath awaiting Freya's response.

"Of course we would!" exclaimed Freya, her eyes glistening with unshed tears of joy. And you can visit us any time you want. You can be part of Kai's life for ever."

Without the need for further conversation, Ella stood up and hugged her sister in an embrace filled with enormous love and gratitude.

☐

That night, Freya recounted her conversation with Ella to Greg. He was as taken aback as Freya, but every bit as delighted as her at the prospect of being able to look after Kai indefinitely.

"She says his father was a one-night stand in Miami," repeated Freya, realising this was the flaw in the plan. "How do you feel about that?"

"What do you mean?" asked Greg, unsure of his true response.

"Are you happy for her to think that is what happened, or do you think she deserves to know the truth?"

"I think she's been through enough and if she wants to believe in the one-night stand version of events, then let her do so."

"What if she suddenly remembers what really happened?"

"I'm not sure it would alter her decision to leave him with us. In fact, it would probably make it easier, knowing I'm his natural father."

"That's true. But what if she wants to take him back? Your name isn't on the birth certificate."

"I've already looked into it. I think adoption is necessary for me to formally establish paternity and give us legal security, and emotional security for Kai, of course. And from what you've said, it seems that Ella is keen to go down that route, and has no intention whatsoever of taking him back."

"Can you believe it?" sighed Freya. "How everything has turned out, I mean. How a nightmare situation, with us nearly losing everything, has ended up with us achieving our dream of becoming a family."

"Only because your sister nearly died, remember..." added Greg bluntly. "She was a good mother before it happened. We mustn't forget that."

"I will never forget that, Greg. And somehow, I can find it in my heart to forgive both of you, now that I have Kai, for something that almost destroyed everything. Don't you forget that."

Epilogue

Delray Beach – Two years later

"Happy Christmas, sleepy head," murmured Freya in Greg's ear, as he began to stir. "We might have a bit of time to ourselves before Kai wakes."

"Happy Christmas to you too," he replied, wrapping his strong body around her petite form.

The fairytale had continued to unfold, with Kai being the light of their lives. He had given new meaning and purpose to their lives. The gallery was going from strength to strength, but Kai added another dimension that gave everything more meaning. Now at three years old, he was into everything, and as bright as a button.

Before long, Kai was awake and ready to open his presents. "Shall we have them after breakfast, poppet?" suggested Freya.

"No, Mummy. Please can we open them now."

"What about Auntie Ella and Uncle Marcus? Don't you think we should wait for them to wake up?" laughed Freya, knowing her suggestion was futile.

"I tell you what, little man," suggested Greg. "Why don't I see if Santa has got a special before-breakfast present for you to open? I'll bring it upstairs with a cup of coffee for Mummy, shall I?"

"Yes please, Daddy," replied Kai, bouncing on their bed.

As he entered the kitchen, he was taken aback to see Ella sitting at the kitchen table with a coffee at such an early hour. "Morning! Happy Christmas. I didn't expect you to be up yet."

"Merry Christmas to you too. I couldn't sleep."

"Too excited to see what Father Christmas has left for you under the tree, eh?" he joked.

"I couldn't sleep because I was thinking about Kai."

"I see…" Greg held his breath, wondering what was coming next.

"I was thinking how lucky he is, to be living here with you in this wonderful part of the world, surrounded by so much love."

"He is our world, Ella. Not a day goes by when we don't thank you from the bottom of our hearts for what you've done for us."

"I know. Everything worked out in the end."

"I think it has. Another coffee?"

As he turned away from her, she smiled to herself as she looked at his strong profile, at his tousled blond hair that matched her son's and knew from the bottom of her own heart that she had made exactly the right decision in handing her son over to his father and her sister. Looking through the window framing a scene of endless blue, the sky meeting the water in a seamless horizon, she knew that she would be able to stay in her son's life forever, albeit from a distance – a mere ocean apart.

ABOUT THE AUTHOR

Born in Staffordshire, Carol began her first career in banking after graduating from Leeds University with a degree in Modern Languages. Whilst raising her two daughters, following a move to rural Somerset, she completed a further degree in English Language, and at the age of 40, embarked on her second career in teaching English. Since retiring, three years ago, she has been fortunate enough to fulfil a lifelong ambition to become a novelist, inspired by her travels abroad and spending weekends on the Dorset coast.

An Ocean Apart is Carol's second novel.

Printed in Great Britain
by Amazon